To Max,

FINDING MY HIGHLANDER

ALEIGHA SIRON

*Something to heat up
your nights! :)*

Tirgearr Publishing

Aleigha Siron

Published by Tirgearr Publishing
Ireland
www.tirgearrpublishing.com

ISBN 978-1-910234-25-9

A CIP catalogue record for this book is
available from the British Library.

10 9 8 7 6 5 4 3 2 1

DEDICATION

I dedicate this book to my husband, Robert, the best partner, helpmate, and genius techie, who weathered my tantrums about the evils of technology every time I hit a glitch or crashed the computer.

ACKNOWLEDGEMENTS

I wish to thank all the friends and family who championed my writing career through its many twists and turns over the years. You know who you are.

I owe a very special thank you to one of the many "nieces of my heart," Jenny Donadio, for her steadfast encouragement and early organizational assistance. Your vote of confidence from the "younger generation" was and still is a warm hug.

To Faye McGay, my long-time friend, for her aide in the first of many edits.

And to Chess Edwards, the most centered Life Coach on earth, who helped open the doors more fully to my creative and meditative processes.

Praise and thanks to Kemberlee Shortland and the folks at Tirgearr Publishing for redirecting me when I went off track. Your early guidance resulted in stronger character development as well as a much-needed boost of encouragement to keep working on the book.

Finally, a special thank you to the fans and lovers of romance who believe it is always possible to find that "happy ever after" ending.

Chapter One

Modern Day, San Francisco

A thick bank of fog rose above the horizon swiftly advancing toward the cliff where Andra stood, the wild and windblown sea below. She snuggled into her mother's cloak. Barely a memory of her mother remained, but she always felt her presence when wrapped in the familiar wool. The Celtic embellishments stitched along its hem matched the filigree on her mother's sapphire ring, now worn on Andra's left ring finger.

The heady tang of ocean air and wind-torn cypress and juniper that grew in twisted profusion on the ridge and cliffs north of Golden Gate Park penetrated her meditation. A smell so familiar and healing, it ushered in thoughts of earlier times when she would cling to her father's hand and climb the rocky escarpment while he spun magic tales of Scotland, Highlanders and knights of mystery and courage.

Her father always insisted their family's long history dated to the early kings of Scotland, but Andra considered that idea pure fantasy. She touched the Celtic cross at her neck with its embossed dove images at the four stations, worn in remembrance of a child she had lost several years ago. Now, at twenty-seven years of age, she must say farewell to her father, the last of her family. Not yet though, not yet.

A deep sigh rippled through her. "Well, Dad, here we are. I took a leave of absence from the pharmacy; Bill can handle things for a while. I'll depart tonight on the overnight flight to your beloved Scotland. Honestly, I'm not sure I'm ready for this final journey with you, Mom, and my precious Danny, but it was my final promise to you. We Camerons always keep our promises, a lesson you instilled and I remember. So, go I must, to scatter these ashes in our ancestor's land. Who knows, maybe I'll finally find my very own Highlander, as you had always hoped."

With a heavy heart, she sat down on a maroon and tan wool plaid. The sudden, strong scent of juniper touched by salty air floated across her tongue. She opened her mother's old, brocade carpetbag and removed a maplewood funeral urn. Cradling it in her lap, she traced the trinity knot engraved on the smooth wooden surface, then lovingly splayed her hand over the urn containing her family's commingled remains.

She reached into her bag and removed a clear box containing a black *sgian dubh*. The beautiful, sheathed dagger had a long history in the Highlands. Its name coming from the hilt made of hard, jet-black, bog oak, but also because warriors wore it in a covert location, strapped under the arm or tucked into a boot. This one, with a silver pommel cap and silver tip on the leather sheath, belonged to her great, great (too many greats to count,) grandfather from her father's side, or so the legend went.

As a young girl, she had begged her father to allow her to help clean it. Finally, when he decided she understood the proper reverence as he often reproved, he allowed her to polish the silver and steel, and oil the leather and wooden case where it was stored. It became a cherished ritual shared for many years.

"Dad, can you believe it, I even managed to obtain clearance to carry the *sgian dubh* into the cabin with me as long as it's in an air-sealed container. The museum at Castle Ruadhstone has agreed to house the artifact for display during my stay in Scotland. You would not believe the weeks of wrangling and writing it took to obtain permission."

Andra pulled out the blue, green, and heather plaid, neatly folded and wrapped in a linen covering. The fine piece of woven wool came from her grandmother on her mother's side. She ran her fingers over the soft fabric thinking of the many years it had passed from generation to generation. Her grandmother had told her its age equaled that of the *sgian dubh* resting in its box by her lap. What complicated histories. She never could keep them all straight, but loved their stories just the same. Without a doubt, there were many embellishments from generation to generation; lending the tales a mythical air and retaining only the thinnest thread of truth. Now, she was the last of once proud and extensive families, at least as far as she knew.

The fog was thickening, and the wind picked up. Andra stood and carefully removed the cap from the urn. She tilted it slightly so only a small measure of ashes sifted into the wind and murmured softly, "Dad, in this place where you and mother fell in love, where I was born, where Danny drew his few precious breaths, I leave this dusting of ash so something of each of you will remain here with me upon my return." A gust of wind took the trickle of ashes over the headlands and out to sea.

She slid to the ground and closed the lid. The ruby nestled in the raised bevel of her dad's ring, worn on her right middle finger, flashed when a prism of light struck through the clouds. It seemed the moment should be an epiphany of sorts, but of what she didn't know. She rubbed her thumb over the intricate Celtic knots that covered the band and choked back tears.

A suffocating weight stopped her breath, as though one of the boulders on the hill behind had slipped its mooring and crashed against her breast. The air around her felt thick and wavering. Her stomach roiled as she replaced the urn in the aged carpetbag. Before she finished repacking the remaining items, the earth beneath her shifted and rolled dizzyingly.

"Damn, another earthquake!" Reaching to brace against the tree at her back, she searched the cliff edge for possible danger from falling rocks. The air shimmered as the rumbling grew stronger, a loud roar filled her head, and a dark chasm opened beneath her. Thrown into a whirlwind, her body stretched and tumbled feeling both weightless and dense as iron at the same time. The atmosphere sizzled and cracked, as though a great heaving beast awakened. The air around her grew heavy enough to crush her bones. Surely, she was dying. Excruciating pain penetrated every fiber of her being until everything swirled and blanked out.

Chapter Two

Andra came around slowly. Her head ached and felt wet and sticky. A wave of nausea swept over her when she sat up. Though not usually squeamish, she thought she might throw up when she touched the lump on her forehead. Her hand came away bloody and blood trickled down the side of her face and dripped off her chin. The *sgian dubh* lay on the plaid under her, its Plexiglas box smashed. Her side throbbed where she must have landed on it. She rolled onto her knees and took slow, deep breaths through her nose, blowing out through her mouth trying to calm her shaking body. Aside from the lump on her head and blood flowing down her face, a dark foreboding gripped her.

"Duh? What do you think is wrong! You smashed your skull on the bloody boulder you're leaning against. And, I'm talking to myself, again." Friends and family frequently chided her for the constant singing or talking diatribes she engaged in with herself.

That wasn't the problem though. Something else was strange, very strange. She must have been out for a while because last she remembered it was early afternoon but now, twilight descended. A deep feeling of disquiet settled over her, and the hairs bristled across the back of her neck. She brushed away the broken pieces of plastic and grabbed the sgian dubh.

"Damn, damn, and double damn. I'm going to miss my plane and this gash probably needs stitches." Her vision fuzzy, she tried to orient herself. A rich scent of heather and herbs and damp earth filled her nose. No boat whistles pierced the air. No sirens shrieked in the distance. No ocean scents reached her nostrils. For that matter, where was the ocean?

4

"What the hell! Did I just fall off the cliff? No, because then I'd be on the shore." She shook her head. "Urrrgh, don't do that you idiot. Don't move, just breathe slowly." She attempted to quell her anxiety by speaking aloud as her surroundings were entirely too quiet.

Moving her head cautiously, Andra observed a thick, dark forest that rose to the peak of the hill behind her. Dense tree growth and scrub continued down past her left beyond the boulder she leaned against and thinned out slightly in front of her. A filmy mist feathered through the trees. To her right, glimpsed through sparser forest, the ground rolled into mounded hills covered with bushy plants that smelled of heather and other unfamiliar scents. Thick, grayish-white fog swirled over the distant hills, moving like a specter in her direction.

"I must be hallucinating," Andra groaned. "Perhaps I'm unconscious and dreaming." Yet the ground felt solid enough. The air, heavy with mist and strong earthy scents, smelled totally unlike the briny windswept cliff where she thought she should be. She placed her hands on the ground at her sides just as a low rumbling started again.

"Another earthquake?" This quaking was not the same. Whatever the cause of this rumbling portent, it was heading toward her and coming on fast.

"What the..."Andra blinked her eyes in disbelief. It appeared as though the horsemen of the apocalypse were thundering through the trees, and she was about to be trampled under their pounding hooves. She rose up on wobbly legs, her bloodied right hand raised in front of her, the sgian dubh tightly clutched in her left hand.

The horses ground to an abrupt agitated halt. A man, dressed in a kilt, smoothly dropped to his feet even before the dappled gray beast he rode on had come to a full stop a few feet in front of her. *A kilt, really.* Even covered in grime he was a magnificent specimen. Close to six and a half feet tall, broad shouldered, every inch of him banded in generously honed muscle.

To his right and slightly behind stood a monstrous steed,

carrying a man doubled over and tied to his saddle to prevent his plunge to the hard earth. Andra's injuries did not compare to the grievous wounds suffered by the man bound to his horse. Two other slathering horses ridden by equally foreboding men, stood behind the man on the ground and his wounded comrade. The injured man and one of the mounted men wore kilts, like the one worn by the man standing; the other mounted man wore tight pants and a linked-metal vest with leather straps holding numerous weapons.

The air assaulted her nose with the smell of dirt, horse, sweat, and…blood. She must have taken quite a smack to her head. The images battering her brain simply wouldn't solidify into anything resembling rational thought.

The man on the ground spoke, but she couldn't make out his words. He spoke again. "Lass…?" His voice vibrated over her skin with a gentle, burring tone he might have used to calm a panicky horse.

"Wh…where am I? Who…who are you? Wha…what's happening?" Her voice, breathy and hesitant, rose in pitch toward a fit of hysteria.

One of the men in the back moved forward, coming alongside the injured man. "A filthy Sassenach. She's likely a spy." He spat to the side, his face dark and threatening. Arms the size of thick tree branches gripped his reins. His face, streaked with dirt, sweat, and blood, wore a scowl meaner than any she'd ever seen

"Sass-Sassenach?" she whispered. She understood his derogatory reference to the English, had heard it enough in the many tales spun by her father over the years.

The giant on the ground moved slowly forward, his hand still reaching toward her while he spoke to the mean-looking one. Gaelic. They were speaking Gaelic. Though she knew a few passing words, mostly curses and a few endearments, she was certainly not proficient enough to speak intelligently or grasp their quick pattern of speech.

Her gut gripped, her head throbbed. She closed her eyes, wishing the hellish nightmare away. When she opened them again, nothing had changed.

"Stop where you are," she hissed at the man facing her. She widened her eyes, tried to focus on the scene in front of her, while glancing from one man to the other. "I know Judo," she sputtered. She raised her pitiful dagger as if that could do anything to stop these men. The one who had called her a Sassenach growled something in a threatening tone as he inched his horse in her direction. The fourth man moved up beside the injured man's horse.

"Wake up, wake up, wake up, wake up!" she screamed in her head. No, she'd screamed it out loud!

Thick, dark-blond hair, streaked with lighter strands from time in the sun, fell into the eyes of the man standing on the ground. He had a strong chin covered with several days' growth, a wide forehead and high cheekbones smudged with dirt and grime. Questioning brows arched above piercing, dark-blue eyes. He stopped his approach but maintained an intense penetrating focus on her face.

He spoke over his shoulder to the mean one and issued a command. Again, she did not catch the words, but his tone left no question that he commanded the group. As he advanced ever so slowly, she matched his movement with backward steps.

"Shush, be at ease, lass. I see you're injured, we'll nae harm you."

"Leave the Sassenach, or better yet, kill her. She'll tell our enemies we passed this way. We have no time to deal with her and must get Lorne to safety." The mean one spoke English, scowling with obvious hostility directed at her. The quiet one said nothing but watched the others closely.

"She's bait—a Sassenach trap!" The mean one's horse jittered around as the man scanned the trees and hills.

Her back stiffened as if all her Scots ancestors had suddenly risen behind her. "I am no damn Sassenach. Who are you and where in the hell am I?" she screamed. "Is this some bizarre reenactment scene?" She already knew the answer to that question. The man bent over and tied to his horse had real wounds. No theatrical makeup could mimic the blood streaming down his legs, or the blood and grime streaked across the others' clothing and limbs.

Screaming seemed to be the only way she could speak now. "My name is Andra Heather Adair Cameron, daughter of Brian Cameron and Gillian Adair, descended from the ancient kings of Scotland." She had no idea if any of those tales of ancestry were true but what did it matter at this point. This hallucination could not be real. Surely, she'd cracked her skull, and now floated in this bizarre, nightmare realm.

All the wind left her lungs; she had screamed them clean. She dropped to the dirt, bent forward, and vomited. Humiliated, and concerned she'd suffered a concussion or worse, she found it impossible to unscramble her brain or utter another sound.

Chapter Three

Kendrick watched the lass fall to her knees and empty her innards. The head injury still trickled blood down her face. It looked serious enough to have addled her senses. He had no time to waste assessing her unexpected appearance, nor her injuries, nor her unfamiliar English dialect, nor her peculiar form of dress. They must get to their hiding place in the hills. Lorne could not survive much longer on his horse, if he survived at all.

He moved to within a foot of her and knelt down. Kendrick would not leave an injured, defenseless woman alone in the wilderness even if she were a Cameron. "Dinnae fear us, my name is Kendrick MacLean. Tell me, where is your home, where are your kin, your protectors?"

He noted her fingers glittered with expensive rings, diamond studs adorned her ears, and an exquisite, gold, Celtic cross hung at her neck. This was no common woman, definitely a lady, or perhaps a noble, as she claimed. Surely, such evidence of wealth meant that that degenerate, Cormag Cameron, was not a relation of hers.

She didn't answer him. Delicate long fingers gently pressed against the lump on her head, and came away smeared with streaks of blood. Still bent forward on her knees, she moaned, shook her head, spat and wiped the back of her hand across her mouth, and then riveted him with wide, terrified eyes.

Softly but more firmly, Kendrick tried her name. "Andra, we cannae stay here. Enemies may be fast on our trail. My brother is grievously injured, and a storm approaches. I won't leave you here alone and I cannae wait to find your kin. I swear on my honor I will help you, but you must leave with us immediately."

He reached forward and lightly touched her arm. A shock of energy shot through his hand. She hissed, pulled back, and fell onto her backside. Terror-filled eyes, the color of moss in a shadowed glen, brimmed with unshed tears and locked on him. He stilled, his hand suspended just above her. Holding her gaze, he reached under her arm, lifting her as he stood. She wobbled but didn't pull away this time. She's definitely addled, but he could do nothing about it now.

Keeping his eyes on her face, he called to his cousin, "Rabbie, gather her things into her plaid and strap them to your horse, we head for the caves."

A sharp whistle brought his horse forward, huffing, and tossing its bridle. Andra flinched at the animal's approach. "Relax, Thunder is well mannered." He hoped to soothe both horse and woman with his calm voice. As soon as his horse stood beside them, Kendrick mounted and lifted the woman to sit her in front of him. Though solidly built, she felt feather light in his hands. He wrapped one muscled arm tightly around her waist. She winced and sucked against her teeth but did not fight him. Her warmth penetrated the underside of his arm and her fresh scent invaded his senses.

"Struan, grab Lorne's reins." The horses chuffed and stomped their feet for a moment, then surged forward in full flight up the hill into the darkening forest.

The woman quaked in his arms; her lips, blanched of color, trembled as though she wanted to speak, but she said not a word. She held herself taut as a bowstring, exhaustion heavy across her tensed shoulders as she attempted to keep herself apart from him.

The forest thinned to large swaths of scrub fern and heather that sprouted around the base of scattered boulders large enough to conceal a horse and its rider. Sparks flew from beneath the horses' hooves as they grappled for purchase on ground that had transitioned to a hard, stony surface.

Eventually, the woman relented to Kendrick's grip and tentatively leaned against his chest. He wanted to encourage her ease but feared any words would tense her again so he remained silent. *That's good, lass, relax. You're safe.*

Finally, they reached their destination, hidden between high, craggy cliffs swathed in mist and slipped into a cleft between two large outcroppings. Soon they passed single file into the deeper blackness of a cave. Flexing thickly muscled thighs to guide his horse through the tight, stone passage, Kendrick felt Andra stiffen and pull away from his body. He whispered in her ear, "Dinnae fash yourself, all will be well."

Kendrick dismounted then lifted Andra to the packed dirt floor and moved her against the solid wall of the cave. Her knees buckled. "Steady now, I'll come back to you in a moment, I must tend me brother. For your safety, do not leave the cave," he cautioned, more gruffly than he intended. He took a moment to study the fine form of her face. Dazed moss-green eyes stared somewhere over his shoulder as though through a fog, lost and unfocused.

* * *

Andra leaned her head against the cool, damp stone. *This can't be happening. It isn't real.* But the odor of sweaty horses and men and the coppery tang of blood certainly smelled real. The hard-muscled mass that had kept her from toppling off his horse certainly felt real. More real than anything she had felt for months, perhaps years, but her mind couldn't connect this experience to a meaningful reality.

As Kendrick walked to the back of the cave, she closed her eyes and slid to the floor. The past few hours would not congeal into anything that made sense. "Well, Dad," she groaned, "either I'm suffering delusions and the wildest hallucinations, or I am in Scotland, but I know not when, where, or how." For a moment, she swore she could hear his laughter, scolding her to *buck up Andra, and go with the flow.* It was one of his favorite admonishments, always delivered with a chuckle.

Battered, bruised in body and mind, Andra questioned her tumble through...what? Space, time? Impossible! But perhaps not, how else could she explain her present circumstances? Her shoulders and back ached from the extreme effort it had taken

11

to hold her body stiff and separate from Kendrick's during their frantic charge through the night. Yet she still felt the thrill of desire that had infused her when she finally relented to the grip of those strong arms and sagged against his hard chest. *What was that about?*

The man called Lorne moaned. She felt a disturbance of air as they carried him past her and deeper into the cave. Keeping her eyes closed, she leaned against the cold wall until the sound of water sluicing over stone entered her awareness, and amber light drifted over her closed lids. When she opened her eyes, she noted someone had lit several torches, and she could see they were in a large cavern. To the rear of the area, water softly cascaded over a segment of the stone face, passed into several drop-down pools, and disappeared into a crevice hidden in the shadowy dark.

Water! Her mouth and throat felt parched, and her head ached. Water would help. She pushed against the wall until she could stand without fear of falling. The men were busy with the injured warrior, horses, and dragging dense foliage to cover the entrance they had come through. She moved slowly toward one of the lower pools, knelt down, and splashed cold, rejuvenating water on her face. It felt like a touch of heaven in the middle of this nightmare. She leaned forward and stuck her entire head into the shallow depths, expelling air bubbles, then drank deeply like a dog lapping at a pool in the desert. When she sat up, the quiet one stood to her left side.

"Lass, can I help you?" His voice was softer than the others, his stance relaxed, composed, despite the dirt and blood splattered over his massive arms and clothing. He seemed to be a quiet, gentle man, though physically as imposing as the others.

"You could bring me my bag."

He moved his hand from behind him and cautiously extended her mother's old carpetbag. "Do I need to check it for weapons?" A slight crinkle lifted the corner of his mouth. A piece of leather cord tied wavy, light-brown hair at the nape of his neck and tight braids spilled alongside sharp, scruffy cheeks. His eyes were dark and shadowed.

"Thank you…it's Rabbie, correct?"

"Aye," he nodded.

Andra granted him a guarded smile. "I'll pull no further weapons if you promise to be kind." The slight attempt at humor from both of them eased the tension coiled in her gut.

He swept an arm gracefully in front of him and bowed, "Always, m'lady, as I learned at me mother's knee." Then he left her to tend the horses.

She searched her bag for the washcloth, hand towel, and first aid kit she always carried when traveling. The washcloth came to hand first. She dipped it into the cold water and wiped the dried and clotted blood from her face and hair. Then she dunked her head in the pool several more times.

"I seem to be awake," she whispered, just for the comfort on her own voice. "My surroundings feel solid enough," she pounded her fist on the dirt, "so it must be real. Accept it, Andra, and decide what to do next."

She could hear the men speaking Gaelic, hushed yet clearly distraught about the condition of their clansman. They gathered near another pool of water several yards from where she knelt. She watched them over her shoulder for a few minutes struggling to fit the scene into her new reality. A million questions rose in her throat.

"Not now. Patience and observation are what's required. All will be revealed in time." *What a stupid cliché.*

Should she offer her help with their friend; would they accept it? She could not sit here and do nothing when one of them was seriously injured. Besides, anxiety always spurred her to take action. Her father had always said, *"Move, keep busy, and don't let dust gather under your feet."* With her father's words ringing in her ears, she approached the men cautiously, keeping her eye on the mean one, Struan.

"May I be of assistance?" She stood with her feet firmly planted on the hard-packed, dirt floor, her head held high, one hand pressed flat against her side, the other rested on the cross dangling on her chest. It took an extreme effort to control her trembling body. Her palms moistened with sweat. She steadied her focus on Kendrick. His strong hands moved carefully over his

Keep your eyes on your job and clean away the muck.

She wanted to speak with them, but didn't know how to begin. If she even looked at Struan, he glowered at her. Completely focused on his brother, Kendrick more or less ignored her, so she concentrated on cleansing and assessing the leg wounds. Her ministrations revealed a few, less-serious slashes across Lorne's calf. On inspection, she felt certain they could bind them without stitches. When she looked up, the men had begun cleaning a large gash along his ribs. It looked gruesome, and her stomach lurched. It took a moment to steady her breathing. Kendrick poured whisky over the wounds and Struan started to suture, but the patient no longer responded. His chest rose and fell in a halting fashion, and yet he did not moan or move.

The scent of strong whisky burned her nose, mingling with the smell of blood and filth. She breathed shallowly, repressing a gag. "His leg will also need stitching."

With a nod of his head Struan huffed, "There is another needle and gut, just be certain you clean the wound."

They expected her to suture. "Oh! I have never sutured a wound. I'm certain I would make a mess of it. But I'll clean it thoroughly for you."

Struan harrumphed, grunted, and snarled, "What good was your *first aid train'en* then, if you cannae even stitch a wound?"

A well of annoying sounds and insulting comments, Struan drew out the words as if scum coated his tongue. Even so, his hand remained steady as he expertly stitched Lorne's flayed flesh. Obviously, these men had considerable experience with wounds of this nature. Andra ignored his baiting and continued to clean Lorne's legs but watched surreptitiously, thinking she might need to acquire that skill.

Searching through her bag, she found a tube of antibiotic cream. Her hand fisted over the tube. The ointment couldn't hurt and might help, but how could she conceal it and use it at the same time? She must not allow them to examine the tube closely, or they'd think she was a witch. A burning fire under her feet would be her reward, especially if they found the stamped expiration date. "Damn!" she hissed.

Struan snapped his head up, auburn hair curled wildly around his face, his brow furrowed as he growled, "What is that you say, wench?"

She ignored Struan and focused on Kendrick. Handsome, rugged, all virile male, just glancing at him made her weak in the knees. His dark-blond hair fell across a bronzed, well-proportioned face with a straight nose and full lips. A small cleft in his chin lent him a hint of boyish charm. Large, powerful yet gentle hands examined his brother's neck, shoulders, arms, and torso—for bone fractures, she assumed.

Watching him, she found herself wanting to feel those hands on her. *Whoa, from where did that thought come?* She needed to examine her sanity and rein in her wild imagination.

Her voice trembled when she spoke, "Kendrick, will you permit me to use some healing ointment on the bandages before we bind his wounds? I will use it on my own cuts and scratches. It is quite safe and may help prevent infection."

Kendrick studied her with focused concentration that shot to her core; it felt as though he reached to her very soul. "You'll need a few stitches on your head as well. Let me tend to them and then you may add your ointments."

Andra sat as still as possible while Kendrick applied a few stitches along her hairline. The pain made her dizzy and nauseous. At least the heat of his presence offered some small distraction, though not enough to prevent a few tears or repress her hisses as the needle pierced her skin.

As soon as he finished, she opened the tube inside the bag and wiped ointment on her finger. She applied it to her forehead laceration first. Then with her back to the men, she squeezed out a generous portion on strips of linen and placed them over Lorne's wounds while Struan bound each one.

Andra and Struan silently switched places when he moved to stitch the thigh. She retrieved her thick, cotton washcloth, rinsed it clean and wiped away the matted blood and dirt from Lorne's face and head. Kendrick glanced with interest at the washcloth but said nothing to her.

"This long cut along Lorne's temple may require a few stitches," she said. The man shook violently under her hands, and his teeth chattered loudly. "We must finish quickly and warm him or our efforts will have been wasted."

Kendrick glared at her as though he wanted to smack her for stating the obvious. He swallowed hard, nodded, and abruptly went to start a fire in a stone circle farther back in the cave while Struan finished tending to Lorne. Someone had placed straw pallets near the fire pit.

Once he completed the stitching and binding, Struan bent to lift Lorne. Placing her hand on his thickly muscled arm Andra stopped him. "Wait, if you and Kendrick each lift one end of the plaid, I'll slip my hands underneath to support his back, and we can move him more safely to the pallet."

"I will assist you." Rabbie said. Intently focused on Lorne and the other two men, Andra had not heard Rabbie return.

Struan shot her an angry scowl, his muscled arm tensed under her hand, but Kendrick intervened. "'Tis good advice."

They lifted Lorne in his plaid and laid him on a pallet next to the now-glowing fire. Rabbie placed several blankets and a fur covering over Lorne's quaking body. Andra brushed her hand across the injured man's forehead. He was hotter than fire and shaking so severely she thought he might bite through his tongue.

"Where's my bag?" As if this whole situation hadn't panicked her enough, the fear that he might not survive clutched at her chest. Kendrick brought her bag without question or comment, just another penetrating stare.

Her hand wrapped around her trusty bottles of ibuprofen and acetaminophen, a runner's go-to for relief from aches and pains. She always carried a bottle of each everywhere she went. Keeping the label covered she tipped four acetaminophen and two ibuprofen tablets into her hand and asked for a cup of water.

She tossed three tablets down her own throat, lifted Lorne's head onto her lap, tilted his head back, opened his mouth, suppressed his tongue, and tossed the other pills into him.

"Kendrick, please help me administer these tablets. If you rub his throat while I dribble in water, we may be able to induce a swallow reflex."

"What's that you're giving him?" Struan snarled.

"It's medicine to help reduce fever and head pain. As you saw, I took a few myself. They may help and couldn't hurt him." His suspicious tone was making her nervous.

Finally, Lorne choked and swallowed the pills. Andra sat back with a sigh while continuing to press a cold compress to his forehead. He shook so violently she could have sworn the bones in her own hands rattled as she held his head.

Take slow, calming breaths. It seemed she constantly needed to remind herself to breathe. A damp sheen of sweat covered her forehead even though the temperature had dropped precipitously. She felt clammy, and her head pounded ferociously. It was imperative they do something to get Lorne's body temperature under control.

Andra stood and faced three, fierce Highlanders. She knew what had to be done, but cringed with worry for her safety should she even suggest it. "Listen to me, he is freezing, yet burns with fever." Three sets of startled brows rose at her tone and demand for attention but she rattled on. "His condition is very grave, and it's imperative that we stabilize his body temperature. I have a suggestion which may help,"

She paused to take a deep breath, exhaled and rushed on. "I need a solemn oath from each of you," her eyes drilled each man, "on your honor as gentlemen, give me your solemn vow, your promise that you will not harm, nor molest me in any manner." Unflinchingly, she searched each face.

All three mouths dropped open with outraged sputtering; Kendrick spoke first and none too happily. "Och, Andra, why do you question our honor, we are Highland warriors. We dinnae molest defenseless women."

Struan interjected. "Just like a bloody Cameron to accuse us of the worst behavior while 'tis your clan that harbors the most despicable heathens on God's earth."

19

Exasperated with Struan's constant grumbling she spun on him. "My clan? I have already told you, I have no clan. I belong to no clan!" Andra clutched and unclutched her hands. The man had trod on her last nerve. She found herself shouting—again.

"Oh, you're being ridiculous." She stomped her foot in frustration, a petulant and completely uncharacteristic behavior, as her normally calm, controlled demeanor cracked in frustration.

"Just give me your word of honor, if you possess such a thing." Under the circumstances, she should be quaking in her boots, but Andra stood firm. She stared down these massively muscled men capable of inflicting great harm with the flick of a wrist. Though she couldn't begin to say why, she felt no harm would come to her from them.

Their faces expressed offense, but she knew with certainty not all Highlanders could profess honorable behavior. Fists bunched at her hips, she stared at them, refusing to drop her eyes even when Struan curled his burly arms over his thick chest and grumbled something unintelligible while scowling at her as if he would just as soon toss her on the fire.

"You offend us grievously if you think we would harm any woman, especially one who has aided our own. You have my word, madam, no man will harm you in any manner." Kendrick's voice vibrated with an edge of anger. The tallest of the bunch, he stood at least six-foot five, and the rest of them weren't much shorter. Though not petite, Andra felt diminutive next to any one of them. Kendrick, however, was the most imposing man she'd ever laid eyes on in both physique and intensity. He intrigued her.

His eyes flashed a deep, commanding blue in the firelight. A thin, white scar ran along one side of his clenched jaw. She wanted to reach out and slide her fingers along that scar on his jaw. *Why was her mind going off on such thoughts?*

Instead, she wiggled her hand indicating they turn around. "I must disrobe, do not be peeking, nor goggling at me."

All three men repeated the word goggling with raised eyebrows but did as she requested and turned their backs. She hastily pulled her family's ancient plaid from the bag, unlaced her

20

black-leather ankle boots, stripped off her soaked socks. Andra peeled off the leggings and long black skirt, removed her fitted leather vest, and pulled off her favorite heather-colored, turtleneck sweater, hopelessly stained with blood and dirt. Standing in pale-pink satin and lace underwear and bra, she faced the fire with arms outstretched, her plaid unfurling across her back the ends gripped in tight fists.

"Kendrick, come stand beside me with your back bared toward the fire; we are going to heat our bodies and crawl under Lorne's coverings to warm him."

His eyebrows quirked and he stepped toward her with a roguish look on his face. She lifted her left arm to block his view, not that it would help. Since he was nearly a foot taller, he could easily see over the top of her outstretched arms.

While keeping her eye on him she turned to her side attempting to shield her body from his view. In her peripheral vision she watched him remove the upper part of the plaid thrown over his shoulder and pull his shirt off the most sculpted abs she'd ever seen.

Wow! Work out much?

He glanced in her direction as though he'd read her thoughts.

"Turn your head away, please," she said, raising her arm and shoulder higher. Her eyes narrowed in challenge. His brows quirked and tiny, mischievous wrinkles appeared at the corner of his mouth. A guttural noise rumbled in his throat, but he averted his eyes as she'd asked. When her body tingled with warmth, she slid under the blankets and draped herself across Lorne's chest, avoiding his injured right side. She tipped her head back to Kendrick still standing by the fire; his lips parted, a completely amazed expression on his face. "Lie down under the coverings on his other side, but be careful of his wounds."

"You're verra bossy, m'lady, and I dinnae take orders from anyone, especially a woman." Still, he came, all male heat and strength, and crawled under the covers with his back turned to them. The other men took to their pallets and wrapped themselves in their plaids, Struan grunting, while Rabbie quietly chuckled.

After a moment she whispered, "Kendrick, I am not feeling too well myself. My head throbs and I feel a bit nauseous. Please wake me occasionally through the night in case I have a concussion. We should also give Lorne additional tablets in a few hours."

He didn't respond for several seconds and she wondered if he understood about concussions. "Aye, dinnae fash yourself, I will check on both of you."

Andra closed her eyes. *This is just a wild and crazy dream, and I'll wake in the morning refreshed and in my own time.* Another voice whispered in her head, *No, no you will not.*

Chapter Four

Kendrick dozed fitfully for several hours then rolled to study Andra. Her face rested against Lorne's shoulder, one pale arm stretched over his head, slender fingers flashing gemmed rings laced through his hair. Her face glowed in the dim light cast from the faltering fire. Her lovely, slightly parted, rose-tinted lips and high cheekbones mesmerized him. Flawless, lightly bronzed skin indicated time spent in the sun, marred only by the purple bruise and large lump on her forehead. A cascade of burnished brown hair drifted across her face and swirled in tendrils over her shoulders. One shoulder had slipped from the coverings and appeared bound with a thin strap of shiny material the color of blushed skin. Damn if he didn't want that face on his chest, those fingers threading through his hair, his own fingers exploring the soft lushness of her body. She disturbed him, called to him even in sleep, and he didn't like it.

Who are you, lass, and where did you come from? As bold and brazen as she appeared, he admired her tenderness toward his brother and her quick willingness to help. She had asked him to wake her in a few hours, but loath to disturb her rest, he watched her sleep.

As though she felt his gaze, her dark lashes fluttered, and she woke with a start. When her eyes opened, she pulled away, looking confused and disoriented for several moments. She blinked, yawned with that perfect mouth that he wanted to smother with his own and whispered, "So, I'm still here. How long have we been asleep?"

"Aye, lass, you're still here, where else would you be?" She didn't answer. "It's near dawn. You've slept mayhap a few hours."

She studied him for a moment then lifted her face to Lorne and pressed her hand to his forehead. "His fever is still high. Has he woken at all?"

"Nae, he remains still and quiet but has ceased his trembling."

She slid from the covers, pulling her plaid with her. As she stood, he caught a glimpse of her full figure garbed in enticing silk undergarments such as he'd never seen before. His manhood surged to attention. *Och, you fool.* Thank heavens layers of covers concealed his response to her.

Turning to the side, she wrapped the plaid around her body, tucking a flap tightly under her arm, leaving her shoulders bare except for that pair of thin silky straps. "We need to get more pills into him." She retrieved her mysterious bag and searched its interior. Returning with several tablets in her hand, she knelt beside Lorne. "Fetch some water," she commanded.

"Fetch it yourself, Andra." Where did she come by such audacity to command him?

She startled at his reprimand and dropped her head, then seemed to reconsider and delivered a laughable attempt at a harsh stare. When he simply lifted a brow and smoothed his mouth into a tight line, suppressing an urge to laugh outright, she stood up, harrumphed, and went to retrieve the water.

"Will you at least help me get these down his throat?" she asked, her voice a soft, lilting tone. Yet she displayed enough self-assurance to meet his eyes directly.

"Aye, that I will, but dinnae be issuing commands to me in the future. A request will be better met."

She smiled sheepishly as if she had no fear of him. Anyone else would have profusely begged his pardon. Perhaps she was a highborn lady as she claimed. They often held themselves in greater regard than was deserved. No matter her status, his head overflowed with questions he needed answered. Eventually, one way or another, she would give him the information he sought.

After they managed to get the pills into Lorne, she popped two pills into her own mouth and then wiped Lorne's face with a cool, damp cloth and laid it across his forehead. Shying away from Kendrick, she pulled her plaid tighter. "Excuse me while I tend to my...er, ah, I'll be right back," she blurted and dashed toward the entrance of the cave.

Every interaction with her was a surprise. She stupefied him, a mystery to unravel and he was verra good at unraveling mysteries. He could think of other things he'd like to unravel, like spooling her out of that tightly held plaid. He would know her story. It struck him as odd how he suddenly wanted to know everything about her. Her possible relationship to the reprehensible Cormag Cameron barely factored into his desire to learn her secrets. Curious, as he rarely felt a need to know any woman beyond a few carnal encounters. Attachments of a more serious nature did not interest him.

He wanted to know where she had come by the odd clothing she wore, and what else was in that strange bag she lugged around everywhere. Strangest of all, how had she come to be stranded and bleeding, alone in the wilderness, draped in expensive jewels? When they'd come upon her, rising like an apparition from the forest floor with her possessions strewn about her feet, he felt an immediate attraction.

Perhaps Struan had the right of it, and she was a witch. He gave little credence to such beliefs, but many men were deeply superstitious. Witch hunts had died down in recent years. Kendrick thought such accusations had more to do with ignorance and avarice. Men in power could easily incite the rabble by blaming an innocent for unexplainable events. In some cases, the rouse allowed them to confiscate land and wealth from the accused. He no longer knew the court's position on the matter since it often changed.

In a voice rough with sleep, Struan interrupted Kendrick's musings, "How fares Lorne?"

"Nae well. His fever still burns and he hasn't moved through the night. The lass gave him a few of her tablets again, but I dinnae ken if they help him."

Struan grunted, "Mayhap you should not allow her continued ministrations. Mayhap she gives him poison." Glancing quickly about the cave he asked, "Where has your *first aid* banshee gone, then?"

"Outside. She needed a moment of privacy. And nae, she gives him no poison. Each time she gives him the tablets she takes a few herself. It is obvious she means to help."

Kendrick stood by the fire, but kept an eye on the front of the cave, his thoughts drifted for a moment. At nine and twenty, he had been laird of their clan for a few years due to his father's deteriorating health. Constant skirmishes with rival clans, stolen cattle, poor crops, winter approaching with barely enough stores to provide for his people, and all the other inherent responsibilities his title inferred, weighed heavily upon him.

Unbidden, his father's constant refrain: *"Ye need to provide the clan with heirs,"* rattled to the surface of his thoughts. *God's teeth!* Why was he thinking about that now? Oh, but he could guess. The thought didn't please him that well, because he was thinking about a particular woman, a Sassenach and a Cameron, no less. A lass with beguiling, green eyes and auburn-streaked hair. How could she be a Sassenach and a Cameron? Nothing about her made any sense.

Rabbie banked the fire, adding smoky peat and strips of wood. Then he went to the horses to search the saddle packs for their remaining dried meat, figs, and oatcakes. Kendrick didn't miss Rabbie's quick, furtive glances cast between him and the cave entrance, his cousin's smirk more telling than words. They'd always read each other's thoughts easily, a habit Kendrick found exceeding annoying at the moment. It would be inadvisable for Rabbie to begin speculating about a potential liaison between him and the lass. He never missed an opportunity to niggle Kendrick to find a new wife. But he didn't want a wife. He might never be ready for another marital alliance.

Rabbie glanced at the front of the cave, "Have you learned anything aboot the woman? Did she say why she was in the forest alone and injured? When I doubled back last night, I found no evidence of anyone following us or searching for her. Only our tracks marred the ground."

"Humph. That tells us nothing." Struan interjected joining them.

"Mayhap, mayhap not. Who can say until she tells us something aboot herself?" Rabbie kicked a loose coal back onto the low flames.

Kendrick continued to watch the cave entrance and didn't answer for a moment. Both men stared at their leader. Rabbie shook his head, the corner of his mouth lifting in amusement until Kendrick shot him a warning scowl.

Rabbie ignored the rebuke. Stuffing a bite of food in his mouth, he continued, "Though her clothing is unusual it is made from verra fine fabrics, those leather boots, and that cape especially. Did you notice the intricate embroidery of Celtic symbols? Mayhap our wee woman of mystery piques your interest, cousin."

Kendrick glared at Rabbie and snapped, "Isn't it time you get out and scout the area? Did you set any snares last night? We could use some fresh meat."

"Aye, I did. I'll leave shortly to see if any redcoats or Cormag's men still roam the area and check my traps while I'm out." Rabbie took another bite of food.

"I'll join you on your forage," Struan said. "I could use a break from this...this..." he sputtered and flailed his hand toward the front of the cave where Andra had disappeared, then abruptly changed the topic. "Besides, 'tis certain we cannae move Lorne for a few days, and we need food. What say you Kendrick?"

"Good." Kendrick only briefly turned toward his men. "Good," he repeated, with a distracted tone, "I will tend Lorne and see what the lass has to tell us."

* * *

Andra paced a path outside the cave. "Why didn't I bring my clothes out with me? Urrrgh! What in God's name has happened? It's clear I'm still here. Wherever or rather whenever here is. Well, there's nothing to do but go back to the lion's den."

Just as Andra approached the cave entrance, Kendrick stepped into the pale light. Was he checking to make sure she hadn't escaped? How could she escape when she had no idea where she was or whether running wouldn't land her in even worst straights? Her chest tightened at the sight of his honed strength and apparent ease. When she breezed past him, her arms clutched around her middle to both anchor the plaid and refrain from running her fingers across his chest. Crazy thoughts assailed her.

She greeted the others with cheery aplomb. "Good morning, gentlemen." Their startled gazes raked down her body to her bare calves and toes, which she couldn't help but curl into the dirt at their scrutiny. A twinge of fear hit her for the first time since their initial encounter. *Was that only last night?* It seemed like ages. She felt exposed standing with her shoulders bared, tightly gripping a plaid that dropped just below her knees. Not smart, especially after last night's little demonstration of heating Lorne's body with hers. But then, she hadn't displayed much intelligent decision making since her arrival.

Rabbie chocked on an oatcake and motioned with his head, "Your clothes are laid across yon rock by the fire, they are probably dry now. Would you like a bite to eat? 'Tis not much, but it will quiet your rumbling stomach." He lifted an oatcake in her direction and discreetly flicked his eyes away from her legs.

She answered with a dazzling smile. "Thank you kindly, Rabbie." Her obvious attempt at friendly banter didn't quell her shaking knees. She squared her shoulders; fear would gain her no consideration with this group. Kendrick pierced her with a hard stare, not blinking or saying anything. Why did he appear so annoyed with her?

The smile slipped from her face. She held Kendrick's stare for a second, then tipped her chin ever so slightly, took the oatcake from Rabbie's outstretched hand, and turned to gather her things. Grabbing her clothes and brocade bag, she rushed back outside. As soon as she moved a few feet beyond the entrance, she sat down and found a clean pair of socks and a clean, dark-green, knit shirt.

* * *

Kendrick followed Andra and watched her from a slightly concealed position beside the horses. The sky was turning a pale shade of violet-gray as night shifted to dawn. When her arms reached to pull on her shirt, he noticed a large bruise that wrapped around her side and across her back. No wonder she had winced when he'd held her in his grip during yesterday's ride. However, she'd never complained, cried, or resorted to hysterics. Not exactly true, but she had exerted some effort at self-control, which spoke well of her strength. The image of last night, when she'd curled her heated body against Lorne's, flashed to mind. He recognized this method of treating severe chills, but never imagined a woman would expose herself in such a manner.

Watching her dress, he admired her firm body, long legs, and rounded backside as she pulled on a pair of snug-fitting trews over bewitching pink-blush undergarments so outrageous his sword rose in salute. Everything fit tightly to her body like a second skin. Standing about five and a half feet tall, she was leanly muscled with full breasts and soft curves. Burnished gold and auburn glints streaked her thick, brown hair, still tangled and disheveled from sleep. Its glossy mass spilled just past the fragile wing bones in her smooth back. He felt lecherous staring at her, but couldn't turn away. His hands tingled with the imagined feel of her silky skin and hair.

Wearing no chemise, or underlying petticoats, she shook and dusted off the slim-fitted, long, black skirt and pulled it over the trews. She laced up a fine pair of short leather boots and slipped on a fitted leather jerkin. Though fully covered, Andra's clothing molded scandalously over her breasts, hips and all other body parts. Perhaps it was a new French or Dutch style, both often scandalous.

"Scandalous be damned," he growled low in his throat, his manhood firming as he watched her wiggle into her clothes. Her beauty and tantalizing figure rattled him. A primal urge flowed through his veins, and swamped him with a yearning he dared not name.

He watched Andra nibble the oatcake while hauling her things over a rocky slope to a small clearing near a stand of pine trees where she sank to the ground.

"What do you think she is doing, casting spells?" Struan

harrumphed as the men came beside him to watch her.

"Nae," said Rabbie. "It seems she sings to her departed. That looks like a funerary urn she's holding. I've seen them on my travels in Europe. Sometimes they use them to return the remains of fallen warriors to their families."

"Strange song and even stranger behavior, and you ken it's a sin to burn the body. Only witches are burned." Struan scowled at the lass. He'd never encountered a woman like her before.

Rabbie interjected before Struan continued. "Nae, they sometimes still burn the remains of fallen warriors when they die far from home. Also, they might burn the remains of plague victims. Mayhap it's a loved one or family member."

"I don't trust her. It's witchery, I tell you." Struan was building up to a full-blown rant about witches. "And when your da and mother hear about her lying with Lorne, there will be hell to pay. He'll be insistin' Lorne marry the daft lass, and I can tell you, Laird Keith will not take lightly to his daughter being set aside."

Even the suggestion stunned Kendrick. "No one will be insisting anything of the sort. Andra only meant to help him heal. There will be no talk of marriage. In fact, none of us will mention anything about last night to anyone. Is that understood?"

Rabbie snorted and pulled the reins of his horse forward. "Best get out and see if anyone is on our trail. Are you comin' along, Struan, or are you staying here ogling the lass?"

Struan grunted, jerked his head, and mounted his horse. "You'll be minding your tongue, Rabbie. Let's get on with it, see if we can find anything out about the wench, and check your snares. We could all use nourishment a bit hardier than oatcakes and dried meat."

Kendrick continued to watch Andra as the men rode quietly down the hill. He felt a deep tug in his chest and wanted to take her in his arms and sooth her obvious distress. "Och! What nonsense. What is it about her that is so disturbing?"

He did not gush over women and their heartaches. He had sealed his heart a long time ago and did not wish to open up to any woman ever again. His first wife came by way of an arranged marriage to quell strife between clans. They only had a year together, but he had come to love her. She was a sweet, biddable lass, and they were both young. However, when she and his newborn son died following the babe's birth, he shut that door—permanently.

He turned back to his brother. Kendrick hoped he would wake today and show signs of improvement, so they could head home before more trouble found them.

Chapter Five

"Dad, I am certain I've lost my mind but from all appearances I have fallen through time and landed in one of your medieval stories of Scotland, rife with fierce and bloodied Highland warriors being hotly pursued by some threat. Rest assured though, I do not plan to play the weak damsel in distress to this band of men. You'd be proud of how well I've managed so far, even if part of me still believes I'm in an altered state suffering hallucinations."

She pulled the wooden urn from her bag and clutched it to her chest, listening to the sound of birds calling up the day, breathing in the earthy smells, the clean air redolent with tangy pine. *How had this happened?* She had been sitting on the edge of a cliff overlooking San Francisco Bay, she released some of the ashes, and an earthquake tossed her through a time portal.

Maybe if she laid out all of her things as she had then, she could reverse the process. She laid down the plaid, knelt on the ground, placed the *sgian dubh* beside her, removed the top of the urn, and reverently touched the Celtic cross at her neck.

"Okay Dad, I'm leaving your ashes on Scottish soil as you asked, you can send me back anytime now." She tilted the urn, held her breath, and let the breeze take a small scattering of ashes. It was a bizarre parody of Dorothy clicking her heals saying, "there's no place like home."

To her dismay, nothing happened. She stopped the flow quickly, retaining most of the urn's contents. She was certain that repeating this action would return her to her own time. If it didn't work now, she might need the remaining ashes to try again. Quietly she waited. Still nothing happened so she began to sing

32

"Dust in the Wind", one of her Dad's favorite songs.

Her voice seized and a sob escaped as her shoulders began to shake. Her father's baritone voice filled her head. *Mo àlainn nighean, - my beautiful daughter - always remember, life is precious and short. Live well and fully before it all falls back to dust."*

Andra heard the horses pass behind her, but refused to look their way, she didn't care if they left her alone. In fact, she'd relish a bit of quiet without them questioning or casting downright hostile glances at her. What had she done to annoy them? Wasn't she the victim here? Well, to hell with it, she refused to play victim or fragile, fainting woman to their fierce, manly gruffness. No! She was strong and self-reliant, quite capable of handling herself. At the moment however, her head throbbed again and a light drizzle fell. Time to get on with it. Nothing would be accomplished moping about or sitting out in the rain and catching a cold.

It took several moments for her eyes to adjust to the dimmer light after reentering the cave. Lorne was still sleeping by the banked fire; she approached him quietly to check his fever, which continued to burn. She rinsed the washcloth with fresh water and gently wiped his face, neck, and arms then reapplied a freshly wrung-out cool cloth to his forehead. At least he wasn't shaking with chills any longer. That must be a good sign.

"Oh hell, what do I know about such fevers and wounds? I've done my best, Lorne." She patted him gently and tucked the furs up around his chin.

When she looked around, it appeared only she and Lorne remained in the hideout. The sound of the waterfall splashing into the largest pool at the back of the cave entered her consciousness. "Well, sir, it seems you are still in the land of dreams and I am sorely in need of a bath."

Approaching the large, dark pool below the waterfall, she could see a very faint edge of light at the top of the rock cliff, but she could not discern the size of the pool as the back portion lay beneath a rock overhang where the waterfall cloaked everything in shadow. She quickly stripped to her underwear and stepped onto the rocky edge while unhooking her bra. A sudden movement of water from the shadows at the back of the pool caused Andra to scream. She lost her footing and stumbled forward.

Emerging from the shadows, Kendrick moved toward her at lightning speed catching her with one hand braced against a shoulder and the other pressed firmly against one breast. Their eyes latched for a few seconds while she struggled to regain her balance. Her hands splayed across his hard, bare chest, the touch scorching. His fingers flexed, increasing the pressure against her flesh. A shocking fire ignited in her; her lips parted as if in invitation before her rational mind and self-preservation kicked into full gear.

Regaining her senses, Andra moved to Kendrick's right, lifted her right leg, and with as much strength as she could muster, slashed her foot into the back of his knee. At the same time, she quickly thrust her arms up and out to break his hold on her body and yelled—*stop*!

Kendrick lost his footing and fell back with a splash. Andra didn't wait to assess possible injury. She jumped out of the water, grabbed her things, and made a wild dash outside. The cover of pine trees where she had previously scattered her family's ashes provided a shelter of sorts, a spot removed where she could calm herself.

"Damn, damn, damn, and bloody damn!" Andra sputtered and gasped, dancing about from one foot to the other as a fine drizzle turned into a full-fledged downpour while she tried to gain her senses and pull on her clothes.

When she fell into Kendrick's arms, her whole body had burned with desire. "What is wrong with me? I'm in the middle of Scotland in God knows what time period with a virile man who sets me on edge with his every glance. Why am I behaving like a foolish teenager?" She didn't ponder that question further. On edge hardly described the heat she felt in his presence. She needed to stay calm and focused on finding a way to return home, not fantasize about a hot Highlander from the wilds of Scotland.

"What in heaven's name am I to do?" she yelled at the gray

sky. She seemed to be doing everything wrong so far, despite all her good intentions.

Yet Kendrick hadn't forced himself on her. He'd simply tried to stop her fall. Had she overreacted? No doubt, he was now seriously angry with her.

"What must he be thinking?" First, she heated her near-naked body in front of a fire and snuggled under blankets with his brother, and now she literally threw her again near-naked body into Kendrick's arms only to execute a perfect swipe and block to knock him back into the water. Women in this time, whatever time it was, did not behave in such a manner. What did they call them? Wanton. He'd think she was a wanton, immoral lunatic.

She'd only intended to help Lorne when she slipped under the blankets with him, and she certainly had not intended the second event as a come-on. "Hell, I didn't plan to dump him in the water," she hissed, "I just ached for a bath." Well, she was getting a thorough rainwater shower now, evidenced by her soaked clothing.

She drove the toe of her boot under clumps of pine needles. Why hadn't he alerted her to his presence before she stripped off her clothing in front of him? "Duh! That isn't so hard to figure out."

Good Lord, but he was handsome, strong, fierce—even a bit amusing. She smacked the side of her head. "Get a grip! And stop talking to yourself!"

Kendrick had not followed her outside. What if he'd hit his head when he fell? What if even now, his blood seeped out in that damn, rocky pool of water? What if she'd accidentally caused him serious injury? Had he drowned? Her thoughts spun out of control. She had a bad habit of taking every scenario to all of its worst possible conclusions.

"Oh my God. Oh my God!" She paced the needle-strewn dirt chewing mercilessly at her lip. The clear image of Struan's leering glee as he tied her to a stake admonishing her for evil intent against their laird filled her jumbled thoughts. Well, no time like the present to face the music, or in this situation, Kendrick's wrath. At the very least, she needed to pull his drowned body from the water. And she needed to get out of the rain before she ended up sick.

"If he's knocked unconscious, what could he do to me, right?" *Wrong, most definitely wrong.* She could envision few circumstances worse than her current situation or the terror her wild imagination unleashed in her thoughts. She groaned and turned back toward the cave.

* * *

Stunned speechless, Kendrick had watched Andra stand on the edge of the pool, disrobing and revealing the curvaceous vision of every man's dream. Though he knew he should step forward or alert her to his presence, he found himself unable to move, mesmerized by the vixen. Just as she unfastened that lacey bit of silk cupping her deliciously full breasts, his conscience spurred him to step out of the shadows. Her startled scream and sudden catapult off the edge had him rushing to intercept her fall. When his hands landed on her shoulder and one breast, he felt a shock like heat lightening travel between them. He held her steady for barely a second before she became a complete berserker and upended him back into the water.

"God's bloody rood, what in the hell just happened?" Kendrick pulled himself out of the water, snatched a piece of linen to dry off with, and started after Andra, his pride and his loins burning with equal intensity. Lorne's rough, parched voice interrupted his pursuit of the daft woman. "Did a fiery water sprite just best me fierce brother?" he coughed.

"Lorne, you're awake. How do you feel?" Kendrick knelt by his brother carefully checking his wounds.

"Like hellfire," he croaked, "but I ken you might just be feeling a wee bit of the hellfire yourself." He coughed, groaned in pain, and closed his eyes. Kendrick lifted a cup of water to Lorne's lips. "Drink." His brother took a few sips then slipped into unconsciousness.

He could do nothing further for Lorne, but he definitely needed to get his wits about him and find Andra. The hand that had caressed her firm, full breast still stung from the warmth of her flesh. She really had felt like a water sprite and moved with such force and power he could almost believe she was not of this world. Seasoned warriors could hardly have executed a more effective disarming. Thank God the other men were not present to see her flip him so easily; he would never live it down. Where had she learned that trick?

Chapter Six

Quickly donning his kilt, Kendrick moved to the cave's entrance and watched as Andra mumbled then smacked the side of her head. She seemed perfectly adept at carrying on her own private conversations. Stomping toward the cave, head bent watching her feet instead of looking forward; she chewed furiously on her full, lower lip. When she finally looked up, her movement ceased abruptly. She stood in the pounding rain like a rabbit frozen in the heather.

"You...you are not injured, then? I...I am sorry...m...my laird. You frightened me. I was not aware of your presence in the pool and merely intended to wash." Her tone betrayed both her irritation and an attempt to mollify him.

She looked contrite enough, he mused. Nevertheless, he kept a scowl plastered on his face. No sense allowing her to think he would tolerate such outrageous behavior. Still, it was difficult to suppress a slight quiver at the edges of his mouth.

All efforts of appeasement dropped from her eyes. "Are you smirking at me?"

"Smirk? I dinnae ken your meaning?" No longer able to contain his amusement, he barked a laugh. "You do remind me of a drowned cat, standin' there in the pouring rain." He flicked his fingers encouragingly. "Dinnae fash yourself, come back to the fire,"

Andra raised a fisted hand, a long, indignant index finger pointing at him as though she were admonishing a bairn. She stiffened her back and thrust up her chin. "Yes, well then, I think you should step back, and let me pass unmolested."

No one of his acquaintance would dare question his honor much less admonish him in such a blatant manner. Yet here she stood besmirching his character once again with no provocation. Well, not much provocation at any rate.

With a voice harsher than he intended, he furrowed his brow, "I dinnae intend to molest you." He didn't force himself on women; the idea was abhorrent to him. Still, his mind had easily conjured an image of her writhing beneath him, more than willing to receive his attentions.

"'Tis just a wee misunderstanding between us, Andra. Come out of the rain, and dry yourself by the fire."

She continued to hesitate.

"Lorne spoke a few words but has slipped back into unconsciousness." He suspected the news would be enough to spur her forward and it did.

"What did he say? I've been so worried. There are so many frightful consequences to head injuries and such terrible loss of blood. Do you know about amnesia? Was he lucid? Sensible? Did he recognize you?"

The woman was a seething caldron of questions and nerves. Despite her agitation, her hand stayed fisted and she brandished her index finger like a wee sword. Keeping a modicum of space between them, she moved forward. Their eyes connected, igniting sparks for a brief moment as she passed.

"Slow down, Andra. Dry yourself by the fire, and I'll answer your questions."

Ignoring him, she knelt beside Lorne and pressed her hand to his forehead. "His fever may be less severe, but to be honest, my hands are too cold to gage his temperature."

Andra lifted Lorne's head onto her lap and dribbled a few drops of water over his lips.

He moved his mouth and blinked up at her for a moment.

"Oh, thank God! Please, take a few small sips of water," she urged.

He moaned, sipped, swallowed, and then drifted off again. She gently patted Lorne's face calling his name. He didn't respond.

Kendrick wondered if she was attempting to hide from him

behind her concern for his brother. It was time for answers. He drilled her with an intense stare, letting her know he would brook no further avoidance. "Who are you, lass? How did you come to be in our path yesterday?"

Her furtive glances at their surroundings and hesitancy to look him in the face suggested an attempt to evade or at least divert him from his questions.

"I don't…" she paused, took a deep breath. "I do not know how to answer that, sir." Unflinchingly, she lifted her eyes to his. Her jaw stiffened. This was a statement as direct as though she had screamed it, her refusal to cower under his scowl. Time seemed to stop and the sound of water splashing against rock only intensified the silence between them. He crossed his arms over his chest and waited.

"I mean to say, I am not certain how I got there, or even where I am now, except you and your men speak Gaelic, and as I believe you've already stated, it must mean we are in Scotland. However, I do not seem to remember anything else; I do not even know the day or year." She touched her hand to her head and winced in pain.

He kept his face devoid of all emotion. Any feigned indication of discomfort on her part would not sway him from his task to gain what he needed to know.

"Aye, we are in Scotland. 'Tis the year of our Lord 1705." Her startled reaction puzzled him. A frightened look crossed her face and straight, white teeth clamped onto her bottom lip as she reached up to caress the cross on her chest while her eyes dropped to the dirt. He noticed she often touched the cross when she was nervous. It made him wonder—did she seek forgiveness for the lies yet unspoken?

"You're claiming a loss of memory, is it? And yet, you seem to remember your name, Andra Heather Adair Cameron." He harshly bit off her surname. He hated Cormag Cameron and his band of ruffians. He couldn't subdue the question burning his brain: if a connection to his nemesis proved true, what would he do with her? "Which clan Cameron do you belong to?"

Two little creases formed between her eyes and nose and her mouth scrunched into a twisted expression of confusion. "I—I do not know of any clan Cameron or of any kin in Scotland. My father was a pharmacist, er…apothecary, a man of science, a chemist…" Her attempts to explain seemed to addle her. She gulped and rushed on, "My mother passed when I was very young and my father always kept me with him. We traveled extensively to far and exotic lands in search of knowledge about medicine and science. As he lay on his deathbed, he asked me to return the family's ashes to Scotland. How I arrived here, wherever here is, I am unable to explain."

Her voice trailed to a near whisper. "Besides, you would not believe my words as I scarce believe any of this myself. It's all just a jumble in my mind."

That last remark grabbed his attention. "Unable or unwilling, that is the question, isn't it? And why would I not believe you if you spoke the truth? Furthermore, you ken 'tis a sin to burn the body, unless it's the body of a witch. And some consider dabbling in the healing arts a form of witchcraft." He didn't believe such nonsense, but decided the suggestion would provoke a more truthful response from her.

Kendrick stared at her, his face a stony mask. He knew she prevaricated. How did a person not know of their clan's origins, or the location of kin in their homeland? Even if she didn't know her clan, how would a woman travel alone to Scotland with her family's ashes, especially a woman speaking in that strange English dialect?

It was unconscionable, no woman ever traveled about unescorted. And what Scotsman would fail to teach his daughter his native tongue or the history of his ancestors? Her explanations defied logic and her continued subterfuge angered him.

"Enough with the artifice. We both ken your words are false. I ken you are withholding the truth, and I'll not stand for it. You will answer me and tell me the truth by one means or another." With a harsh, biting tone, his voice reverberated off the stone walls like a boom. He loomed over her, jaw tight, chest thrust out, hands on his hips in his most intimidating pose. A flicker of fear crossed her face and then just as suddenly dropped behind green eyes ablaze with defiance.

She sucked her mouth into a tight line pulling the bottom lip under her teeth. If she kept nibbling at that lustrous mouth, it would soon be shredded and bleeding. He could not discern her thoughts as she continued to stare at him, baiting his anger, with Lorne's head nestled in her lap.

"Dinnae think you can hide behind my brother's body and not answer my questions. Are you a Cameron spy?" They had warred with the Cameron clans for generations. The Camerons sided with the Sassenach when it suited them or when they could gain lands or titles from the association. But that didn't explain why she had so readily divulged her surname? If, however, her relations did not have filial connections to Cormag's, he could always ransom her back to them. Unfortunately, she now knew of this refuge in the hills, and he would not allow her to divulge that information to their enemies, not even to some of their allies. The situation required careful consideration.

He took a threatening step toward her. "Or mayhap you're a witch, as Struan insists?"

She gently laid Lorne's head on the ground and rose to face him. They stared at each other over his brother's prone body. Her brazenness intrigued him. That she dared stand toe-to-toe with him in a battle of wills took courage and baffled him more than a little. Though he wouldn't admit it to anyone, he admired her spitfire attitude. Still, she might also be a wolf in a lamb's coat. He could not trust her nor let his guard down for an instant. It wouldn't be the first time an enemy used a beguiling woman to obtain information or weaken an opponent.

* * *

Although Andra felt an urge to drop her gaze, she refused to show such weakness. That would not help her. Neither of them spoke nor seemed the least bit inclined to yield. Even though she could not win this trial of wills, she could not allow an accusation of witchcraft to go unaddressed.

"Do not denigrate my family or my father's name, sir. He was a good and honorable man of science, and highly respected among his peers."

Suddenly the cave seemed too confining. An overwhelming urge to run tingled down Andra's spine, but where would she go? He towered over her, obviously intent on unnerving her, and his looming presence succeeded in unsettling every nerve. She bristled at his threatening posture as a fire erupted in her belly. Despite a normally calm, peaceful nature, she refused to acquiesce to threats. On the other hand, she did not want to anger him further. She needed to appease him in some manner if she wished to survive the night

"Laird MacLean." Her voice came out deep and challenging, not in any way placating as she had intended. He raised an eyebrow at her tone. She modulated her voice as best she could and tried again.

"My laird, I apologize if my answers do not meet with your commands. I am doing my very best to answer as truthfully as I am able. Might we please sit a moment and try again without you threatening and questioning my every utterance?" She found the stunned look on Kendrick's face almost amusing. Almost.

"You are a most audacious woman," he responded, his voice rough and growly. "Every word you utter is an accusation against me, yet you are the one withholding information. In case it has slipped your powers of observation, we have been speaking and 'tis you who's evasive. You only need to answer my questions—truthfully."

"I am not..." she swallowed a lie about to slip out. "I am doing my best. This is all so confusing. One minute I was sitting quietly with my family's things saying a final farewell and the next minute I'm on the ground, the horses of the apocalypse charging toward me. I remember nothing else. I have absolutely no idea how I ended up in that wilderness." She waved her arms around the cave. "None of this makes any sense to me."

He watched her face closely, too closely. She sputtered for a moment, feeling much like a rabbit caught in a snare. *This is hopeless.* No matter how hard she tried to insert as much truth as she could, if she disclosed the truth, he'd consider her insane, or worse, believe his accusation of witchcraft. She dropped her head to her hands and swayed from side-to-side.

He probed further, his tone mocking, "Describe this place where you sat so quietly?"

"On a high cliff facing the ocean on a far distant shore," she groaned at how ludicrous her response sounded, even to her.

"Talking to you is like pulling teeth. On exactly what distant shore might you have been while uttering this fond farewell?" His unrelenting, sharp tone of voice intensified.

"Please Kendrick, my head throbs, and I can't tell you more. It is not clear to me, and God knows, I wish it were. I cannot answer what I don't know or remember. I am at your mercy and beg patience. You have my word, I will continue to try and remember what happened in order to provide the answers we both seek."

"The answers are right there in that stubborn head, Andra. Just speak them and we'll be done with this. I will nae harm you, you have my word, and I stake my life on my word."

Her eyes widened, and an annoying flush heated her cheeks. Rainwater still dripped from her hair and clothes. She shivered from the cold as much as from their confrontation. To continue would accomplish nothing. Exhaustion from her attempts to appease the man rendered her mute.

"You could drive a man to violence, you ken."

She flinched at his threat and took a tentative step back.

He also took a step back, clenched, and unclenched his fists, as though to refrain from grabbing her to shake out the truth. "Get out of your wet clothes before you become ill. I do not wish to add another sick person to our party. I have no time to care for you as well as Lorne." On that sour note, he turned away from her.

Well, the arrogant cad, what made his word more honorable? In truth, she couldn't argue the issue. She must forge a believable story to keep the peace until she could return to the twenty-first century. After all, if she arrived here, surely there must be a way to return.

Andra grabbed her satchel and moved to the shadows at the back of the cave for privacy. Her thoughts strayed to their earlier encounter by the pool and a hot quiver ran through her. She looked back to assure herself he wasn't watching her.

Dark-blond hair tumbled loosely around his head and fell below his nape onto a strong, straight back. He sat facing the entrance like a glorious, marble statue, all muscle, and power. Quickly pulling on dry clothes, she shook her head to clear the rising, irrational, and very heated thoughts.

Chapter Seven

Kendrick went out of the cave periodically while Andra kept the fire banked and tended his brother. Several hours passed in relative quiet. Lorne drifted in and out of consciousness, occasionally opening his eyes and sipping water. He'd thank her with a cracked moan or grunt and then drift away. Andra managed to get him to swallow a few more of her medicinal tablets and took a few herself. Kendrick kept an eye on her but discerned nothing further from her behavior. He decided to try again.

"Lass, what can you tell me about yourself that might help me understand how we found you alone in the wilderness?"

Her cheeks puffed and she blew out a frustrated gust of air. "Honestly, I wish I could explain that to myself but I simply can't." She paused and lifted a cup, "I've made some tea with a spot of whisky for Lorne. Would you care for a cup?"

"You're changing the subject, Andra. And where did you acquire this tea?"

"No. I'm not changing the subject. I brought a small amount of tea with me, and frankly, there is precious little of it left. I'm simply offering to share as a prelude to relaxed conversation. I call this my 'hot toddy', Lorne and the others seem to enjoy it."

Kendrick raised an eyebrow. "Thank you, I'll accept, but I still want you to answer my questions."

"Fine, ask away." She smiled sweetly and handed him the cup.

"Well, your clothing is rather—unusual. Where did you come by them?"

"My clothes? What's wrong with my clothes?" Her hands splayed at her sides. She looked down at her garments. An exasperated sound escaped her pouting lips, but she didn't comment further.

"They are—revealing," Kendrick responded. His eyebrows arched sharply. "Some might think scandalous."

"Oh? Revealing?" She looked down again. Little worry lines creased the bridge of her nose. Regardless of any explanation she might give, he could not imagine her clothing an acceptable mode of dress anywhere.

"I am well covered, nothing is revealed. They are my travel clothes. As I said, my father and I traveled to many lands, even to the far East."

The way the fabric clung to her rounded curves left little to the imagination. He needn't engage his imagination anyway because she'd already fully revealed her lush body, though not intentionally. His strong attraction to her warned him not to linger on those images. Continued questions regarding her state of dress and appearance would only result in firing his desire, so he redirected. "You've been to the land of the Saracens?"

A blank expression confirmed his suspicions. She was attempting to fabricate a story. He held up his hand struggling to control his anger. "Nae, dinnae say it if you cannae speak the truth."

"I can't tell you what I don't know myself," she blurted testily. "I've already explained my travels with my father." Turning in a piqued flounce, she busied herself tending to Lorne and tidying the area, completely ignoring his presence. It took every reserve of patience not to grab her shoulders and shake the daylights out of her. Yet something told him if he grabbed her, it would not be to extract information, so he stepped away.

* * *

Twilight descended too quickly. Struan and Rabbie had yet to return. Was this a good or bad sign? How long did a reconnaissance mission take? Kendrick had grown ever more vigilant and followed her to the entrance of the cave whenever she went out to tend to personal matters.

"You know, I am quite capable of going beyond those trees

and boulders to attend my needs without your supervision. I'll not run off into the night. Where could I go when I don't know where I am?" She goaded him, but could not stop herself.

He gazed at a point beyond her shoulder with an implacable face, and then turned his dark, penetrating eyes on her. She flinched slightly, but covered it with a thrust of her chin and returned his stare. He wouldn't best her in this staring contest, no matter how formidable his expressions.

As usual, she broke first, "Are you concerned for Struan and Rabbie? Should they have returned by now?"

He scanned her hair, her face, settling on her lips a bit longer, and then his eyes raked down her body. His scrutiny did not reveal any of the earlier humor she'd detected. Why did he feel the need to intimidate her with his stern regard or more likely, lustful appraisal? She squared her shoulders, readying for another onslaught of intimidation.

His expression suggested he didn't miss her challenge, which only seemed to pique his interest further. "They are warriors," he said, "quite capable of handling themselves. I'll go hunt a rabbit or game for our dinner. Lorne needs fortifying broth if he's to gain his strength. We must ride from here soon. 'Tis not wise to linger long in this location." His words were clipped and abrupt.

She wanted to ask why staying there was a bad idea, but decided against it. Despite what he'd said, he didn't move but returned his attention to her. Tension rippled over his body as though he battled some internal dispute. Finally, he snatched the horse's reins and started to pass by her. With a light touch to his forearm, she halted him. A rock-hard bicep flexed under the pressure of her fingers and heat shot through her hand.

"You won't be gone long?" She hated the tremor in her voice.

"Nae, not long." He started to pull away, but she clutched his arm more tightly.

Eyeing a bow and quiver of arrows strapped to his saddle, she dipped her chin to them. "Could you leave me that bow and arrows? Just in case." A cool breeze blew between the boulders at the entrance carrying the smell of rain.

"Nae, I will not. You have your *sgian dubh* in yon bag. I'll not provide you with weapons to shoot us down on our return. You'll be safe. I'll conceal the entrance with the brush and tree branches when I leave."

She snapped her hand away and flashed a furious frown at him. How dare he accuse her of being a threat? Hadn't she been helping in every way possible? She had tended his wounded brother with the same care she might extend her own brother, if she had one. Obviously, she should hold her tongue because if she were in his position she wouldn't trust him either, but she lashed out anyway.

"So you won't give me a weapon for our defense but you'll entrust me with the care of your brother. How can I protect us if someone comes? What if his condition worsens, and I need your help?" Her voice escalated in pitch from anger and more than a touch of fear. "Perhaps I should just run off, leave the lot of you to your own devices?" An empty threat to be sure.

"Why do you constantly challenge and defy me?" A scowl deepened the lines on his forehead. It was obvious he was not accustomed to anyone, especially a woman, a Sassenach no less, questioning his commands. If he thought she had been challenging so far, an even bigger surprise awaited when she found a way to return home. On the other hand, based on current circumstances, she'd more than likely be the one surprised. Shocked to her toes, no doubt.

He gripped her shoulder with a firm hand. "You'll be staying here tending to Lorne as I instruct you. God help you if any harm befalls him. Do you understand me, Andra?" His fingers bit into her shoulder as he gave a firm, warning shake. She didn't think he meant her any harm, but she was tired, aggravated, and frightened, which she certainly would not admit to him.

She lifted her face to his in defiance, fire meeting fire; a conflagration exploded between them. She would not be cowed and stood her ground, trying desperately to conceal her trembling. Before either of them turned away his hand moved to the back of her head, his lips crushed onto hers, his tongue probed her mouth and God help her, she returned his kiss with her own ferocity as he pulled her more tightly against the hard planes of his chest.

She clutched his shoulders to steady herself. The intensity of their encounter was a revelation, one she'd best not examine too closely. Reluctantly, she pushed him away, urging herself toward some modicum of control. Neither one of them spoke. She felt adrift when his hand dropped away. Cool evening air doused the heat between them.

His gaze strayed to her mouth. In response, she parted her lips, still wet from his probing. She licked the strange taste of whisky and mint left there from his kiss, and his eyes darkened under heavy lids. Swiftly, he moved out of the cave, threw the brush across the entrance, and left without another word.

Andra wrapped her arms around her middle and watched him disappear into the blackness. Suddenly her world felt very empty.

Lorne coughed roughly, drawing Andra's attention from the blistering confusion of her emotions. "You're awake. Do you think you can take a bit of tea?" She had a few herbal tea bags in her case. Her trusty, well-packed case carried a wealth of things she would sorely miss once those supplies disappeared, should she fail to find a way out of this era. No! She could not allow her thoughts to dwell on that problem; it required enough fortitude just to get by hour to hour.

With a gravelly voice unused for the past few days, Lorne asked, "So, I was nae dreaming, I really did see a spirited water sprite take my brother in hand. How long have I been unconscious? It seems I've missed some interesting entanglements." He laughed, which caused another harsh spat of coughing.

"Rest your voice for a minute. I'll fix you a cup of reviving tea." Andra smiled as she searched inside her bag.

"Och, lass, tea is nae a fit drink for an injured man." He croaked out of parched lips. "Bring me yon flask. A bit of the *uisge beatha* is what I'm need'n."

She did as he bade but also filled a cup with hot water from the pot over the fire and steeped the tea bag. Lorne needed as much fluid replenishment as possible. It couldn't hurt to add a drop of whisky to the tea if it would encourage him to drink. She even relinquished one of her precious packets of honey and voila, she'd made a traditional hot toddy. She sipped it first to gage the temperature and then helped Lorne lean his back against her so he could sip the concoction.

"Mmm, my fiery sprite, 'tis just what my weary bones be need'n. The angels' brew to be certain." He continued sipping and examined Andra with curious eyes. "Well now, who are you and how do you be kenning my brother? He seems quite smitten. 'Tis an uncommon state for our usually stern, reserved laird. He prefers distance and rarely looks on a lass with such—interest." He paused and leaned against her, his eyes closed.

She thought he'd fallen asleep again and moved to place him back on his pallet when he clutched her wrist. "Your name? Or should I continue to call you Sprite?" He turned slightly so he could see her face; his expression betrayed a hint of humor. His eyes, a lighter shade of blue than his brother's, turned just as penetrating when he focused his attention on her.

It seemed he'd observed quite a lot in his moments of lucidity. Including that embarrassing moment when she flipped Kendrick into the pool and ran from the cave in a near naked state. Was there to be no end to her self-inflicted mortification?

She moved from behind him to stoke the fire. "My name's Andra." When she turned, his intense scrutiny and furrowed brow suggested a barrage of unspoken questions.

"And you are a Sassenach?" He flicked his fingers toward her hands. "Would it be Lady Andra, then, and what would be your family's name?"

She looked at the rings on her fingers and felt a deep pang of loss for her parents. "It's a long story for another time. Right now, you need to finish that drink and take a few more of these tablets. Let us see if we can rest a while, and we'll have that chat later." Leaning on his elbows, he finished the tea while watching her with eyes stark with pain. When he fell back, she pulled the covers snugly around Lorne and returned to her own pallet by the fire.

"I think 'tis an enchanting story you have to tell, Sprite," he said in a tired, weary voice. "I look forward to learning all your secrets, and the secrets between you and my brother. I'm verra good at uncovering secrets, you ken." Closing his eyes, he drifted into a deep sleep, the first restful state she had seen him in since the beginning of this madness.

Andra lay in the dark, staring at the burning coals. Everything was happening too quickly. Why she was reacting with such heated passion to Kendrick, a man from over three hundred years in her past about whom she knew nothing?

That wasn't true. She'd witnessed his concern for his brother, and on occasion a flash of humor, although he tried to conceal it under all that lairdly bluster. He'd been extraordinarily kind to her under the circumstances. His roguish appearance and strong physique appealed to her. She also knew he did not trust her one wit.

The blatant desire that flared between them when his lips had touched hers before he left still rattled her. It was so out of character for her to fall head over heels for a man she barely knew. For any man, actually. This sense of freefall baffled her. What could explain her bizarre behavior? She wouldn't even try to analyze Kendrick's reactions to her.

Had it only been two days since her slip through time? It felt like weeks. Did time accelerate when you pierced that mystifying veil?

"Well, out of time, out of character, I suppose. Oh, God I am losing my mind," she whispered to the chill air.

Chapter Eight

Andra wanted to sink deeper into sleep but something more disturbing than nightmares pushed her to wakefulness. Shivering and cold her eyes opened to rest upon the last glowing embers on the fire then flicked through the darkness surrounding her. Once again, the shock of her circumstances slammed her senses leaving her disoriented for several minutes. How long had she been asleep? Aside from Lorne's quiet snores, the cave appeared empty. She could barely see the entrance. She added some sticks and peat to the fire and checked on Lorne. He appeared to be sleeping more easily and after their few words, she believed he would recover. A hand to his forehead confirmed that his fever, though still warm, was substantially lower, approaching normal.

She rose quietly and went outside to tend her needs. Pushing past the brush at the entrance, she lifted her face to a sky bright with stars. A pale sliver of moon hung on the horizon above an inky black forest. She couldn't ever remember such quiet. The small sounds of critters scurrying under leaf cover entered her awareness. An owl hooted and she spied the white underside of its great wings gliding across the craggy escarpment. It swooped down and snatched an unsuspecting mouse in its talons. She felt a bit like that mouse, just a scuttling little creature snatched by the razor talons of a mysterious destiny.

Her fingers drifted to her cross and then to her lips where she could still feel the pressure of Kendrick's kiss. Prickling heat infused her skin. "This is ridiculous," she whispered to the stars. "I'm suffering from Stockholm syndrome; it's that business of developing an incomprehensible attraction to one's captor."

Where was he anyway? Where were the other men? How long had she slept? Questions hammered into her brain one after another. She suspected it might be near dawn as the first chatter of birds rose from the trees. Raising her arms in a wide stretch and sucking in a deep, cleansing breath, her nose filled with the faint smell of smoke.

"Where is that coming from?" All her senses went on alert. Was there another camp nearby? If enemies were pursuing them, could the smoke be from their campsite? She climbed to the top of the ridge. A strong wind carried the sharp, acrid smell of fire, though she couldn't see flames. She questioned whether she should leave the shelter of the cave. She could not ignore a possible threat and Lorne still slept.

Chills rippled over her skin, and not from the cool air. "I'm strong. It's sensible to know what dangers we face." Andra ran miles every day up and down the hills in San Francisco. She had studied self-defense. If nothing else, she needed to consider reinforcing the brush concealing the cave's entrance.

A path of sorts, most likely a deer trail, wound up the hill. She decided to follow it. After tying her long skirt into a knot high on her hip, she stretched out her long, legging-covered limbs and moved into an easy slow gait, taking as much care as possible not to trip.

The sky turned from a shade of dark slate to a deep grayish-purple, then dusty gray. Her vision grew accustomed to the faint light. The smell of fire grew stronger the farther she ran into the woods until the air hung heavy with smoke. Stretching her gait, she increased her speed. The old, familiar burn of a good run seared her legs. Something wild and frightening coiled in her gut, but she could not escape the urgent need to run faster and faster. Eventually plumes of dark smoke billowed over the hill ahead. Keeping the upper part of the ridge to her left, she skirted around trees, and through brambles and tangled underbrush that scratched at her limbs.

When Kendrick had departed last night, she was certain he went in the opposite direction, so she didn't think he would be at the end of her mad rush. Something beyond reason drove her on.

Alert to every sound—the pounding of her feet on the soft earth, the late or early movement of wildlife scattering in the undergrowth away from the fire, the sudden cessation of birdsong—all penetrated her awareness with a cloying dread. Then the sound of people struggling and the anguished cries of fear assaulted her. She worked her way through thick brush to the top of the hill and peered down on an unholy horror. Covering her mouth, she choked back the scream that almost escaped her throat.

Flames engulfed several small crofts and the surrounding fields. The dying shrieks from inside the walls of the burning cottages tore the air and mingled with the moans from those fallen outside. Everywhere she looked lay mangled bodies. A company of English militia and a few men wearing dark, Scottish plaids were viciously murdering the people who struggled to crawl away. A couple of men dragged the limp form of a woman tearing away her clothes.

Andra's knees buckled as she ducked down and slunk behind a tree. Bile rose in her throat. The metallic taste of blood flowed over her tongue from biting hard on knuckles jammed in her mouth to prevent a terrified scream from escaping.

Andra turned away from the hell below. About to flee, a movement in the trees caught her eye. Two children ran for cover through thick brush and the shelter of darker forest. She ran after them, hoping to help them hide or escape. Her speed and long stride brought her beside them quickly. They opened their mouths to scream, but only the shrieks of the dying filled her ears. Her heart pounded fiercely in her chest until she thought it might explode. Gulping deep breaths of choking air, she realized it would be foolish to speak. The children might think she was with the English who were destroying their homes.

She raised her hand to her lips and whispered, "Shushshsh," pointing in the direction from where they had fled. Then she pointed in the direction she had come from and motioned they should go that way. A girl of perhaps twelve or thirteen years of age clung desperately to the hand of a small boy about four years old. The girl's eyes were wide with terror, her lips trembled, and the boy at her side started to whimper.

Andra shushed them again and lifted the lad to her chest, patting his back. His small arms instantly gripped her neck and he hid his face on her shoulder. She tucked his legs around her waist, then grabbed the girl's hand and ran as fast as possible, dragging the girl with her.

Never had she run so fast yet felt so slow. How many miles had she run before reaching this nightmarish scene, seven, eight, maybe more—bringing those murderous bastards far too close to their hideout. She ran and ran until she could run no farther then stopped, sucking great gulps of air. She looked behind praying no one followed them.

She could hear the pounding of horses' hooves but the sound came from in front of them rather than from behind. Had the murderers managed to get ahead of them as they ran? She whipped her head in every direction searching for an escape when strong arms lifted her onto a horse. She dropped the young girl's hand but managed to hold onto the boy clutched to her chest when Kendrick's voice penetrated her terror.

"Be still, you foolish woman, and hold your *wheesht*." He said something to the boy in Gaelic she did not understand, but it stilled him in her arms. Through her hazed and scrambled brain, she recognized Struan as the other rider. He firmly held the young girl in his lap. Kendrick's arm crushed across her and the boy as she struggled to get air into her lungs. They rode over the hill away from the direction of the cave and the mayhem behind them and into a thicker forest of trees.

They traveled many miles further than she had run. The men maneuvered the horses along a torturous route winding through a steep valley thick with mist, crossing several small streams until they turned up another steep incline. At the hill's summit, the fog dissipated to reveal a rider on his horse.

Rabbie walked his mount toward them. He circled to their rear and swept away their tracks using long lengths of brush and tree branches attached to the back of his horse. Soon, they were once again skirting the rocky scrabble leading up to the cave. All sense of time and direction had slipped away. No one had spoken a single word. A rumble of thunder and foreboding dark clouds moved fast in their direction, promising another storm would soon reach them. At least a good rain might wash away any trace of their passing. When they entered the cave, Struan set the girl aside and pulled clumps of brush and trees across the entrance.

Rabbie dismounted swiftly and removed the boy from Andra's arms, whispering soothing Gaelic in his ear. Kendrick swung down and pulled Andra after him. His hands gripped her shoulders tightly and he shook her brutally. His eyes glowed with heat and anger. A rigid band of sinew clenched with tension along his jaw.

"Are you mad, woman? I leave you with precise instructions to stay in the cave and care for Lorne. And what do you do? You abandon my brother, tear off into the night, and nearly bring yourself into the hands of our enemies."

He shook her forcefully again, "Are you one of them, then. Do you seek to bring them to our hiding place and have us murdered?"

She sputtered, then tightened her mouth and hardened her glare. With a quick thrust of her arms, she tried to break his hold, but he anticipated her maneuver this time. At the same moment she raised her arms, he flung her back with such force she flew like a leaf and landed hard on her rump. The children were huddled beside her like frightened, weeping kittens burrowing against the wall.

Jumping off the ground with a need to vent her terror and frustration, she ran at him flailing balled fists against his chest. "You stupid–boorish–brutal–bastard" with each word she hit him again and screamed in his face. Everyone and everything else faded away. Just the two of them remained, facing off in heat and fury.

* * *

Kendrick gripped her upper arms, expecting her to quiet. Instead, she moved into him and once again tried to flip her leg behind his. Needing to get her under control before he lost all semblance of rational thought, he lifted her off the ground, her arms pinned to her sides. She kicked at his groin and missed her mark, landing a booted foot on his unyielding thigh. Despite her struggles, she was no match for his strength. He easily spun her around as if she were only a stick. He tightly wrapped his forearm under her breast, and he pulled her roughly to his chest. He yelled at Rabbie to bring a rope and gag. Andra struggled fiercely, and managed to release one hand, which she used to claw and scratch at his arms. She continued kicking against his legs, landing a few blows that would undoubtedly leave bruises. When she started to shriek, he placed one hand over her nose and mouth. After a few tense moments, her movements slowed and she passed out.

Rabbie came toward Kendrick, his hands palm up in front of him as if calming a wild horse. "What possesses you, cousin? Hand me the lass."

Kendrick's breathing came rough and hoarse through his throat as he stared at his friend. His jaw ached with tension; his mouth clamped tight enough to break teeth.

What was wrong with him? He never lost control, not even in the heat of battle with men raging in full combat. Kendrick did not permit himself to experience fear, not for himself, his men, not even the people in his care. He had schooled long and hard to bury that emotion behind the skill and experience gained in many battles.

He had allowed fear to grip him twice before, once in his first battle. It had cost the lives of a few good men and friends. The second time happened shortly after he had assumed the role of laird. His father's illness prevented him from continuing in that role and he seemed ready to relinquish the responsibilities to his eldest son.

Kendrick always knew he would eventually bear that mantle. Unfortunately, many calamities befell him in those early years as laird. The clan suffered significant financial losses from the Darien Scheme, which sought to establish a Scottish colony in Panama. Kendrick had been the one to suggest they invest their reserves in that scheme, even before he'd become laird. There had been poor crop returns for several years, causing food shortages throughout the land. In addition, within a few months of becoming laird, Kendrick's young wife and son died following the bairn's birth. After that event, overwhelmed with feelings of inadequacy, he seemed to lose his mind for a period.

For weeks at a time, he had rambled through the hills, drinking to excess, and wenching when the opportunity presented itself. No matter how far he roamed, he never found the oblivion he sought, or a release from his sense of failure. Reivers attacked the borders of his lands, stealing cattle the clan could ill afford to lose. Men were injured or lost, perhaps due to the lack of his direction and leadership.

His father had tried to manage in his absence, but his health deteriorated even further, and Lorne had not yet returned from university. He had been of little use to himself, much less to his clan and kin. Finally, Rabbie and Struan found him in the hills and engaged him in fierce hand-to-hand beatings. He withstood the worst of their lashings, and they refused to leave him alone. Either he would return to his home, clan, and responsibilities, or they swore to surrender their own lives in their effort to bring him to heel.

Fear and love. Two emotions no warrior could allow to reign; a lesson Kendrick took to heart once he had recovered his sense of self. From then on, he determined never to allow himself to succumb to the weakening sentiments of fear or love again. He had long buried his heart and emotions behind steel barriers.

Yet, when they had returned and discovered Andra gone, his anger burned like a hot brand in his gut. The crazy, mad woman, who seemed to fall out of the sky into their path, tested every reserve of patience he possessed. Intriguing, secretive, maddeningly obtuse, she definitely fired his loins, which disturbed him no end. He strived to convince himself the woman presented nothing more than a troubling puzzle to solve, but he failed.

When he'd raced over that hill, nostrils burning with the smell of fire, the sound of battle-crazed men in the distance, the screams of women rending the early dawn air, fear had gripped him like a vice. Then he saw her, head snapping around wildly in the smoky half-light, hair flying out in a tangled mess, with two children clinging to her limbs. He could have wept with relief and he never wept.

"Laird?" Rabbie moved to take Andra and softened his voice, "Laird?"

Rabbie never addressed him by the honorific title "laird" unless upset with him or trying to prove a point. Rabbie was Kendrick's second cousin from his father's side but as close to him as he and his brother Lorne. In fact, no one came closer in friendship and esteem, with Struan a close third.

Kendrick swung Andra into his arms pressing her limp body against his chest. "Nae cousin, nae, I'll tend to her myself. You see to the bairns and have Struan tend the horses."

He could feel their astonished faces follow him as he walked to the pool at the back of the cave. He sat on the edge of the rocks thinking how only a day ago she had been standing in this exact spot disrobing in front of him, enticing him with her every move. He ripped a piece of cloth off the bottom of his shirt and wiped her face with cool water. When she started to come around, she struggled against him. He held both wrists in one hand and pulled her tight against him.

"Calm yourself, lass; it's over now, you're safe." He kept his voice soothing and low.

Eyes venomous with anger glared at him. "Safe! Safe! Safe from whom? Safe from those murdering men, safe from you?" she spit out.

Grinding his teeth, the muscles in his jaw grew almost painful as he reined in his temper. He battled between the urge to throttle her or pull her into a fierce, protective embrace. Throttle won or at least a verbal throttling.

"Listen, Andra, and listen well. I am not a violent man unless necessary, but those are my men. I am their laird. They must trust me to lead them into battle, through the verra gates of hell when required. I will not allow any lass, no matter how comely or distressed she appears, to interfere with my authority or the safety my men."

Her mouth dropped open. Did she find him shocking? *Good. She needed a shock.*

"I expect absolute obedience from my people and my men. Do not disobey me again. And never attempt to knock me down or strike me for you will not win and only injure yourself. I gave you my word we'd protect you despite the fact that your story reeks of perfidy. You will not be endangering everyone with your foolish recklessness. When I give you an order, you will follow it."

She blinked at him her mouth agape. "I am not your property, nor one of your men to jump and obey your every command!" she seethed through her teeth, tugging valiantly against his grip.

"Now there you're wrong, Andra. You are my property until I say otherwise. If you dinnae start answering my questions, or you run off again, I will tie you up until we reach my castle. If you give me your word, which I am not sure is worth anything, I will refrain from tying you up tonight. Those poor bairns have just witnessed the murder of their kith and kin. They could use a woman's gentling." His arms tightened around her rather than loosened.

She flashed a furious scowl at him. "What the hell do you think happened here? I woke, I smelled smoke, and no one was here. It seemed reasonable to investigate. And those bairns might not have escaped without my help."

They locked eyes in another silent battle of wills. She blinked up at him, her body still shaking under his grip, but rather than show deference, she kept her chin thrust in defiance. He could see he'd accomplish nothing further tonight and needed to step away from her heat and his own intemperate mood. He stood, gently but firmly set her on her feet, and strolled over to his men.

* * *

Well, it would seem this fight was over. Andra didn't know whether to cry or kick the man in his finely muscled, departing derriere. "Urrr, men!" she hissed.

But his words slipped back into her head: *I will not allow a lass, no matter how comely...* So, he thought her comely—distressed (which was true), and accused her of duplicity all in one breath. Okay, she'd grant he thought her duplicitous or evasive, but she struggled with a problem he couldn't even fathom. Adrenaline still pumped through her blood from fear, exhaustion, and a weird exhilaration from the feel of his strong arms around her. *Well, that would never do.*

She stamped her foot, and with stumbling steps walked to where Rabbie sat on a pallet by the fire, giving the children something to drink. A tartan plaid draped across their small shoulders, and he spoke to them in soothing tones.

He looked up with a crooked half smile. "Are you well m'lady?"

She tilted her head and studied him for a moment. "Well enough. How are the children?"

"Frightened, but calming down. You did a brave thing helping them to escape."

"Some people don't share your opinion." She dipped her chin toward the bairns, "Do they speak English?"

"Dinnae worry, they will understand you, but they are reluctant to speak." He nodded his head, and walked to join the men seated beside Lorne, talking in low voices.

Andra sat and wiped the children's faces with a cool, wet cloth. She held out her arms to the lad, and he went to her easily. The boy still whimpered a bit, and the girl stared off into space, her face a frozen mask. Andra cradled the lad's head against her chest, wrapped the other arm around the girl, and began to sing "All The Pretty Little Horses."

The men were a wall of silence behind her, even their movements had ceased. Andra blocked them from her mind and finished the song while rocking the children held in her arms. Her eyes closed, and tears streamed down her face. She sought to erase the horrors of this night and guide them all to restful sleep with the soothing melody.

Chapter Nine

Andra woke with a start to sounds of movement in the cave. Each time she woke, she experienced a moment where she thought everything had been a terrible, dreadful dream. Then reality smashed a fist into her consciousness; she remained in another time and place. The realization came in the form of children snuggled close against her. The girl's hand draped protectively on the boy's back. Trying not to disturb their sleep, she moved away slowly.

As she walked toward the exit, Lorne entered the cave, one arm across Struan's shoulder with Struan's burly strength supporting his weight. He walked with agonizingly slow steps, but at least he walked.

Outside the sky remained dark. A faint tinge of violet suggested the approach of dawn. When she started to pass the men, Struan grunted and stopped her.

"Where do you think you be go'n?"

A frustrated groan escaped her lips. "A moment of privacy is all I need."

"Then I'll be accompanying you. Just let me settle Lorne." His voice commanding and rough, as though he'd swallowed a mouth full of gravel.

"Dinnae scare the lass with all that bluster." Lorne looked at Andra, a smile on his face. "Best let him stand guard, there's nae tell'en who may be aboot. Besides, Struan is a wee bit cranky in the morning."

"Seems to me he's always cranky," Andra huffed, but she waited for him by the cave's entrance.

* * *

Kendrick and Rabbie were not present. Andra decided not to inquire after them and busied herself with the care of the children. Relinquishing a pack of her strong breakfast tea and another packet of honey, which she opened away from prying eyes, she prepared to break their fast. Everyone enjoyed the honeyed tea, even Lorne and Struan, who took theirs with a dram or two of whisky.

"Well now, finally something worthwhile from that there witch's satchel of yers," Struan commented. Though he goaded her with a slight hint of humor, an accusatory expression remained on his face. A retort rose to her lips, but then she thought it best to avoid confrontation and ignored him.

The children still wore their dirty, torn night shifts, were barefooted and covered in cuts and scratches from their escape through the night. Andra convinced them to relinquish their clothes for washing in exchange for warm plaids.

After she had thoroughly examined and cleaned their injuries, Andra's last two pairs of clean, dry socks adorned their feet. "What dae ye call these again?" asked Kyle, an amber-eyed, freckle faced charmer with hair the color of autumn leaves. He wriggled his toes, endlessly fascinated with the snugness of the socks several sizes too large, but they kept his feet warm and dry.

"They are called socks where I come from."

The boy assessed her with a frown on his forehead. "Ye say yer nae a Sassenach but ye talk funny, like a Sassenach but nae the same."

"Oh, have you talked to many Sassenachs, then?" she chided him lightly.

"Nae, but ye dinnae speak like a proper Scots lady." He sighed, looking at her with penetrating eyes for one so young.

"Well, I am Scots through and through, though I have been away for a verra long time. I haven't been in Scotland since I was a verra wee bairn and have nae memory of it." Andra added a few Scottish terms to put the children at ease.

The girl, Senga, slender and quiet, with hair the same rich color as her brother's and eyes like dark, round chocolate drops, had not said a word to her. Andra worried about Senga's silence,

64

but she would not push her to speak before she was ready.

The children were both far too thin with dark circles under haunted eyes. Wherever Andra went, Senga meekly followed head down, arms limp at her sides, but she would not speak or look directly at anyone other than her brother.

Once thoroughly washed, the many cuts and scratches tended, with warm socks on her feet and one of Andra's long knit shirts pulled over the girl's slender frame, Andra wrapped her in a warm dry plaid and sat her between her knees. Brandishing her horsehair brush, she untangled the girl's long tresses with smooth, even strokes. It was a soothing task, one Andra could barely remember between herself and her mother.

"How old are you, Kyle?" Andra asked.

"I be five years. And me sister be ten and four. Me older brathair died," he puffed out his cheeks and expelled a sad, little sigh.

Humming a soothing lullaby, Andra brushed Senga's hair while Kyle leaned against her side rubbing his little fingers over the smooth leather of her vest. Every so often, the boy hummed along with her, hopelessly out of tune…His voice halted every few bars with soft sighs. She plaited the girl's hair into a long French braid and tied off the bottom with a thin strip of linen formed into a bow.

"Well now, aren't you the most beautiful, young lass in all of Scotland?" The praise elicited a dip of the girl's chin. If it dropped any further, her neck would snap at the back. Gliding her fingers along the girl's hair, she wanted so much to pull her into an embrace, but the child would not welcome it. "I'm here if you want to talk with me," she whispered.

She had never been around children so quiet. The grievous shock they had suffered would scar any child and silence many for life. A pain pierced her heart. Her ministrations aroused an ache, never far from the surface, for her own lost child whom she had held for only a few hours before he died. Even now, she could still feel his slight weight absent from her ever-empty arms. When the children went to explore the waterfall and pools, Andra turned to attend Lorne's injuries.

"You have a way with the bairns. Do you have any of your own?" he asked.

Instinctively her hand pressed against her lower abdomen.

" 'Tis a painful memory that presses on you?" He placed a hand gently over the hand she rested on her thigh.

A wrenching recollection moved her to change the subject. "Do you think they have other family who will care for them? I wish I could assure them everything will be well in time." She truly ached to snuggle these babes and give them assurance, but she knew the history of this time. Nothing would ever be easy or all right if the children were now orphans. Yet, if they had kin somewhere, surely they would offer care and shelter. Her father had always regaled her with stories of the Highlanders' honor and love of family.

She lifted her eyes to Lorne's, "I must seem very foolish." In that moment, she knew she would do everything in her power to help them locate any remaining family. There had to be something she could do for them before she found a way to return to her own time.

"Dinnae fash yourself. Highlanders will not abandon bairns to the elements. If no kin are found, our clan will provide for them."

Chapter Ten

After carefully searching the area around the sight of the previous night's butchery, Kendrick and Rabbie set about burying the dead. Nothing remained in the crofts to salvage for the children. The burned ruins of three small crofts and a byre held nothing of value. A few scattered, tools rusted and dented by age and use, proved useful for digging the graves. Vermin still ravaged the slaughtered remains of a few. If there had been other survivors, human or animal, no evidence existed. They found a scrap of Cameron plaid clutched in a dead woman's hand. They both growled in their throats and cursed the bastards and all the Sassenach who raped and pillaged their land.

Under a cerulean sky mounded with frothy clouds, they worked with quick efficiency. The English could be anywhere nearby and discovery would not bode well for them. Nevertheless, the dead needed burying and words spoken over their remains. Despite a slight chill in the air, sweat dripped from their chests and arms.

Kendrick's thoughts kept returning to the previous night and the image of Andra rocking the bairns and singing that haunting song. Her clear, sweet voice still rang in his head. No matter how hard he tried to close himself off from his attraction to her, the woman seeped into every fiber of his being. Every maddening, irritating, or generous thing she did unfurled another thread of mystery and wove straight into his long-cold heart.

She claimed her name was Cameron but insisted she did not know her clan. Could this be true or had she rescued the children over shame for the brutality of her clansmen? He did not want to believe a connection existed between her and Cormag Cameron or anyone associated with him.

"What do you think of the lass, Rabbie? Do you think there's a connection between her and our enemies? Perhaps she is trying to escape them."

Rabbie wiped sweat from his forehead and remained thoughtful for a moment. "She is a conundrum to be certain. While she's reluctant to answer your questions, she tries to help where she can. Her clothing is unusual and her jewelry expensive. The lass has been kind, thoughtful, reserved, and at times outlandishly amusing. She has more than a little fire in her, and I've never heard a sweeter voice. She could make the angels weep.

"I am inclined to believe she speaks the truth and doesnae ken her Scottish clan, which I agree, is quite peculiar. The fact that she speaks but a few words of her native tongue is the most troubling thing to me."

Rabbie glanced at his cousin, whose gaze scanned to the heavens. "Do you think to divine the answers from the sky, then? She is comely to be sure. You better be careful. I think she has caught you in her web." He chuckled, an attempt to add a bit of levity to an otherwise onerous day.

Kendrick harrumphed in response and applied himself to their task more rigorously. He could not explain the feelings exploding in his chest to himself, much less to anyone else. He admired the amazing gentleness Andra had displayed with the children, and when she sang to them, a hard lump had formed in his throat. In all his travels, he had never heard a song like the one she'd sung last night.

On their return trip to the hideout, they dipped into a nearby loch to wash the burnt stench from their clothes and noses. Kendrick ran his hands through his wet hair. "At least we can have some meat tonight. I'm near famished." A few squirrels and rabbits retrieved from Rabbie's snares hung from their saddles.

"My stomach growls louder than a wildcat." Rabbie chuckled, and then grew serious. "What are we going to do about the Cameron menace?"

Kendrick abhorred the idea of starting a clan war over the loathsome Camerons. There had been more than enough strife to beleaguer the clans. Constant skirmishes with the Sassenachs and the border clans who sought alliances with them kept everyone on edge. Many Highland clans hovered on the brink of starvation.

"I'm not exactly certain. Though I'm not in favor of taxing our people further, we must find a way to settle this matter with Cormag and his clan for the last time. If he seeks war, he will soon find it. I plan to discuss it with father and meet with our allied clans as soon as possible."

"Aye, there has been much to beleaguer us; not to mention the loss of wealth in the failed Darien Scheme. It was good you stayed away from that misadventure."

"I lost my share, cousin, but there's no sense worrying over the past. There's more than enough trouble brewing. Especially now that Queen Anne has passed the Alien Act, one more blow preventing our ability to trade with the southlands, the French, or the colonies. There's plenty of talk about bringing back the Prince. Yet other clans grow weary and consider a union with England the only solution."

Kendrick grew silent and stared toward their destination.

"You're thinking about her, I can tell. It appears a pretty, green-eyed lass has kindled her own sort of trouble with you."

"Leave it be, Rabbie." Thoughts of her consumed him, but he certainly wouldn't admit his growing obsession, nor would he discuss the matter with his cousin.

* * *

Andra was tucking the children under their blankets when Kendrick and Rabbie entered the cave. She acknowledged their entrance with a brief glance over her shoulder. Rabbie flashed a brilliant smile at her, which she returned. A stab of jealousy hit Kendrick and he shot her an angry scowl. She blithely ignored him, turned away, straightened her back, and rested her pert, little butt on her heels. One minute in her presence and she already attracted and irritated him. It felt like a sharp barb had lodged in his brain.

Senga reached out and tentatively touched a finger to Andra's hand. "What is it you need, Senga?" The girl turned her face away.

Kyle answered. "Will ye sing for us, Lady Andra?"

Kendrick noticed all the men turned toward the little group when Kyle made his request. Andra bent forward, kissed the wee ones' cheeks, and sang. When the words, *"Amazing grace, how sweet the sound that saved a wretch like me,"* rang out everything hushed but her crisp soprano voice, which seemed to bind their souls in a song-like prayer both tender and profound. When the verse, *"'Tis grace has brought me safe thus far, And grace will lead me home,"* something hard knocked in his chest. Kendrick noticed the other men dip their chins, and clasp their hands in front of their bodies in a pose of suspended reverence.

As the last note reverberated through the cave, she kissed the children, snugly tucked them into the plaids and whispered, "Good night, sweet lambs."

Andra appeared to collapse into herself and struggle for breath. When she turned toward them, her face twisted in anguish and her eyes glistened with moisture. Tears spilled over the rim of her lashes and streaked down her face. Bunching her skirt in her hands, she darted into the night. No one stopped her. The men looked away from each other as though embarrassed or confused over what to do.

After a moment of hesitation, Kendrick followed her outside but stayed back a few feet, uncertain how to approach. A terrible torment seemed to possess the lass. She shook with pitiful, wrenching sobs and pounded the ground with her fists crying out to her father. "Please Dad, please, please, send me back home. Oh God, how can I survive here?"

What could she possibly mean by those words? It didn't matter; he would untangle her words later. For now, an overwhelming urge to wrap her in his arms swamped him. He felt an urgent need to protect and shelter her from whatever caused such searing pain. It took every ounce of reserve he possessed to permit her this release without interference. The brave, obstinate, defiant lass she'd seemed up until this moment bled into the ground along with her tears. He could not leave her in this disheveled heap, sobbing into the dirt.

Approaching cautiously, he knelt and touched her shoulder. "Lass?" She flinched but did not pull away. After a few moments of hitching sobs, she turned into his arms and clung to his neck. She cupped his stubbled cheek with a cool hand and pressed her face into his shoulder.

He wiped her tear-stained face with his thumbs, and brushed back silky strands of hair that always managed to escape her braid. Resistance was impossible. He kissed her hair, her forehead, her eyes; he tasted the salt on her cheeks and lips. Gently at first and then with riveting passion they pressed into each other, grasping, claiming. His desire for her penetrated his bones straight to the marrow.

With eyes wide open, she searched his face, perhaps seeking words he knew not how to give. With an expression full of aching need, she lifted her lips to his and granted him a quenching kiss. Never separating from his mouth, she pulled him beside her onto a bed of pine needles and fallen leaves.

"A stór, you taste sweet and salty." Kendrick suckled her lower lip, invaded her mouth with his tongue.

She matched him stroke for stroke. His hands traced the line of her neck, across her chest, along her ribs, squeezing at the curve of her waist. She turned into him more fully. He continued his exploration along the full roundness of her hip and tight buttocks. Her hands moved across his arms, shoulders, up his neck and tangled into his hair.

Some part of his thoughts screamed, *"This is not right. You should not compromise her in this vulnerable state."* Nevertheless, he wanted her, craved her touch, and needed her passion as much as she needed his. Ignoring the reservations tugging at his conscience, he ravished her mouth and slipped his hand under her shirt to cup her breast. A breast holstered in the same silky contraption she had worn by the pool. He remembered the pink blush of color that almost matched the flush on her milky skin. His thumb circled over the puckered bead under the silken fabric.

She moaned and lifted fully into his palm.

Pulling his shirt out of his plaid, she slid soft cool hands over his abdomen. Long, slender fingers raked through the wiry hair on his chest then followed the thin line that continued down past his belly. She stopped just past his waist and sat up to wriggle out of her vest. They spoke no words, each pulsing with intense need.

He helped pull her shirt over her head. Even in the dim light, her skin glowed like polished pearls. He pressed his lips to her neck, nipping and drawing kisses down her chest and took the tip of her breast, silk material and all, into his mouth. Her hands reached behind her back to unfasten her silky undergarment. She pushed him away and let her full breasts spill out.

"I rather enjoyed the feel of you through that silken holster." But the heat of her unadorned, rosy flesh was far more enticing.

"Shush," she quieted him. Unpinning his plaid, she pulled his shirt over his shoulders, fumbled with his belt to release his kilt, sporran, and the dirk strapped there.

Kendrick briefly held her apart from him. He was no monster to take advantage of her in a moment of extreme distress. "*Mo chuisle*, I burn for you, I do, but I will stop if you wish it. Just say the word. Are you certain you want to continue?"

Every fiber of his being wanted to claim her completely, wanted to plunge into her soft, heated folds and drown in the taste and smell of her. In spite of this urgent need, he held still, waiting for a response. He needed her acceptance.

Her voice was a husky whisper as she placed trembling fingers to his face. "This is so…unlike me. It has been a very long time since—," she continued to feather sweet kisses over his face and neck as she spoke and he could barely concentrate on her words. "I do not want to question it. All I know is what I feel. I want…" She faltered, and then laved her tongue along his neck and whispered, "I want this moment, this fire exploding between us. This madness is the only real thing worth having in a crazy, unreal world."

She nipped his earlobe sending a bolt straight to his loins where he hardened and thickened with need. Then she stood to pull off her skirt and those tantalizingly tight fitting trews. His hands cupped her breasts, then followed the descent of her clothes over full hips and down strong, firm legs, helping to push them away from her feet.

He tugged his plaid under them to serve as their bed. She stood before him naked, shivering, yet her flesh felt hot under his hands. Her fingers snaked through his hair while his rough hands rubbed over her taut buttock. One hand slipped across her hip and traced a finger along what appeared to be a long scar on her abdomen.

"How did you receive this injury, lass?" It was a significant scar; he wondered how she'd survived such a wound. When he opened his mouth to speak again, she touched her fingers to his lips to quell his questions. He pressed his face against her belly, kissing and nipping along the pink ridge. His hand slipped high between her thighs and a finger delved into her moist heat. His thumb rolled over her pleasure bud eliciting a throaty gasp from her lips.

Andra closed her eyes and lifted her knee to his shoulder, granting him access to her sensuous core. Piercing him with a look of pure need, she leaned against his hand supporting her lower back and buttocks, and flung her head back. He kissed and bit her inner thigh, flicked his tongue through her slit and tugged on her pearled nub. She moaned, gasped, and pulled his hair as he brought her to a crescendo of passion with his mouth.

The explosion caused her to vibrate in his hands, and he waited a moment for her to recover. He pressed his face against her warm belly and then pulled her down, under his body. Holding himself over her, his turgid shaft pressed against her wet entrance, he asked one last time, "You want me, Andra? Say it."

She wriggled under him pushing his throbbing tip into her folds, "Yes, yes please, now Kendrick, I want you. Now."

Her answer, heavy with desire, clutched at his soul. In one fluid motion, he entered her. He stilled to let her grow accustomed to his invasion. She lifted her hips and thrust hard bringing him to the hilt of her womb. He withdrew slowly, then thrust back, lifting them to higher and higher pinnacles of pleasure as their pace increased. Compelled to connect completely, he kissed, licked, and grasped her to him and she responded in kind; each consumed by the intricate dance of need. Their movements synchronized, and despite the newness of their acquaintance, it felt as though they had been engaged in this dance all of their lives.

"Andra, *a stór*," he moaned with a deep growl in the back of his throat, for she was already a treasure to him, even though he might try to deny it.

"Harder, Kendrick, more." she panted. Her legs wrapped around his hips and she raked her nails across his muscled back. The sound of his name called out in the throes of passion pulsed in his brain. He wanted to hear her call to him repeatedly.

"Say it again. Tell me you want me again."

When she cried out his name, he swallowed her voice, his tongue demanding and thrusting in rhythm with his hard shaft. Their vigorous joining, ravenous and without restraint, demanding in its fierceness, culminated with one, final explosion as they reached their climax in unison. He failed to withdraw before releasing his seed. Something he never did. She didn't seem concerned and consideration of the possible consequences faded from his thoughts when their passion had swept him up like a turbulent wild wave on a stormy sea.

He collapsed on top of her. The sweat from their bodies melded and cooled in the night air. The scent of sex mingled with the smell of mint and lemon, a scent that was hers alone. He tried to pull away thinking his weight too much, but she wrapped her arms and legs around him, clutching him tightly to her body. He reached behind and pulled a portion of his plaid over them.

"*Mo chuisle*. You have undone me completely." He lifted on his elbows and brushed damp hair away from her face, kissing her softly, gently touching her, still imbedded in her heat.

* * *

Andra thought she should be embarrassed, but she wasn't. For the first time in her life, she understood how sorrow, fury, and a fearful rush of adrenaline required a sexual release. Refusing to argue with herself over the insanity of her behavior, she relinquished all thought to his heat and the exquisite feel of his lavish invasion.

Their coupling had been more intense than anything Andra had previously experienced. She'd known very few lovers. Of course, Ray, the father of her child, rotten as he had turned out, was the worst. They had met in their last year of college. He had stolen her heart, then smashed it irrevocably with his thoughtless indifference. Following the car accident that claimed their baby's life, he visited her only a few times in the hospital and then disappeared. She never saw him again. In recent years, however, she had kept busy, helped her father with the pharmacy, worked on producing her own line of scented oils and body lotions, and stayed away from men and the painful memories they evoked.

There had never been a lover like Kendrick. Perhaps the extreme circumstances of where and when she found herself could account for her behavior. She did not care about the why, she felt sensually alive, as she hadn't in years, perhaps ever. The raw heat and sexual release helped burn away her pain and fear.

Her hands thrilled at the solid feel of him. His spicy, male scent, the musky smell of their loving and the heady aroma of pine surrounded them. The crisp, clean air held the scent of rain and damp earth. She was drowning in these new smells and sensations. Their sexual encounter might be the most reckless thing she had ever done in her life, but she'd not regret a single second of it.

Andra returned his light kisses and ran her hands through the sweat-soaked strands of his hair. "Perhaps we should dress and go back before someone comes looking for us."

He chuckled, but he did not pull away. "Nae, they'll not disturb us, my sweet."

A weighted sigh escaped her swollen lips. "Thank you, Kendrick."

"You thank me?" he sounded incredulous. "Why do you thank me for disregarding your virtue? For taking advantage of you in a moment of pain and distress?" He brushed his mouth against her forehead and gently cradled her face with hands that could easily crush.

She laughed at his musing and then realized he was serious.

"Well, I think I needed that. Perhaps we both needed that release."

"Aye, mayhap so. Do you often release your anxieties in such a manner?"

She tensed under him the moment the words escaped his mouth. "No, I do not! Don't let it swell your head, Laird MacLean." There was no doubt she'd needed that carnal release, but in hindsight, recognized it might reduce her standing with this powerful man. She pushed her fists hard against his chest, trying to roll away.

He tightened his hold on her. "Nae, Andra, forgive my foolishness. I meant no disrespect. It was a bad attempt at levity. You'll learn that about me. I'm not good with the witty repartee."

Her fingers reached to stroke through his hair and along his jaw. "I think we both craved that release, laird."

"Kendrick," he corrected. "After what we have just shared, you must call me Kendrick. Aye, I believe you're right. We both needed that passion. I'm truly sorry to have spoiled this perfect joining. Please forgive my—please accept my apology for any harm my words or deeds may have caused you."

She could hardly believe he asked her forgiveness.

He showered kisses over her face. "I'm thinking these past few days have unsettled you, Andra. Most women would have succumbed to weeping and wailing especially after the scene you witnessed yesterday. Have you witnessed battle before?"

Even now, he probed for answers about her past. "No Kendrick, all my battles have been of a different nature. What I witnessed last night was too terrifying for words. One could hardly refer to it as a battle—it was a complete massacre. If you don't mind, I'd rather not revisit it, especially now."

"Of course not," he soothed, pressing his lips to her temple. "You're a most amazing woman. I understand your need to relieve tension from these past days, and I'll not regret our joining. I hope you'll have no regrets either."

She patted his cheek and gave him a quick smile. "No regrets, Kendrick. Life is too short." *Where in the hell did that come from? All my relationships have been full of regrets. Well, no more.* Perhaps this was a turning point, no more regrets, no more self-recrimination. A good adage to live by, one with which her father would agree.

"We should go back," she repeated with barely a whisper and turned her head away from his renewed kissing and the swell increasing between her legs. She needed to regroup, gather her thoughts.

He hesitated a moment, pressed a kiss to her forehead, then rolled away and helped her up. They dressed in silence and dusted themselves off, brushing the leaf and pine debris from each other's clothing. When he gripped her butt and pulled her into his arms for one final, bruising kiss, evidence of his renewed arousal pressed firmly against her belly. Her nether regions wept in response. The man fulfilled every fantasy she'd ever held about lusty Highland lairds, and then he gently released her.

Though their arms brushed as they walked, they did not use their hands to touch. She stepped a few paces ahead of him when they reached the cave, and he permitted it. She entered with her head held high. Gliding past the men, she went to the pool in the rear of the cave. The men halted their conversation as she passed, then resumed talking as if nothing were amiss.

What must they think of me? Females were not so brazen in this time. In fact, women who slept with men outside of marriage were mistresses or whores or bar wenches, which was the same thing. They were chattel, had little or no rights, lived hard, grueling lives and frequently died early in childbirth. So why was she throwing herself at this man with complete abandon? She chose not to examine the answer to that question too closely.

The emotions welling inside her felt as foreign as going to Mars, or to a time as completely removed from her prior life as she could have ever imagined. Passion, fear, anxiety, inexplicable joy—how could one feel all that at the same time? Though she didn't want him or the others to have a low opinion of her, she refused to consider this recent diversion a mistake. Would it affect her safety with them? Possibly. Of course, it doubtless didn't matter, Kendrick being laird, could do as he pleased, and no one would take issue with him. Nothing could undo the deed and as she'd told him, she would not regret their loving. For now, she'd leave these worries for another day because it felt like her bones had turned to slush, and the sleep she so desperately needed might finally come.

Chapter Eleven

The following day passed in relative quiet. Andra and Kendrick exchanged a few discreet glances but did not converse other than a brief morning greeting before the men went on patrol. Andra stayed busy, tending the children who were still very withdrawn. Lorne improved steadily, despite being very weak. An easy banter was developing between them.

"Lass, I believe you owe me that story now. Your mystery intrigues me, and I assume we should be calling you m'lady, 'tis that not the truth of it?" He glanced at the rings on her fingers and the cross at her throat.

"Andra will do," she said, folding her hands into her lap.

His lips quirked into a smile but there was no humor in his eyes. He searched her face for answers but she had none to give and turned to check on the children.

He continued, "As Struan says, you seem to have a wealth of mysterious things in yon bag of yers, and you dress—well, unusual let us say. You speak with a strange tongue, like a Sassenach, but different. Struan tells me you're a Cameron as well. Now that is a frightful combination, being a Sassenach and a Cameron."

His dark-blond eyebrows hitched to the middle of his forehead, belying his attempt at casual regard. "How do you reckon we trust you when they are our fiercest enemies, a pack of reiving cutthroats who join the Sassenach when it suits their thieving purposes? From your own telling and your unusual accent, you seem to be both. Now, I dinnae wish to appear ungrateful for the help you have rendered on my behalf, but you can understand why these questions need answers. Surely you can tell me more of your kin or travels?"

She studied him carefully. Oh, how she ached to tell him the truth. Her head tilted slightly to the side, "I know you have many questions. As I've told your brother, much of what has happened is beyond my understanding. I do not know of any kin in Scotland. My father took us away when I was a baby, not even as old as Kyle is. My mother had already died. When my father lay on his deathbed, he requested I bring his ashes to Scotland. It is true that my family name is Cameron. Nevertheless, I do not know these Cameron of whom you speak. In fact, other than you and Kendrick's men, I know no one in Scotland. It is as much a mystery to me as to you."

"You speak aboot your father's ashes. You ken, what that suggests?"

She maintained steady eye contact when she responded, hoping that would help "I understand, but sometimes while in strange places, one must comply with their customs for safety purposes. And I could not travel such long distances transporting my father's dead body." Even to her ears that sounded like a paltry excuse.

Lorne grunted, shifted his position, and seemed to ponder her answer. "Hmm—you traveled to heathen lands, then?"

"On occasion, my father traveled with other men interested in learning about botanical plants and their medicinal properties." She hoped this answer would assuage his curiosity and not lead to further questions that might endanger her security. Didn't her kindness toward him and the bairns reveal her in an unthreatening light? Hadn't she displayed appropriate appreciation and deference? Well, except for last night. That proved to be appreciation of a completely different nature.

She deftly redirected their conversation. "Let's clean your wounds and change the bandages. If you are careful, you might want to get up and move about. It may prevent that leg from stiffening too severely."

"Ah, I see you'll not answer my questions now. Do not think to avoid our inquiries indefinitely. I like you, Andra. I think we'll become friends and eventually you'll give up those secrets you hold so tightly. 'Twould be best for all concerned if you did so sooner rather than later."

"Mmmm." Andra continued to redress Lorne's wounds. "I'd like nothing better than to answer all of your questions, but I can only provide answers to things I remember clearly. It does seem my memory became scrambled after I hit my head."

Lorne let the matter drop. The men returned later that night, accompanied by a man named John. The man stood several inches shorter and had a less pleasing countenance than her rescuers, but he equaled them in muscled strength. A bushy, unkempt beard and wildly windblown hair partially obscured his face. Yet he possessed the same Highlander focus—fierce and penetrating. He eyed her with avid curiosity as Kendrick introduced John as a member of the MacLean clan.

Andra had cooked the rabbits in a stew using dried oats for thickening, which she served to the men in crude wooden trenchers. They all ate voraciously while the men discussed leaving on the morrow. Other than a nod in her direction when she placed the meal into their hands, they did not include her in their conversation, though they did not hide their discussion by asking her to leave or by quieting their voices.

"I am willing to stay with you, Lorne, if you think you need more time before riding," offered John. "Now that me and the men have recovered most of the cattle, the Camerons seem to have withdrawn to their filthy castle again, lousy bastard's—er—beggin' yer pardon m'lady."

Evidently, John knew of her Cameron last name. He didn't seem to know what to make of Andra. None of the others offered any explanations about her presence, and she had no idea what they might have told him prior to his arrival.

"No offense, they are nothing to me," she said, "but you might want to consider your language when you speak around the little ones."

The astonished expressions on their faces made her want to laugh, but she refrained. Kendrick started to say something, then stopped when she turned away, leading the children to their pallets.

There would be no repeat of last night's events; she decided to keep her distance from Kendrick. What could she say to him? "*Oh, please forgive me for ripping off your clothes last night. I am just a wild, lustful woman out of time and place who's completely lost her mind!*" Not likely. Besides, in the light of a new day he seemed neither interested nor disturbed by the event. And why should he? As a hot, hunky Highland laird, women probably threw themselves at him all the time. She got what she needed, he got what he needed, and that would be the end of it.

Nevertheless, thoughts of his warm hands and mouth on her body made her nether regions wet with desire. *Stop it this instant, Andra.* She could not and would not become another sniveling conquest. Men of this era were likely to be as bad or worse as men from her time; she'd be just another notch on the proverbial belt.

She only needed to survive long enough to return home; yet thoughts of home only filled her with a grinding emptiness. Who was waiting for her? No one of importance needed her. Dad's partner at the pharmacy was more than capable of handling the business without her assistance. Her private line of hand creams and bath oils was not a burgeoning business that required her immediate attention. She turned her mind from these sad stressful thoughts. Instead, she sang to the children.

* * *

Listening to Andra sing brought the previous night's tryst to Kendrick's mind. He had bedded many women in his life, had even been married, but the intensity of their coupling profoundly disquieted him. His desire for her increased every time she glanced his direction. The scent and sight of her conspired to make him hard, distracted, and filled with a need that went far beyond slacking his lust.

A demanding ride scouting the countryside earlier that day had done nothing to reduce his urge to return and claim her again. All he could think about was the feel of her under him, the softness of her skin, and the intensity of her lovemaking. Yet, the confounded mystery of her appearance, and continued reluctance to trust him with her story disturbed him more. He must unravel those mysteries before he allowed himself to taste her passion again.

He stood abruptly, "We'll pack up and leave before first light. We can stay tomorrow night at Red Jack's Inn. John, you'll scout ahead, secure rooms at the inn and reconnoiter for enemies in the area."

"Do you think that wise, Kendrick?" asked Struan, always the cautious one. "How do you intend to explain yon lass and bairns at the inn?"

"I'll think of something. Besides, even at a slow pace, it will be hard on Lorne, and I don't want to leave him here. He'll need a bed to rest in before we make the last push for home."

"Och, dinnae fash so over me," Lorne grinned. "I have Lady Andra's tablets. No doubt, the lady herself will watch over me. I'll manage well enough. She has proven more than capable, wouldn't you agree, Kendrick?"

It appeared as though Andra had drifted off to sleep next to the bairns, but Kendrick suspected she listened carefully to their banter. He did not want his brother or anyone else to presume an attachment between him and the lass and pierced Lorne with a quelling stare. His brother only chuckled and rolled over.

They had always enjoyed sparring with both weapons and words over the years. Now, however, Kendrick was not amused with his brother's obvious prodding. No doubt Lorne had noticed his veiled glances and discomfited avoidance of Andra. Though no one had commented on the previous evening, his brother rarely missed anything when it came to the lasses. "You best rest while you can, wee brother. If you fall off your horse on the morrow, I might just let the beast drag you back home."

Chapter Twelve

Long before light creased the sky the next morning, they packed and saddled the horses with quiet efficiency while Andra returned the cave's supplies to their storage place. It was no easy task for Kendrick and the men to hoist Lorne onto his horse. His brother's lips pressed tightly over his teeth and sweat covered his forehead and dripped down his neck.

Andra approached Lorne once he sat on his horse. "Take these, and drink this entire cup of water." Lorne hesitated for a moment but she pressed four tablets into his palm, "Don't be stubborn. This is going to be a hard day, and they will help with the discomfort."

"Thank you, m'lady."

"What's with the m'lady again? My name is Andra," she reproved gently.

Kendrick wanted her to ride with him, but then again, he didn't relish the awkwardness of holding her for the long ride ahead. He asked Rabbie to hand Senga to him, but the girl grabbed Andra's hand and turned away from Kendrick.

"We each must ride with one of the men," she explained to the girl. Senga looked to Rabbie and reached for his hand, but when he turned her toward Kendrick, she balked again. Andra lifted Senga's chin, but the girl refused to meet her eyes. "Could you ride with Rabbie?" Senga's shoulders slumped, but she nodded acceptance.

Struan already held Kyle on his lap. John had departed hours ago, and sharing a horse with Lorne would only cause him more pain and difficulty. That meant Andra must ride with him. She turned that defiant chin his direction, her brows raised in question. What was she waiting for, an engraved invitation?

"Do you object to me riding with you, Kendrick?" She looked him straight in the eye refusing to flinch under his stern gaze. Fire sparked beneath those deep green pools of liquid enticement.

"Nae, lass, I've no objection." His voice sounded gravely as though he hadn't spoken for days. This would not do. In one swift movement, he gripped under her arm and swung her in front of him. He pinned her sideways to his chest as he had done following their first encounter a week ago. *Had it really only been a week?* It seemed like an eternity.

She cast him a scowl over her shoulder, adjusted her seat, and swung her left leg over the horse's head to sit astride in front of Kendrick. "This will be more comfortable for both of us, if you don't mind?"

Mind? Her skirt rode up scandalously exposing those tight, black fitted trews, and though her cape covered everything sufficiently enough, he found it damned disconcerting. He did mind, but wouldn't tell her so. No matter how much he attempted to divert his thoughts from the heat of Andra's thighs against his or her firm derriere pressed to his groin, ignoring her was a useless effort.

He certainly would not explain the aching need he felt to touch her, to fold her into a comforting embrace, to possess her completely. Nor would he tell her that riding with her would distract him from his need to stay fully focused and alert as they rode through territory rife with possible enemies. On the other hand, he wanted her near him where he could smell her sweet lemon-mint scent. What could he say to distract him from his want of her?

A multi-colored, silk scarf wound tightly around her neck. The colors were a swirl of blues and peaches. It resembled silks from the far east that he'd seen in the French court. The tips flipped over her shoulders and lashed against his cheeks.

"Did you acquire this scarf on your travels?" What a stupid question. It sounded ridiculous. Since when did a laird concern himself with women's fashion? Nevertheless, if he could get her talking mayhap she'd disclose information he needed to ken, and it might distract him from the bulge pulsing uncomfortably between them, clamoring for release.

"It was a gift from my father when we visited Paris."

"So, you have been to Paris? Was your father known at court?"

"No…no, my father went there to study with other men of science and medicine."

More subterfuge. He grunted and asked no further questions.

Between scudding mounds of white clouds slashed with golden rays, the sky turned a brilliant, clear blue. Familiar scents of heather, pine, rich earth, and clean crisp air filled their lungs. Exquisite in its ruggedness and beauty, his homeland always imbued him with a deep peace. Yet today, the sights and sounds surrounding them were not sufficient to distract him from the woman in his arms.

* * *

After riding for several hours, Kendrick ordered them to stop for a brief respite in a clearing surrounded on three sides by forest. On one side of the clearing grew dense gorse, thickly clumped wild ferns, and tangled underbrush, on the other stood a tight clump of trees. Andra hurried the children to attend their needs then checked on Lorne.

"You can take a few more of these tablets now," she told him.

"I thank you, m'lady—Andra. I do think the pain would be much worse without them. What are they exactly? Did your da make them?" Every time she used the medicines from her bag, she danced with danger of discovery.

"No, they were not made by my father but he used them often when treating illness and fever." Before he could engage her further, Kendrick ordered they remount.

Phew! Another bullet dodged. It's getting more and more difficult to maintain this pretense. Eventually she knew she'd slip, and then what would happen?

They rode for several more hours and arrived at the inn shortly after dark. John awaited them by the stables. "They have two rooms above stairs. Some of us can stay in the loft above the horses," he informed Kendrick.

"What of the men inside?"

"Locals, according to Red Jack. They're already deep in their cups. You'll find a rear stair behind the kitchen. Red Jack thought it'd be best to take them through there rather than subject the lady and bairns to the men's rough behavior."

Kendrick dismounted in one swift movement. Andra slid off the opposite side before he could pull her into his arms.

Addressing John, Kendrick said, "Rabbie and I will bed in the room with Lorne, allowing one of us to guard the other room through the night. You and Struan tend to the horses and stay in the loft after you've eaten. Have Red Jack send food and ale to the rooms, and then replenish our supplies with what the kitchen can spare for tomorrow. We need to leave before first light. Alert me if you see or hear anything suspicious."

One small torch lit the wall outside one door; the door to the other room was across the hall. Inside, the rooms were small and directly above the storeroom and kitchen. Each contained one bed pushed against the wall and covered with a thin plaid. The wood plank floors were rough and without rushes or other covering. A small brazier sat in one corner with a few sticks and peat inside. A window covered with a rag was on the opposite wall. One rickety, wooden chair and a table, barely larger than a modest serving platter, stood to the side of the window where a single candle flickered beside a ewer of water and a chipped bowl.

Rabbie helped Lorne into the room on the right. Andra took the children to the room on the left. "Home sweet home!" she said, dropping her bags, but her tone held little humor.

A pervasive smell of mold, sweat, and old cooking lard assaulted her nose. The covering on the bed looked none too clean. Andra removed the thin cover and shook it out the window before replacing it.

"Well, at least there don't appear to be fleas or other crawly things hopping about."

"Mayhap not what you are used to, m'lady, but 'tis the best we can do for tonight. I will have another pallet brought up with the food." Kendrick leaned against the doorframe, his arms folded across his chest.

"Oh," Andra startled. She thought he'd entered the other room. "No matter, we'll be quite fine for the night, won't we children?" She waved her hand in a dismissive manner. Kyle sprawled across the bed and Senga sat beside him with her head down, silent as ever.

"On second thought, perhaps a pallet for me would be wise; the children can sleep in the bed. It looks a bit small for all three of us."

"Aye." Kendrick answered. Andra could feel his eyes follow her as she wandered to the table, poured water in the bowl, and rinsed a cloth to wipe the children's hands and faces. While she tended the children, Kendrick stood stoically against the doorframe, watching her every move. What did he want? Why didn't he leave?

They had ridden the entire day with barely three sentences exchanged between them. She was exhausted and her nerves frazzled; she didn't need his unrelenting attention. Just then, the innkeeper's wife appeared at the door with food. A young lad trailed behind carrying a pallet and extra blankets.

"Och, me dearies, ye look plum tuckered ye do. A bit of me hearty barley stew and some ale will fix ye right soon enough. 'Tis long I've nae seen ye, Laird MacLean. Now here ye be with yer lovely wife and her bairns. And poor Lorne, dear lad, injured and all. To be certain ye've had a time of it." She bustled about the room, placing food on the table that looked about to topple over. When done, she put her hands on her hips, and assessed Andra and the bairns with obvious curiosity.

Why hadn't he corrected the woman and told her Andra was not his wife nor the children hers? Demurely folding her hands, she stood ramrod straight in front of the children. She could play a part with the best of them, but she knew her accent would raise too many questions. So, she nodded her thanks and smiled congenially but held her tongue.

Kendrick took her hint, "Ye have our thanks, Mrs. Riley. You always did make the best stew this side of heaven."

She blushed and looked at him with adoring eyes. "Och, be

gone wif' ye' and yer sweet tongue."

"As you say, everyone is tired from our journey, and we must depart early on the morrow, so we won't be keeping you from your duties. I'd appreciate it if you could prepare a few loaves of bread and provide wine and ale for the remainder of our journey." He handed her a few coins from his sporran and patted her arm as she reluctantly left the room, clearly disappointed not to learn more.

Everyone seemed either smitten with his charms or frightened by his ferocity. "Will my accent present a problem for us?" she whispered to Kendrick after she heard the woman descend the stairs.

"You never ken who may be listening. It's best not to raise questions that we, or should I say *you*, don't want to answer." He cocked his eyebrow and a slight curl tipped the corner of his mouth. He was not being hostile, simply relentless. Still, he didn't move from the doorway. Was he trying to agitate her?

This was neither the time nor place for another discussion. "If that will be all, I think we need to take our rest now." With a flick of her wrists, she shooed him out of the room.

Andra thought she heard Kendrick outside the closed door listening as she whispered to the children. Little Kyle ran a constant stream of chatter interrupted by occasional yawns. "Will ye sing to us again?" he pleaded.

"We don't want to disturb the other customers. Perhaps I'll hum to you while you drift off to sleep." Before she finished the song, Andra heard the Innkeeper's wife and her lad speak with Kendrick. "Yer wife has a lovely voice. She be a most bonny lass."

"Aye, that she does, Mrs. Riley. Thank you again for the supplies." Footsteps descended the stairs, and Andra heard a door close. His presence in the room across the hall both comforted and distracted, and she wondered if he had similar thoughts.

Chapter Thirteen

They broke their fast before dawn and traveled for several hours with only the sound of birds in the trees and chatter from Kyle to disturb the quiet. They made their first stop after passing through the forest and onto a landscape of rolling hills covered in heather and gorse where a sparse scattering of alder and birch trees grew.

A silver birch tree and a mass of scraggy willow shrubs clustered along the edge of a rocky burn that spilled over a steep embankment and into a swift moving river. "This is a good place to rest and take refreshment." Kendrick said as he called the riders to a halt. "We should arrive at the castle by nightfall if we dinnae tarry long."

"Are you sure I will be welcomed by your people?" Andra had been reluctant to ask this question, but the prospect of meeting Kendrick's family and clan made her stomach tighten and neck throb with tension.

Lorne and Kendrick were standing together when she asked.

"Och, your singing alone will make you welcome." Lorne said. "You sing all the time, lass, 'tis very pleasing to the ear. Mayhap you weave magic with your bonny voice."

"I don't sing all the time. And there's no such thing as magic." She responded with more asperity than she'd intended and rolled her shoulders to loosen the tension his words triggered.

Kendrick laughed, "Aye, you do sing all the time. All morning you've been humming like the wee birds."

It wasn't the first time someone had mentioned her incessant humming and singing but their laughter flustered her. "Well, I'll

90

just have to curb my enthusiasm in the future."

She looked around at scenery straight out of a fairytale. Mist drifted over purple-covered hills, snuggled between an abundance of wild fern and thistles she spied a few bearberry bushes kissed with the first flame of fall. High craggy peaks caught clusters of clouds in the distance.

"Although, I must admit this enchanting vista does call to my voice." She twirled in a circle with arms outstretched above her head and sang the words from "The Sound of Music" with sufficient exuberance to gain a nod from Julie Andrews herself. A brilliant smile covered her face as she waltzed toward the trees singing her heart out. When she turned to check on the children, she noticed Senga move too near the edge of the embankment above the river. The horses stood near her drinking from a stream that spilled over into the wider more turbulent expanse of water. Lorne was brushing down one of the steeds with a handful of dried grass. She started to call Senga away from the edge when something rustled the brush on the other side of the stream causing the horses to shy toward the river, knocking Lorne on his backside. As the men ran to grab their mounts and help Lorne, Senga spun away from the skittish horses, lost her footing, and tumbled over the edge.

With no thought to her actions, Andra made a mad dash toward the river while kicking off her boots and tossing her mother's cape aside. She dove into the fast moving water. Spinning and sputtering, she gasped for air when she surfaced. Then she saw Senga rise out of the turbulence several feet away and go under again. The men yelled to her from the shore but Andra stayed focused on her efforts to reach the floundering girl. She kicked her legs hard against the current and dove under the murky churning water toward where Senga's plaid swirled on the waves.

She could barely make out a form in the murky water ahead and rose for one final breath before diving under. Catching Senga's wrist, she pulled her to the surface and wrapped her arm around the girl's chest. Senga hung against her like a dead weight. The swift current had carried them into deep water at the river's center, dozens of yards from where they had entered.

As she fought against the pull of the current, she aimed for an area where the embankment dropped to about a foot above a narrow rocky shore. Kendrick guided his horse into the water at that spot. Fighting the current with faltering strength, she struggled against the swirling eddies. Pulled under again, still gripping Senga against her, she kicked hard toward the shore. Her lungs and limbs burned with fatigue. Suddenly, a strong hand grasped her shoulder and heaved her and Senga out of the water.

Once on shore Kendrick drew Andra tight against his chest. "What possessed you to do that? You could have drowned."

Andra shoved away from his embrace with all the power left in her and dropped beside Senga. He knelt behind her his hand on her back, "She's gone, lass, let me take you away."

He tried to pull her from the girl but Andra slapped him off. Breathing into Senga's mouth, she began chest compressions. After a few attempts, Senga coughed and Andra rolled her to her side patting her back.

Rabbie and Struan reached them just as Senga coughed up the water. Struan crossed himself, "You bring the dead back to life? You are a witch!" His eyes grew round and wary.

Coughing and barely able to catch her breath, she gasped. "No Struan, I learned… (gasp)…this…(gasp)…traveling…with my father." She took another ragged breath, coughing and sucking air. "If you can get the water out of the lungs quickly, then air refills them and normal breathing resumes."

She looked up as Struan started to back away hands raised in front of him, a stunned and fearful look on his face. Fully aware of the superstitions and witch burnings that ran rampant in this time, she could not ignore his fear.

Exhausted and hurting in places she had never felt before, she managed, with Kendrick's assistance, to gain her feet though they hurt like the devil.

"Now you listen to me, Struan. You pray to the same God as I, and God helps those who help themselves. You're big, braw warrior and have a few wits about you most of the time. Hear me about this. That girl was not dead! She most definitely would have died very soon if I hadn't pushed the water from her lungs. Furthermore, perhaps this is a lesson you should learn."

Advancing toe to toe with Struan, she poked a finger into his chest as he continued to back away. "You're a bloody, damn superstitious brute, do you hear me!" Her throat felt like she'd swallowed shards of glass but she continued. "If you paid a bit of attention and allowed yourself to learn something new instead of being so bloody arrogant, you might save your own sorry arse or that of one of your men should someone fall off their bloody horse in the water and find their lungs full of water."

One hand on her hip and the other fisted with one finger pressed into his sternum she continued, "Which is it, are you a man of common sense and able to learn a new thing or two, or are you a witless man consumed with superstition to the point of blindness and ignorance." Struan's mouth gaped in shock. She could guess from his stunned expression that no woman had ever dared to curse or accost him in such a manner.

Andra's voice had risen to a high shrill. Her body shook uncontrollably with cold and exhaustion, but she would not back away. Consumed with the need to pummel some sense into the man, she hung on. If that failed, she would scream and pull out her hair and become the banshee he thought her. Hell, maybe she was a banshee after all.

Struan's scowling face turned beet red. He attempted to cross his arms over his puffed out chest but she refused to remove the finger poking into him and grabbed a fist full of shirt and plaid.

With an exploding voice, he gripped her upper arms, lifted her into the air, and shook her hard as if she were no more than a sopping wet coat. "Stop your cursing and screeching and calm yourself, you wild banshee! I'm not tak'in kindly to your slander'in words and insults. Your language is fouler than a sailor's."

She dangled in the air, his grip bruising her arms, but at least he was not backing away with a look of terror on his face. Anger was better than fear.

Chapter Fourteen

Kendrick watched the explosion unfold, reluctant to intercede at first. A spitfire to her core, he couldn't help but admire Andra's tenacity. At the same time, he wanted to smash Struan's face for daring to touch his woman. *His woman?* He shook his head and refocused.

Standing behind her, a grave expression on his face he commanded, "Release the lass, Struan." His voice demanded an immediate response.

"She is a wild one, I'll grant you that, but what she says has merit. I have seen another use this method to revive someone who had fallen into water. And look, the girl recovers her breath," he said, gesturing toward Senga who continued to cough and shiver; her little brother crouched next to her, patting her back with his small hands.

When Struan set Andra on the ground and released his hold, she stuck out her tongue and scrunched up her face. A childish expression likely intended to relieve her anxiety. To everyone's surprise, Struan made a similar face back at her. Half a breath later, they all burst out laughing. Struan, who rarely smiled except at the bairns, startled everyone with his antics, and the tension dissipated like the rivulets of water dripping from Andra's clothes. Finally, she collapsed flat on the muddy bank spent and unmoving.

Young Kyle pleaded, "Will ye not help me move Senga so she won't fall in the water again?" Rabbie and Struan guided the children away and Lorne followed.

Exasperated, Kendrick ran his hands through his wet hair shaking his head. "Are you mad, woman? What am I to do with you? First, you run off in the night toward the smell of smoke and rescue children from men intent on murder and mayhem, and then you jump into a raging river. De you think you are invincible, lass?" Actually, his chest swelled with pride. She behaved as bravely as any warrior, but far too recklessly for her own good. God's bones, how he desired her.

"Then you attack and challenge Struan's wits and sense. For a moment, I feared Struan would do you harm, and I'd have to injure one of my best men in your defense. What possesses you, Andra?"

"Possesses me? Urrrgh, not you too." Andra sat up, slinging mud from her hands, eyeing him with a serious expression. "Would you really injure Struan in my defense?"

Kendrick didn't answer, not certain he wanted to pursue where this discussion might lead. She tilted her head with a deeply creased brow, "I know he doesn't trust me, but I'll not stand for him calling me a witch when all I've done is help. There are no such things as witches. It's just idiotic, superstitious nonsense."

"Aye, we're in agreement there, but you are unlike any woman I've ever met. Surely, you understand why others might harbor suspicions. Even with me, you continue to hold your secrets." The fact that people were superstitious and willing to cast aspersions far too readily concerned him and didn't bode well for her future. Too many questions remained unanswered, but he did not consider her a witch. She made herself an easy target though, and trouble would find her like the truest arrow.

He helped her up and brushed away the mud and debris from her soaking wet clothes, which clung seductively to her firm figure. The feel of her under his hands tempted him. When she tried to step away, she winced in pain and fell against him in an attempt to gain her balance.

Holding her steady, he noticed blood pooling at her feet. "Och, you're bleeding." In one swift motion, he lifted her into his arms. A full erection rose under his plaid the minute he pressed her against his chest. Willing his thoughts to her injuries and not his desire to plunge into her wet folds, he carried her to dry grass.

* * *

Andra clutched his neck and rested her face against his shoulder. She could feel his erection press into her hip. Her mind turned to their encounter the night after she had rescued the children, and liquid heat surged to her core with want for the man. Without a doubt, she would repeat that coupling in a heartbeat, but not in the middle of the day surrounded by all these people.

What was wrong with her? She had nearly drowned, been called a witch—again, faced down a gruff warrior, and all she wanted to do was tear off their clothing and let Kendrick smother her with his mouth and pound into her until all the fear and uncertainty disappeared under his searing touch. Based on the hardness pressing against her, he might be of a same mind.

The children returned to sit with Andra, each holding a hand. Concern creased their foreheads while Kendrick washed and wrapped her feet in strips of linen.

"Senga, we must remove these wet clothes before you become ill. Rabbie, please bring my bag and we'll see what we can find for Senga." He complied without question.

She pulled out her washed, but sadly stained heather-colored sweater and the matching cashmere pashmina. Maybe one of the women at the castle could help her remove the faded bloodstains. They must have a lot of experience with that type of stain.

"Give us a moment of privacy, please." The men turned to break camp and ready the horses. Quickly, she stripped the girl out of her clothes and pulled the sweater over her head. She wrapped the pashmina around her waist like a skirt and flipped the end over her shoulder like a great kilt then belted it all together, successfully hiding most of the stains.

"There now, you're dry and look as lovely as a field of heather," she said, smiling at the girl. Senga squeezed her hand but did not look into her eyes.

"'Tis true sister, yer verra bonny." Kyle stood and took his sister's hand, then bent over and kissed Andra on the cheek.

Tears welled in her eyes and she nearly choked on her words.

"Rabbie, do you have a dry plaid to wrap around Senga? We need to keep her warm."

He came to take the children, soothing them with softly spoken Gaelic.

Kendrick leaned against a tree observing Andra as she administered to the children. His presence agitated her more than she wished to acknowledge and her attempt to ignore his serious perusal failed completely. She could hear his breathing, smell his scent, feel his every glance, and she needed to redirect her thoughts immediately. She reached to pull on her boots and hissed in pain.

He moved to her side, "Leave them off. It will not do to have your feet swell inside the leather. And speaking of getting out of wet clothes, you need to do the same."

"Yes, of course," she unwound the soaked silk scarf from her neck and removed a dry shirt from her bag. When she tried to raise her arm, she yelped in pain.

Kendrick dropped to his knees. "What pains you?" He ran his strong hands around her neck, across her shoulders and down her arms, applying mild pressure. He lifted her arms away and moved his hands down her sides, hesitating for a split second when they slipped past her breasts. When he touched the side previously injured when she'd crushed the Plexiglas box after her tumble through time, she cried out in pain.

"Lie down," he commanded, his voice full of concern. He leaned her back to the ground. Without asking, he pulled up her shirt and examined her side.

Andra could barely catch her breath and it was not due to the injury. His rough hands sparked tiny pinpoints of fire where he touched and probed. She wanted those fingers probing elsewhere and could not get a coherent word past her lips.

"You've reinjured your ribs, and mayhap cracked a few. We best bind you to prevent further injury." He helped remove her shirt and said not a word about the pink, satin bra but he took a long moment to slide his gaze over her breasts and she noticed his kilt tent between his legs. He positioned his back to shield her from the men and bound her ribs in strips of linen torn from his own shirt. Then he helped her don her last clean, dry shirt. "Do ye think ye can ride, lass?"

"Yes," she replied, sounding more certain than she felt. If he kept this up, he'd not have a strip of linen remaining on his shirt. The heat from his hands at her waist made her ache for him, and his deep, blue eyes seared her. If she gazed into those liquid pools, he would see her unfettered desire.

She averted her face and dipped her head to the side, "Thank you, Kendrick. I think I'll manage well enough. Could you bring my cape, please?" He rose swiftly and walked away, taking the heat of the world with him.

* * *

If his men and the children were not waiting for them, he would have taken her right there, wet and aching. He would have claimed her as his own and plunged his burgeoning member deep into her heat. He needed to rein in his emotions before this rampant desire caused him to do something he might regret. That first encounter was one thing, a bit of battle lust on both of them, but he still knew nothing about the woman.

Kendrick fussed with his horse taking a moment to allow his arousal to abate. When he returned to Andra, he lifted her off the grass and set her back on his horse. When he tied her boots to the saddle, he again took note of their quality.

"These boots are verra fine and the precise stitching and material of the soles is not like any I've seen before." He waited for her to say something, but her focus was on some distant place. She always avoided talking when he commented on her clothing or the jewelry she wore. Why would she not trust him just a wee bit— tell him something, anything meaningful to dispel his doubts?

In a short while, the river fanned out and split around a small island. The current had slowed to a gentle meandering making it an easy place to cross the horses.

Andra, nestled against his chest, glanced around. "This is a beautiful glen, the faded heather and clumps of golden-amber grass sway like gentle waves on a sighing sea," she said.

Kendrick joined her perusal of his land. "Aye, we are on

MacLean lands now. 'Tis the most beautiful spot in all the Highlands." He didn't bother to suppress his pride. The closer he drew to his home, the more he could feel the stress from the last days slip away.

Andra started to shiver. "Are ye cold, Andra?"

"I'm fine," but her jaw clenched in an effort to keep her teeth from chattering. "How much farther before we reach your castle?"

"Not far, we'll be there in a few hours." Kendrick pulled his plaid around her shoulders.

"Mmmm, you are so warm." She snuggled against him and a surge of possessiveness swelled in his chest. Sleep finally dragged her under its forgiving veil, and she relaxed into his embrace.

Looking down at her plump mouth slightly parted as a light snore escaped her throat; he felt an urgent need to shelter and comfort her. He found her beauty beguiling, evident even while covered in dirt and debris; but her gentle and fierce protection of the children held him in thrall. Her willingness to face difficulties with strength and offer help to strangers at her own peril surprised him. Something in his chest thrummed and kicked. *Mine,* his mind shouted.

After a while, Lorne pulled beside his brother and spoke in a quiet voice. "Almost home, brother. It looks like fatigue has finally claimed the lass. What do ye plan to tell our parents and the clan about her? The clan's not likely to welcome a Cameron, you ken."

"I have sworn my protection. That will be enough for anyone to ken for now. I'll discuss things with Da and Mother. Mayhap they've heard of her father or kin." Kendrick changed the subject, "How do you feel brother? You've said little on the ride."

"I've been worse. Those tablets Andra gives me help considerably. I'm certain I could not have made it without them. I thank you brother for allowing her ministrations. Perhaps the fairy folk dropped her in our midst to aid with my recovery. She's a fine, bonny lass, and if I weren't betrothed, you'd have a fight for her affections."

Kendrick clicked his tongue, "Och, what affections do you speak aboot, you daft fool. Aye, she is bonny enough, but you well ken I'm not looking for an attachment. Besides, you'll have your hands full with your own sweet Edana. Need I remind you she anxiously awaits your return? One lovely lass should be enough to keep you quite busy."

Lorne laughed at his brother. "Your discomfort speaks louder than words, brother. I haven't seen a woman penetrate your cool reserve in a long time. Don't bother to deny that you've already formed an attachment to her."

Kendrick cast him a stern look but didn't argue the point.

During the last hours of their ride, a crash of thunder rumbled overhead and lighting opened the night sky. By the time they finally crossed the drawbridge and entered the lower bailey, it was already full dark and the weary travelers were drenched.

John had ridden ahead and advised Lady Beatrice of her family's approach. She stood regally at the keep's entrance beside her exuberant daughter, Isabel. Several stable lads grabbed the horses' reins as the men and their passengers dismounted and climbed the steps to the keep.

When Kendrick tried to wake Andra, she moaned but did not open her eyes. As he wiped the hair from her face, panic gripped him.

"Rabbie, let me hand Andra to you, she's burning with fever." People died every day of slight fevers and she had been through one shocking trial after another since they had first found her.

He jumped from his horse and took her back into his arms taking the steps to the keep two at a time. He kissed his mother's cheek in greeting still clutching Andra tight to his chest. "Could you send the healer to my chambers immediately? The lass burns with fever."

Despite the late hour, the keep buzzed with activity. His mother issued orders to her maids and told Isabel to return to her own chambers. "I'll not have you felled by fever as well, child."

"Oh, must I, mother? I could help Kendrick."

"Absolutely not! We'll let Jane tend her. Ye may visit her when she recovers and her sickness poses no danger to you. Take the children from Rabbie and get them settled in the nursery."

Isabel relented and directed her attention to Rabbie. Glancing at him from beneath fluttering lashes, she asked, "And who is this charming lad and lass?"

Chapter Fifteen

The following day Kendrick and Lorne went to their father's chamber. It was difficult to see him in his reduced state. His once muscular frame had withered to flaccid skin and bones, and his coloring had sallowed.

"So, I hear you've brought a Cameron into the keep. Do you plan to ransom the lass if she recovers?"

"Nae," The brothers answered in unison. Kendrick took over. "It seems she has no memory of her kith and ken in Scotland though she remembers her parents. Her da took her from Scotland as a wee bairn. After her mother's death, she traveled with him until his recent death left her with no remaining kin. There is much aboot her we dinnae understand. However, she was verra instrumental in Lorne's recovery from his injuries and took care of the bairns. I couldn't justify leaving a wounded, disoriented woman alone in the wilderness."

"I see, 'twould be wrong, of course. Have you learned of the bairns' family?" his father asked.

"Aye, as best we could determine, they're all dead. The lad says there are no other kin and the girl never speaks. Rabbie believes they are distantly related to the Dunbar's so mayhap Alith kens of them."

"De you think Andra's connected to Cormag Cameron and his band of rogues and thieves? You cannae be too careful when it comes to them, you ken. Dinnae trust the lass." Monroe started to cough harshly into a square of linen he held in his hand. The cloth came away covered with blood.

Monroe looked at the cloth with disgust. "'Twon't be long before I meet my maker. I am proud of you sons and ken you'll take care of the clan well when I'm gone. I had hoped, however, to see you married before I depart these earthly realms, Kendrick." He coughed again.

"You must decide on a bride who will benefit the clan and give you heirs. Find a strong, capable wife of breeding age that will bring men and arms to us. You have left this too long, son." He started coughing and struggled mightily to regain his breath.

"Dinnae fash yourself, Father. I fully accept my responsibilities to the clan and won't fail you." His thoughts flashed on Andra. It shocked him to realize he wanted her by his side. Unfortunately, there was no sense broaching that impossibility.

* * *

Since their return to Ruadhstone castle, Andra's fever continued to rage. She didn't regain consciousness, but thrashed about in her bed, then fell silent for hours with almost no movement. She moaned and called out words no one understood. Her chest wheezed despite all efforts by the healer to calm her breathing. Even though the demands of the keep and clan business kept Kendrick busy, he checked on Andra's progress as often as possible and sat by her bed late into the night.

Climbing the stairs to the tower early on the third day, he came upon Lorne and Rabbie talking quietly in one of the alcoves cut into the wall between floors.

"What's amiss? Is it Andra?" He could tell by the frowns creasing their brows that the news wouldn't be good. His mind and gut twisted at the thought she might not survive.

"We grow concerned about Andra's condition." Rabbie explained, staring through an arrow slit to the bailey below. "Lorne and I were discussing the possibility of finding Andra's wee tablets and administering them to her. They appeared to be of great help with Lorne's recovery. Or mayhap one of us should try her method of warming a fevered body to reduce the shakes that wrack her."

As usual, Rabbie attempted to add levity to the situation, but Kendrick's thoughts immediately turned to their first night when they had climbed under the coverings, one on either side of Lorne. The sudden desire to cradle her heated flesh in his arms surprised him.

"Damn, I should have thought of the tablets before." He pierced his men with a stern stare. "And no one will be climbing into bed with Andra," he said, biting off the words with more agitation than he intended. "No, 'twould be most improper and would give mother an apoplexy if she found us thusly."

Incredulous at their suggestion, he paused, rounding on them with a scowl. "You dinnae speak to Mother about that night did you? You ken if anyone learned of that, well—it wouldn't be acceptable. Not to mention the problems it might create with Edana and The Keith."

Should any one of the men disclose the events of that night, there would be consequences he didn't want to consider. And he definitely did not want the impropriety of that night to suggest an attachment between her and Lorne. Though he could not explain why, he did not want others to deem Andra a loose or wanton woman. Until he had a better understanding of her history, he needed to quell the gossip, or at least not add to what had already spread through the keep.

"Nae, of course not." the men exclaimed in unison.

Lorne continued. "We'll find her tablets in a wee container in her bag which is in the armoire. If you send the maid out for a while we could find them easily enough."

"I will handle this. You need to get on with your business before we draw unwanted attention."

His chambers were stifling hot. A fire roared in the hearth, someone had shuttered the windows and tightly closed the drapes blocking any light or breeze from invading the room.

"How fares the lass?" he asked the maid, Vera. His mother had placed her in charge of sitting with Andra when the healer was not present. He had enjoyed Vera's favors on a few occasions, but their dalliance had ended more than a year ago. She was a devious and untrustworthy chit, one he wished he'd never bedded. Now, he avoided her whenever possible. She batted her eyes coyly and sidled up to him in a suggestive manner. It didn't sit well with him that she watched over Andra. "Leave us," he commanded with a scowl. She hesitated for a brief moment, then huffed out the door.

He searched Andra's satchel, feeling as though he invaded her privacy. A foolish thought since he had the right to examine anything she brought into his home. Inside her bag, he found neatly folded items of clothing and several containers including one made of a clear, shiny material with a strange closure on it. Inside it, he found a number of items he could not identify and set them aside to examine more closely at another time. He also found two bottles made of a hard, white material with something printed on the surface and a pliable tube, which he recognized as the source of the ointment she had applied to Lorne's injuries and to her own. These things made the mystery of her presence even more perplexing.

A brusque knock sounded before the door opened and closed quickly behind his brother. "Have you found the tablets?" Lorne noticed the bottles inside the clear container and said, "Aye, those are the ones. I watched her closely when she opened her bag to extract them for me."

Kendrick pulled on the metal tab at the end of the clear package and found it opened along a set of rigid cog-like metal teeth. He pulled the tab back and forth a few times. "Quite an ingenious device and this is verra strange material," he said, rubbing his thumb across the plastic case. After pulling out the bottles, he handed the package to Lorne to examine.

Affixed to the outer part of the bottles were paper coverings, one red, and one blue with large printed names he didn't recognize. The sides of the bottle had lettering so small he could barely read it. He couldn't imagine a printing press or personal hand that could produce such perfect, tiny lettering. After reading the label, he decided on the blue one, though both seemed to address the same ailments. He fidgeted with the bottles for a few minutes, then pulled out his dirk to cut through the hard surface.

Lorne reached to halt Kendrick's assault on the bottles. "Nae, brother, she twisted the tops off in some manner."

Kendrick saw that there were two spots on the cap. When pressed, he found the top unscrewed with little effort. He lifted Andra, dropped the tablets down her throat, and held a cup to her lips. "Swallow these wee tablets, Andra." He pressed his hand to her forehead, which burned like the fires of hell. "Come back to me *mo leannán.*"

Lorne clicked his tongue. "So, you call her sweetheart, now? You best take care who hears you blathering sweet words in her ear, brother mine." But Lorne was all smiles. It seemed they'd all come under her spell during their time together.

He returned to examining the other items in the bag. "What do you think all these things are?" He pulled out a package that smelled like mint. There was a small, pale blue round disk. When he dropped it on the floor, it popped open.

"Damn, I've broken it." Lorne moaned.

"What is it?"

Lorne handed him the most astonishingly clear, miniature-looking glass, now marred by a crack through the center. "Put the things away for now, we can examine them another time. I'll stay with Andra for a bit."

"The bottle says to give her two tablets every 4 to 6 hours, but it also has a lot of warnings. Do you think they could harm her?"

"She gave these to you regularly and took them herself when we were in the cave and on the way home. You seem to have survived without ill effects. At this point I think we should try everything at our disposal."

Once Lorne left, Kendrick removed his shirt, slipped behind Andra, pressed her body tightly against his, and pulled the blankets up to her chin. He leaned back against the headboard an ache filling his chest; feelings he had denied himself for a long time crept through to his core, and he couldn't stop them if he tried. Yet try he would.

Andra thrashed about calling out to her da and someone named Daniel. Tears would spill down her cheeks and then she would slip into a sleep so deep he feared she'd never wake. He wondered if the other name was that of her husband or lover. The thought of her in someone else's arms clawed under his skin, an itch he wanted to scratch at until he drew blood.

Chapter Sixteen

When Jane, the healer, came to check her patient, Kendrick had just administered the third dose of Andra's tablets and wiped her brow with a cool cloth.

"I brought some willow bark tea and broth if she can swallow a wee bit," Jane offered. "Why don't you break your fast and get some fresh air m'laird?" Jane had been with their family for many years and had replaced Alith, the woman who'd been healer since his grandmother's time. Ancient and beyond the ability to continue the rigorous demands placed on a healer of a large clan, Alith still assisted gathering and preparing herbals and medicines. Everyone called her Auntie or Lady Alith.

Kendrick went to the outer bailey and took up his sword to practice with Rabbie.

"Any change yet?" Rabbie asked, taking a swipe at Kendrick.

"Nae," Kendrick blocked and thrust with such force he almost knocked Rabbie off balance.

"I ken you want to vent your frustrations. Well then, let's see what you have, cousin."

Rabbie would accommodate his need to release the tension that spooled off him like a tightly coiled whip. They began a fierce practice battle that demanded all their strength, skill, and focus.

An hour later, Isabel approached the men with Senga and Kyle in hand. Panting and drenched in sweat Rabbie glanced aside, allowing Kendrick the advantage, and he knocked the sword from Rabbie's hand. Well matched in their abilities, Rabbie and Kendrick usually ended their mock battles in a draw.

"Well done, cousin, but 'twas only your sister and the bairns that caused a moment's distraction allowing you the victory."

Kendrick spun around. "What brings you here, Isabel?" His heart thudded in his chest, fearing bad news.

She graced the men with a brilliant smile and replied, "Andra is awake and asks after you, brother."

With wide, determined strides, Kendrick headed toward the keep. He wanted to run directly to her, but went to wash first. It would not do to display the urgent need he felt to see her awake and mending.

When he entered his chambers, he found his mother sitting next to Andra wiping wet, stringy clumps of hair away from her face. She turned to her son. "Her fever finally broke, but she is verra weak. Cook will send fresh broth shortly. Dinnae tire her over much, Kendrick."

His mother patted Andra's hand. "I will check on you later. What you need now is rest."

Kendrick took his mother's place on the chair by the bed, scooping Andra's hand into his. "You've suffered a raging fever and gave everyone quite a scare." Watching her face closely, he added, "I invaded your things and found the tablets you gave to Lorne during his recovery. The wee writing said to use it for fever, and it seems to have helped."

He noted the apprehension on her face and felt a slight flinch in the hand he held. The tablets were not the only thing in her bag that confounded him and required further explanation.

She nodded. "Thank you." Then she adroitly changed the subject, "Your mother said Senga and Kyle are well and that Lorne improves greatly." She spoke with a gravelly voice, and wheezed and coughed as she spoke. Though the fever had broken, her breath still rattled her chest. Some questions could wait a few more days, but he would have answers to a few now.

"My sister has the bairns well in hand. They ask for you every day." He paused a moment then plunged ahead, "You frequently called out in your delirium." Her shoulders tensed.

"You were asking for your da and someone named Daniel. Do you remember who this Daniel might be?" Regardless of who the man might be, gaining this information might help him unravel Andra's secrets. Silence settled over them while he awaited her answer. He didn't want to learn of a lover or husband but had to know.

Andra's hand moved protectively across her abdomen. A gesture he'd often seen women make when they were breeding. "Andra? Does that name mean anything to you?"

Tears slipped over her lashes and she looked down at her lap. "It's a common name is it not?" she whispered. She would not look at him.

He waited patiently for several minutes before responding, "Aye, 'tis common enough, but why in particular do you think you called it out while delirious?"

An exhausted sigh escaped her lips, and her shoulders slumped. She lifted moss-green eyes, glassy with tears. With a hand still pressed against her abdomen, her voice hitched, "Daniel was my son." She turned away as a sob shook her. "If you don't mind Kendrick, I feel the need to rest. Please."

Kendrick flinched. Was—past tense. Had the bairn died? This explained the intense tenderness and protective instincts she displayed toward the orphaned bairns. But what about the babe's father? Though she had mentioned her father, mother, and now her son, she had never mentioned a husband.

"Are you married, then?" He could barely get the words out and didn't want to examine his feelings on the matter.

Andra kept her face turned away. "No, Kendrick, I am most definitely not married."

The bitterness in her tone was unmistakable. He knew when they had joined outside the cave that she was not a virgin despite being as tight as any woman he'd ever bedded. He would never have guessed she had birthed a child. Obviously, she did not take men to her bed often. What had happened to her? His hands fisted so tightly his fingernails cut into calloused palms.

Swallowing to calm his voice, he asked, "Were you escaping this man who fathered your bairn when we found you?" Had the rake violated her? Abandoned her and his responsibilities to his child, and cast her off to fend for their son alone? With her father dead and no kin to protect her, the evil of the world had visited one tragedy after another on her shoulders.

Tears coursed down her cheeks. "Please Kendrick, I am so tired. We can discuss this later, can we not?"

He wanted to take her in his arms and soothe her pain. He wanted to remove the burden of sadness that weighed so heavily on her shoulders. Yet she was not a beleaguered or ruined waif. She carried herself with a regal certainty and defiant edge. She wore verra fine clothing, though unusual, and a wealth of jewels and gold adorned her person.

He brushed the damp hair from her forehead and kissed her temple, "How can I help you, Andra?"

She shook her head, closed her eyes, and curled into a fetal position facing the wall. "Please, let me rest a bit before you continue your interrogation."

Interrogation! This was not an interrogation. A murderous rage gutted him. He silently cursed the father who had left her alone without a proper protector. He cursed any man who had ever taken her to his bed. He wanted to break and smash things, and to kill the bastard who had injured her in such a vile manner.

He sat quietly by her side, stroking the silken hair cascading down her back until she breathed easier and appeared to sleep.

Angry emotions flayed him from the inside out. He needed to get away from the castle—clear his thoughts. Thoughts that repeatedly settled on this frail and broken woman lying in his bed. He knew he'd only find release through a hard workout or a hard ride. He chose the ride, afraid a mock combat would become all too real.

Rabbie ran toward him as he approached the stables. "A messenger just arrived from The McDuff. They are under siege from the Camerons and their mercenaries."

Kendrick had never felt more inclined to battle. "Bring Struan and twenty-five of our best warriors; we leave as soon as possible."

Speaking with Lorne before their departure, he asked, "You'll check on the lass and see that she is well cared for. And see that

Vera stays away from her room."

"You dinnae want your former trysts gossiping aboot you?" Lorne needled his brother.

"That's ridiculous. The woman is a meddling harpy, always stirs trouble wherever she goes. 'Twould be unwise for her to tend Andra and you ken why." Kendrick jerked his horse's reins to pull away.

"Don't worry; I'll see that Andra is well cared for and that the harpy is kept busy elsewhere." His brother's mouth lifted as though he would continue but he let the subject drop.

Chapter Seventeen

When they met the enemy, Kendrick turned berserker: an avenging angel. Once on the battlefield he gave his gnawing, murderous rage full vent and every whoreson he slashed was in retribution for the hurts Andra had suffered. The battle had been fierce but resolved quickly.

The Cameron warriors made a hasty retreat leaving a few of their dead on the field of battle. While squires and healers busily attended the injured and dead, Kendrick's men gave him a wide berth. They knew better than to engage their leader when his fury was piqued.

Rabbie came alongside him. "Are you well, cousin? You seemed consumed with battle-lust today. Mayhap extreme for the circumstance as you usually just wound enough to scare them away."

His battle rage spent, Kendrick decided to share what Andra had disclosed.

"Aye, Rabbie, I am well enough." He wiped the blood from his sword, placed the tip in the dirt, and rested his hand on the hilt. "The injured will require time to recover before we return to Ruadhstone." His gaze drifted over the horizon in the direction of their home while they stood in quiet contemplation.

Kendrick shook his head. "She had a son," he blurted. "And the whoreson who impregnated her dinnae marry her." He spat on the ground and growled, "What kind of man abandons his woman and son?"

"Och, that explains much. She no longer has the son?"

"Nae, I believe he's dead. She spoke of him in the past tense, but became too distressed for me to press her further." Kendrick rubbed at the dirt on his forehead and brushed back his hair.

"Do you ken the blackguard's name? Is he a member of Cormag's clan?" Rabbie maintained a calm tone of voice as he always did when Kendrick showed distress.

"I don't have any other details. She was far too fragile. I didn't want to cause undue strain that might bring about a relapse with her illness. But I swear on my honor, Rabbie, if I ever find the man, it will be his last day on this earth." Kendrick was falling for the lass and falling verra hard.

"Hmm." Rabbie just shook his head in commiseration and slapped Kendrick's shoulder, "Let's find McDuff, and discover what he kens about this skirmish."

Laird Kevin McDuff, none too happy with this recent attack, blustered in anger as he walked the battlements with Kendrick and Rabbie. "They become ever more brazen with their reiving, threats, and constant attacks. It seems they won't be satisfied until they starve out every crofter and claim all lands adjoining theirs."

"Between their alliances with the Campbells, his hired mercenaries, and Sassenach dragoons, he becomes a growing threat in the area." Rabbie added.

Kendrick rubbed his scruffy chin, "Aye and since the Camerons side with the Sassenach whenever it gives them the slightest advantage over their enemies, they create problems for everyone. Cormag Cameron has always been a ruthless, greedy bastard."

Kendrick, Rabbie, Struan, and Cormag had fostered together as lads. An intense competition always existed between them that intensified considerably when Kendrick married his first wife, Kirstin, a third cousin to Cormag. Cormag had been obsessed with the woman and blamed Kendrick for Kirstin's death, though she had died from childbed fever.

The McDuff watched Kendrick closely. "Struan tells me you found a lost Cameron woman after your last encounter with them. Mayhap they set her in your midst for nefarious purposes. What are your plans for the lass? Will you ransom her in an effort to seek peace? I wouldna advise such a course, you ken, not a one of those bastards can be trusted at their word." McDuff trusted no Cameron and had long been vocal about it.

"Nae, she is not from those Camerons. She's been away from Scotland since she was a wee bairn and says she has no living kin. Besides, I'd never release any lass into that man's hands."

In that regard, Rabbie agreed with Kendrick. However, he suspected Kendrick's desire to keep the woman had little to do with their hatred of Cormag Cameron and his clan. Still, they had much to learn about her and he hoped, for all their sakes, that McDuff was not correct in suggesting an ulterior motive for Andra's appearance. A shudder ran through him when he considered the possibilities should the notion prove true.

Chapter Eighteen

Now that she was recovering, Andra had been moved to her own room several doors down from Kendrick's. Finally, a sennight after her arrival, her condition improved enough to receive visitors. Beyond regular visits from Jane and Beatrice, all others had left her in relative quiet during her recovery. Laying about made her feel antsy, useless; she wanted to get busy again. She had not seen Kendrick or the other men since the day she woke from her delirium, and that made her anxious as well.

Earlier that morning she stared out the window, taking in the view of the castle below. Jane had informed her that she resided at Ruadhstone Castle. The very one she had contacted in her time. Their antiquities director had agreed to house her father's *sgian dubh* in their museum during the visit she had planned. His interest in the artifact resulted in her obtaining permission to carry the weapon in a sealed case on the plane. Of course, that flight had never taken place.

From the vantage point of her window, she could see most of the inner and outer baileys, the front, crenellated gate towers, and two side towers that loomed double the height of the gate towers. All the stone, including the outer and inner walls appeared a dark golden to reddish color that would deepen under the sun to the shade of the red hills visible in the distance. Several utilitarian buildings nestled along the walls of the lower bailey—a blacksmith's shed, weapons shed, stables, and other buildings where workers busied themselves in the tasks necessary to the maintenance of such a fortress. To her right she could see the edge of a deep blue loch, and when the wind blew, the smell of the sea wafted on the breeze. A modest-sized village was just visible through the trees about a mile from the castle gates.

The castle appeared remarkably like the photos in the brochure she had received from the antiquities director. In her time, the outer bailey was a paved parking lot, but the gate and drawbridge, and the inner buildings appeared the same. The castle's director had expressed great pride when he described their management and restoration of many of the original features. How curious that she had ended up in this place, where she had intended to visit, in another time.

Andra had been walking around the room in an attempt to strengthen her weakened muscles when another burst of coughing returned her to bed. Staring up at the canopy, trying to make sense of recent events, she heard a soft knock at the door.

"Enter." she called.

An exuberant Kyle rushed in and jumped on the bed, followed by a stunning young woman with deep-blue eyes and hair the color of dark honey. Senga, reticent as ever, stood quietly behind the young woman, but glanced at Andra from under lowered lashes.

"Lady Andra, it has taken all my strength to corral this wild lad and force him tae let you rest. He's been ever so anxious to see you with his own eyes." A conspiratorial giggle escaped. "Oh, excuse me," the young woman dipped into a curtsey. "I am Isabel, sister to Kendrick and Lorne. Mother tells us you may be able to join us for the evening meal. With your permission, we wish to escort you to the hall and perhaps, if you're strong enough, give you a brief tour of the grounds."

"Your mother mentioned that you had undertaken the task of handling the children. My thanks for your help." Andra noticed that Senga wore a simple, mushroom-colored dress and held an arm full of beautifully colored gowns. Wrapped around her shoulders was the heather-colored pashmina that Andra had given the girl after her fall into the river.

Turning to the young girl behind Isabel, Andra asked, "What do you have there, Senga?" She hoped the girl would finally speak, but Senga only dipped a little curtsey and draped the clothes over a chair by the fire.

Isabel gestured to the gowns, "Mother sent those for you. Kendrick said you only had clothing from your travels, not fit for life at the keep." She plastered her hand over her mouth and gasped. "Please excuse me, m'lady, I meant no offense."

A coy smile crossed Isabel's lips, and she tilted her head slightly as she observed Andra. "Though, 'tis quite unusual for Kendrick to concern himself aboot such matters."

Isabel displayed an infectious exuberance. She was clearly on a fishing expedition to learn about the relationship between Andra and Kendrick. Andra did not intend to disclose anything about that. "Your brother is correct in his assessment of my wardrobe. I'm sure whatever Lady Beatrice has sent will be far more practical than the clothes I have with me."

"Aye, they are quite lovely items, m'lady. If they need tae be taken in or hemmed, the seamstress could easily have an item altered before this evening. Senga and I will help you dress if you wish."

She enjoyed the visit with Isabel and the children, but the one crucial question she couldn't bring herself to ask was—*where is Kendrick*? "It will be wonderful to get out of this room and join your family for the evening meal. I gratefully accept your offer of assistance dressing and a tour, if there is time." Especially the help dressing as she had no idea how to strap herself into the array of clothing displayed before her.

"Truly, I feel weaker than a newborn baby, but am anxious to move about and regain some strength."

"Senga, which of the dresses do you think I should try this evening?" she asked, hoping the girl would speak. Nothing. Not a word. Senga sifted through the gowns and pulled out a wool garment of the softest, summer green with gold thread woven at the neck and along the sleeves. After sending Kyle from the room, they plaited Andra's hair. The unruly shorter hair framing her face refused to stay in place. Isabel left the room, returned quickly with a beautiful set of bone combs, and proceeded to tuck up the loose 'fringes' as she called them.

"Is the corset required?" Andra asked as Isabel held up a bone stomacher. "My ribs and chest ache and I still find breathing difficult." Horrific coughing had wracked her for days and just then, another wrenching cough proved her point.

"Oh, aye, I think you must wear the corset. The only person to forgo one is cook who insists it would cause her food to sour," Isabel giggled.

"That contraption might sour me as well, I'm afraid my bruised ribs will protest most vigorously. Perhaps for now I could forego it, and wear that lovely dark-green jerkin. No one would be the wiser." Though much improved, Andra intended to abandon the corset; certain any contraption that restricted her breath would not benefit continued recovery.

"You're probably correct, if you wear the jerkin 'tis unlikely anyone would ken." Isabel conceded.

When they entered the great hall, Isabel led Andra to the raised dais at the far end of the room. A sudden hush settled as she passed the long row of tables. With a grimace she hoped passed for a smile, she searched the crowd for a particular familiar face. People observed her with curiosity; others with disdainful expressions or outright scowls mumbling comments she did not catch.

Beatrice sat to the right of Lorne. The other men from her rescue were conspicuously absent. A pain fisted in her chest. She hadn't realized how much she missed seeing Kendrick, Rabbie, and even Struan, but Kendrick's absence felt particularly hurtful. She assumed he simply did not want to be in her presence now that they had arrived at his castle. Who could blame him? As laird, more important matters plagued him than the welfare of her woeful self. How would she feel in his situation? These questions rattled through her brain as she struggled to move gracefully through the room. The necessity to remain calm and pleasant, an almost laughable concept under the circumstances, infused her limbs. She simply must maintain the ruse long enough to fully recover and find a way home.

"Welcome, Lady Andra," Lorne rose to assist her to a seat next to his mother.

Beatrice patted her trembling hand, "Dinnae let the gossips disturb you. 'Tis just their curiosity o'er you. You'll win their hearts soon enough." Beatrice smiled sweetly and eyed Lorne in silent communication while Andra took the seat offered.

Before sitting again, he raised his mug, "Raise your cups and let us welcome our guest, Lady Andra, whose ministrations following my recent injuries are the reason I stand before you this day."

Lorne didn't use her last name. Possibly to avert the crowd's anger over her being a Cameron. Besides, she'd heard that that information had already made the rounds of Castle Ruadhstone—more than once.

Lorne winked at her then turned back to the room. He hadn't missed the disgruntled murmurings. "The laird and his kin offer Lady Andra sanctuary and our protection," he continued in a voice that brooked no further discussion or dissent, intent on settling the matter.

Hushed whispers and grumbles hissed through the crowd, but everyone raised their cups and toasted, though none too enthusiastically. One girl sitting at a table to the left lashed her with a stare of pure venom then quickly covered her glare and turned away. The woman looked familiar; Andra seemed to remember her in the sickroom during the fog of her illness.

Beatrice introduced the others sitting at their table. A beautiful young woman with long, golden locks and eyes the color of dark chocolate sat to Lorne's left. Her adoring gaze followed Lorne's every move.

"May I introduce Lorne's betrothed, Lady Edana, and her father, Laird John Keith."

The father spoke with a deep rumbling voice, "We are pleased to welcome the lass who aided Lorne's recovery following his recent injuries." He raised his mug to his lips, but his eyes scrutinized her closely and lacked warmth.

Edana smiled shyly and nodded, "'Tis an honor to meet you, m'lady. I ken we shall be good friends. I am ever so grateful for the care you rendered Lorne." Then she glanced at Lorne, starry eyed, obviously besotted.

"I hope we will be the best of friends." Andra replied warmly. The days ahead would no doubt find her in need of every ally possible.

The aroma of roasted meat and an assortment of roasted vegetables enticed Andra, but a meager appetite permitted only a few bites and small sips of wine. She considered asking why Kendrick and his men were absent, but held her tongue. After the meal, several individuals pushed the trestle tables back against the walls as men took up their instruments to begin the evening's entertainment.

Lorne stood again and raised his mug to gain the clan's attention. "This night it also pleases me to announce the wedding date for myself and my lovely betrothed, Edana. The wedding will take place in a month." The room erupted in rousing approval, much different from the weak greeting her introduction elicited.

"Kyle tells us that you have a lovely voice, Andra. Would you grace us with a song tonight?" Isabel asked sweetly.

Kyle and his sister, seated at a table just below the left side of the dais, had heard Isabel's request and the lad jumped to his feet. "Aye, 'tis true, even the Laird says she sings as sweet as the wee birds. I think she is an angel." His smile beamed over crooked, little, white teeth and his cheeks were rosy blooms.

Andra smiled at him, her heart about to burst. Impossible to refuse his entreaty, she thought for a moment about what song might please this crowd and not sound too strange or out of place. She decided on "My Heart Will Go On," a love song to honor Lorne and his Edana, and hoped it would meet with their approval. After all, the song didn't specifically reference a shipwreck and losses at sea. The song's sentiment easily applied to these harsh times—words about love held in one's heart no matter the circumstances lovers faced.

Chapter Nineteen

Kendrick and his men climbed the stairs to the keep as Andra started to sing. He stopped just inside the door to listen, noticing every face riveted on her.

"Ahh, the lass sings like an angel when she's no yelling and curse'in at you or Struan." Rabbie chuckled.

The vision before Kendrick completely captivated him. Her thick, russet hair glistened with golden and amber light like the threads in her gown reflected the hearth's fire. She faced the dais and seemed to address Lorne and Edana but her words riveted him as if she sang for him alone. The hairs stood up along his arms despite a lack of chill in the air. Damn, he had been in her presence but a few minutes, and already, the desire to whisk her away to his bed filled him with a need beyond anything he could recall. Answers first, he told himself.

When she finished, several seconds of quiet hesitation blanketed the hall and then the clan erupted in applause disturbing a babe wrapped in its mother's arms. The child wailed and Andra turned to the woman and reached for the baby. The woman paused, then handed the infant over. Andra crooned softly and sang a lullaby as she swayed and flitted between the bairns nestled by the fire. All eyes, young and old alike, followed her every move. The musicians picked up her rhythm and added a bit of string, pipes, and a soft tap on a bodhrán drum.

"She enchants them all," Struan grumbled, but a smile tipped the corners of his mouth and crinkled around his eyes.

Andra was still singing to the children when she turned and saw Kendrick at the door. She graced him and his men with a dazzling smile. Her song finished, she handed the quieted babe back to its mother. The musicians began a more rousing tune while the clan yelled a welcome to their laird, and men moved to dance with the women strolling about the hall.

"'Tis time the bairns retire for the night," Beatrice called to the assembly. She went to her son and kissed his cheek in welcome. "Perhaps you should escort Lady Andra to her rooms. It's her first night in the hall, and I fear we have o'er tired her."

When Andra drew near, Kendrick noticed dark-blue crescents under her eyes, and she appeared thinner than when he'd last seen her. He swept a bow and held out his arm, "You look tired, lass. Perhaps it is time to retire for the night."

"I'll admit I feel a bit fatigued." She curtsied awkwardly to his mother and the dais then allowed Kendrick to escort her from the room.

The touch of her cool fingers ignited a fire to his insides. He was grateful his sporran covered the bulge below his waist. "It seems you weave your magic on the clan with your lovely voice."

She looked at him askance. "We're not back to that topic, are we? I thought you and I were in accord on the matter of magic." A smile tweaked the corners of her lips. Her voice held a congenial and flirtations lilt.

Kendrick patted her hand, "Aye, so we are." When they entered her room, he stoked the fire, unsuccessfully fighting his desire for her. He flexed his muscles in an effort to relax the tension rippling across his shoulders.

"I'm glad you've returned unharmed. I'll admit to missing you and the men." The whisper of a smile hovered on lush lips that she moistened with her tongue. In two strides, he had her in his arms and searched her eyes for any sign of reluctance. He needed no encouragement beyond her brilliant smile. He laid a gentle kiss over her wet mouth. Her arms snaked around his neck as she pressed her body into his, and all gentleness fled. He consumed her lips, his tongue invading her with deep, probing strokes. Running his fingers through the strands of her braid, he loosened her hair until it tumbled in a mass around her shoulders.

He released her mouth when she gently pushed her hands against the planes of his chest. "Perhaps we should sit, enjoy the fire, a glass of wine, and a pleasant chat before I retire." She urged them to restraint, but he could see she felt the same desire that roared through his veins.

Kendrick cradled her face in his hands and kissed her forehead. "Och, lass, I think we both would enjoy something more stimulating than a chat and a glass of wine."

Rather than move to retrieve the wine and glasses on the small bedside table, his hands removed her jacket and ran seductively down her sides. "Your gown is fetching and you wear no corset."

He ignored the niggling rebuke in the back of his mind that cautioned control. When he cupped her breasts and trailed kisses down her neck and across the flesh below her collarbone, Andra sighed and gripped his shoulders.

"I thought it too constrictive and knew it would hurt my ribs." she responded breathlessly while easing away from his ravishment.

He took a half step back from her and loosened his hands to a light touch on her waist. He was a cad and not behaving in a gentlemanly manner. Nevertheless, he had not been able to shake his burning desire for her, nor the need to give her shelter and protection. Those thoughts had preoccupied him since he'd last seen her stricken with grief and illness and curled into a ball on his bed.

"You are still sore from the injury you incurred at the river?" he asked, genuinely concerned.

"The incessant coughing over the past week did nothing to reduce the discomfort." Her eyes never left his. "You have caught me off-guard, Laird MacLean. You honor me with your interest in my welfare. However, I think we should take a moment to catch our breath. Don't you agree?"

"You may address me as Kendrick when we are in private, Andra, considering our prior intimacies and the fact that you have repeatedly used my given name." He released her and took up the wine and glasses. "You're right, of course. Please sit and tell me how you've fared in my absence."

They had already shared one amazing night of intimacy, so

why the hesitation now? She wasn't an innocent. She had known a man before and given birth to a son. God's bones, she tempted him, and he desperately wanted to divest her of her clothing and gorge himself on her hot center. He also prided himself on his self-control, which he found nowhere in evidence at present.

Before she took her seat, he raised his hands to pull her back into his embrace but stopped short. That would not be prudent and he knew it, recalling the words he'd rehearsed repeatedly; *answers, you need answers from her before this goes any further.* He couldn't shake the nagging thought that the answers he sought would profoundly affect the future of his clan. *You dinnae want an attachment. You dinnae want a wife, especially one with no acknowledged clan connections, and a Cameron to boot.*

He put the lie to himself again, but in the back of his mind, he knew it was a lie—all of it, except for the itching need to understand the mysteries surrounding her.

* * *

Andra had not yet taken a seat. Kendrick set the glasses and wine on the raised hearth facing the chairs. He started to reach for her again but stopped and silently waited. Even she knew this meeting alone in her room went beyond all propriety. But then again, what did anyone really know about the private, intimate engagements between men and women over three hundred years in her past. Why send away the most handsome, luscious man she'd ever met, a man who plainly wanted her as much as she wanted him. Soon enough she would find a way to leave, but for now, why not enjoy their time together. After all, she was a twenty-first century woman despite this temporary visit to the seventeen hundreds.

Relenting to the desire that flooded her senses, she decided not to deny the moment. Just thinking about their previous encounter made her wet and tingly with anticipation. The second time around could only be better than the first, and their first shared passion had been spectacular. Besides, she had truly missed him.

She smiled her most seductive smile and turned her back. "Will you help me unlace this gown, m'lai—Kendrick?" She

124

remembered him saying he liked the sound of his name when she spoke it. Moreover, this time she spoke it with unveiled longing.

When his fingers touched her shoulders, she noted their incredible strength. He leaned in and took a deep breath against her hair. "De you ken what you ask of me, Andra? Are you sure you want me to bed you again when I can make no promises, and I will not take you to wife? There are many questions I still need answered, and I suspect some of your own you'd wish to clarify."

And there it was—the proverbial bucket of ice dumped on her desire, strumming every fear she held at bay concerning her future should she not be able to leave this time period. Despite the heat from his touch and a blazing fire in the hearth, she suddenly shivered with chill. What would become of her? Who would protect her? She could not become his mistress or even more frightening, have him consider her his whore and pass her off to one of his men once he slacked his lust. Now that he knew about her son, he probably considered her a fallen woman or worse. What was she thinking to invite another tryst?

Her mouth dropped open at her stupidity and she stepped away, pulling her arms across her chest. His words were a flint igniting her anger. "I don't believe I've asked you to wed me, my laird." She harshly bit out the retort.

"Andra, I mean no offense. You know I desire you, and I can see the desire is mutual, but I will not lie to you. It is best we are clear about our standing before things between us progress."

"Of course," she snapped, "you are right, I'm just tired and not thinking clearly. Please, leave me." She squared her shoulders, straightened her back, and lifted her face to his.

A spark lit in his eyes. His mouth drew into a straight line and his jaw tensed. She could see the anger and frustration, but he didn't argue or comment. Without another word, he stormed out, slamming the door behind him.

Sleep evaded Andra that night. She tossed and turned. Just thinking about Kendrick's words made her burn and freeze in equal measure. "I must get my wits about me and find a way to return to my time," she whispered into the dark. Nevertheless, a crack had formed in that resolve though she ignored it completely.

Andra arose from her bed in the still-dark, pre-dawn hours. She pulled on a pair of her black leggings, black slip-on running shoes, and slipped on a plain linen shift and lightweight over gown. Finally, she pulled her leather vest over the shift and tied her hair in a ponytail with a piece of ribbon. It was time to get back into shape and it would start this morning. With her *sgian dubh* tucked into the inner pocket of her vest, she headed to the shed in the lower bailey to find the practice weapons stored there. She located the smaller weapons designed to teach younger boys the art of combat and pulled out a small bow and quiver of arrows. It would work perfectly for her purposes.

"Thank you, Dad," she said to the dark sky. Her father had insisted she learn archery and though she had originally balked at the idea, she quickly grew to love their time spent on the archery field.

Tucking the ends of her skirts into a knot at her side, she began with a good stretching routine. By the time she finished the sky had turned a deep violet-gray, and she could see the hay targets used for bow practice. Movement in the upper bailey alerted her that people had begun their early morning tasks, tending to the castle and its inhabitants. Stretching out tight muscles in her shoulders and arms, she notched an arrow and took aim at the closest target. Concentrating, she let the first arrow fly and quickly re-notched another arrow aiming for the next target farther out.

Chapter Twenty

Kendrick walked the parapet as he often did in the early morning before his clan and the demands of the keep claimed his time. He had slept little the night before. Thoughts of Andra plagued him. After leaving her last evening he went to the village inn, thinking he would slack his lust with a bar wench or some other willing woman. A comely lass accompanied him to an upper room, but when they reached the door, he abruptly changed his mind—something he had never done before.

He could not remove the vision of Andra with her head tilted; that sweet smile, those sultry eyes, her inviting, velvet voice made him grow hard just thinking about it. Then the sudden chilled reversal that arose when she stared him down and ordered him to leave her. She was, of course, in the right, but still...

He spied Andra leaving the keep and heading toward the practice fields. At first, he thought to go after her, but decided she could not reach any place unobserved from his present position. It would be better to examine her movement and discern why she skulked about in the dark.

"Well, well, will our mystery woman never cease to amaze us?" asked Rabbie, watching as another arrow smacked the center of its target even in the low light of pre-dawn. "She's an impressive woman, that she is. Did she disclose anything else last night?"

"Nae," Kendrick snapped.

Rabbie quirked an eyebrow, "Why don't you make her explain the things in her bag for starters? Mayhap it will nudge her to an open discussion."

"Humph. Perhaps a day in the dungeon would loosen her

tongue." However, Kendrick knew he would never throw her into that dank, filthy place under any circumstance, not even if she proved to be from an enemy clan. Besides, her recent illness still weakened her.

"She will withdraw further if I push too soon or too harshly." Yet he did want to push. He wanted to push and push until she disclosed every secret and then he wanted to push his hard manhood into her sweet flesh and claim her once again.

After Andra loosed a few more shots, she dropped the bow and arrows and started running toward the lower gate. Kendrick's muscles tightened. Did she intend to escape? When she approached the inside curtain wall, she picked up her pace and ran a circle around the entire bailey two more times before returning to the weapons she'd left on the grass. Bending over to retrieve the items, she suffered a severe coughing fit.

"What does she think she's doing, tiring herself in such a manner? She's barely recovered from her injuries and illness." Rabbie asked with an incredulous tone.

Kendrick admired her tenacity, though he too struggled to understand her motivation. "She behaves more like a warrior. It seems she intends to make herself fit with punishing trials. Not unlike our men might perform following an illness or injury. One of us must keep track of her at all times until we know what she's doing here and whether she works with someone who plots against the clan."

"Well, if 'tis exercise the woman needs, you should be able to handle that. A bit of frolicking might be something you both could use." Rabbie moved to avoid Kendrick's swing at him.

Kendrick bristled. "Be careful what you babble aboot, Rabbie."

"Perhaps a ride over our lands might help loosen her tongue is all I meant." They both knew it was not what he'd implied.

* * *

Later that morning Kendrick found Andra in the gardens with Jane. "Good day, ladies."

Jane bobbed a curtsey and quickly excused herself gathering

her basket of freshly cut herbs. Andra handed her basket to Jane as well. "Some of the herbs should be dried, but some I will steep and clarify to add to our creams, Jane. I'll join you a bit later."

With a sweep of his hand, he indicated they sit on a bench under an arbor heavy with vines whose leaves dropped in profuse, burnished brown piles. Neither of them spoke for a few minutes.

Andra had no idea how to begin a conversation to repair the rift that had occurred the previous evening. It was a stupid argument. Of course, he couldn't take her as his wife, nor did she want him to. Adjusting to eighteenth century mores presented a challenge, but she did not intend to stay for long.

Finally, Kendrick spoke. "I hear you've been working with Jane making soaps and such. I'm glad to see you settling into your surroundings. Do you feel well today?"

"Yes, thank you." She sounded distracted to her own ears. They were both reticent. *This is ridiculous. We need to be able to speak with one another.*

He seemed as awkward as she felt. He should be apologizing, but then again, she suspected he did not apologize often or easily. Perhaps she should apologize for her blatant capitulation to her desires. They started to speak at the same moment. She stopped and motioned he continue.

He didn't look at her for a second, then turned to capture her gaze. "It's a warm day. I thought mayhap you'd like to ride with me today."

"Oh, I'd love to." An invitation to ride was the last thing she'd expected.

"After watching your...er...exercise this morning in the bailey, I thought you might be well enough."

"Oh, you saw me? Yes, well, I'm anxious to regain my strength and stamina. A ride would be excellent. When might we leave?"

He studied the sky for a few minutes. "We should go soon. The weather may change abruptly later today, and I wouldn't want us caught by the elements so soon after your recovery. Are you sure your ribs can handle a ride?"

"I'm still a bit sore, but if we don't race at breakneck speed, I think I'll be fine."

At least a ride would re-engage them in pleasant conversation. Well, maybe it would. She expected a barrage of questions, but she wanted to make peace. That's what she told herself. In her heart, she wanted something more, something to do with *how* they might arrive at that peace.

They rode out of the bailey, he on his great, gray horse, aptly named Thunder, and she on a gentle, tan mare. Many of the trails skirted fields occupied with men who tended livestock or harvested grain. The golden fields rolled in waves under a soft breeze. Soon they reached a ridge overlooking the ocean. Kendrick pointed out various landscape anomalies, and conversed easily about his clan and the surrounding village and crofts. Every word and expression revealed his pride as he gazed over the land. Visible from this location, the castle's expanse of red sandstone shimmered in the sun. The red hills seemed to have birthed Ruadhstone Castle. Four concentric towers, the outer walls, and the inner structure of the keep looked like a natural part of the rugged landscape of towering spires.

Kendrick pulled them beside a cluster of scraggy pine trees and dismounted. He indicated a pack on the back of his horse. "I've brought refreshments." Taking her waist, he lifted her down, his hands lingering for several seconds before releasing her. He laid down a plaid. "Come, join me."

Sinking down beside him, she lifted her head eyes closed, and breathed deeply, "Mmmm, I love the smell of the ocean."

"Did you live near the ocean?" His nonchalant tone did not conceal his intention to commence the interrogation.

Questions already? What did she expect? "Yes, I can recall being near the ocean on many occasions over the years. My father loved the sea."

"So, you're regaining your memories?"

She dropped her head, her hand drifting to the cross at her neck. "I have many memories, Kendrick. I just can't explain how I came to be in Scotland. My father died. He'd asked me to return the family's ashes to his beloved Scotland. I was preparing to leave on my journey, and that is the absolute last thing I can recall before seeing you and your men riding through those trees."

"From where did you begin to prepare for the trip?"

What had she told him previously? "Truthfully, I cannot recall. I imagine it could have been most anywhere on our extensive travels. I know it was near the ocean, but nothing else is clear in my mind. Do not think that this lapse of memory does not trouble me as much as it seems to trouble you. In ways I can't begin to explain, it terrifies me that I have no idea how I arrived in Scotland."

It did indeed trouble her, but not for any reason he might imagine. The anxiety she felt when she allowed herself to dwell on the matter for too long barely described her terror. His frustration was quite evident, and she knew he was growing angry over her reluctance to disclose more.

"Lorne suggested you might have been in the heathen lands, accounting for your father's ashes. Andra, you can trust me, you ken. I'll not hold anything against you and will do everything in my power to provide assistance."

His entreaties were so intense, so earnest. She reached her hand to cup his jaw. "I trust you, Kendrick. If I could tell you more about how I came to be here, I would."

"What about your son's father?"

That question startled her. Dropping her eyes for a moment, she allowed the painful memories to swamp her but refused to cry. What else could she offer to answer his questions?

"As for Roy, my son's father, there is little to say. He has no claim on me, and I have none on him. I don't know his location, or even whether he lives, nor do I want to know. How or why I ever saw any redeeming quality in the man baffles me, and that is all I would like to say on the matter. I am absolutely certain he will never enter my life again." He had no idea the magnitude of that statement. Especially if she remained in this time since Roy wouldn't be born for centuries.

"I believe you speak the truth, but you continue to withhold.

Just listening to you speak of this worthless rake in your life makes me want to roar like a beast. You may think this is none of my business, but if you or your past poses a danger to my clan, then everything about you is of import to me."

This talk about Roy and her past upset her. When she turned her gaze back to him, she couldn't hide the sadness or the fear that clutched at her. On the one hand, he made her feel desired and safe, on the other hand anxious with his relentless probing.

"I'm so sorry to disappoint you, Kendrick, truly I am. Is it possible to take our time, allow the memories to return at a natural pace? I promise I pose no threat to you and your clan. No one misses me or searches for me. Of that, I'm certain.

She decided she might as well go for broke. "And I'm sorry about last night. I was just so happy to see you safely returned. I feel all at loose ends when you are not near me, as silly as that sounds."

Reaching a hand behind her neck, he brought his mouth to hers in a hungry, demanding kiss. Twining his fingers through her braid, he loosened her hair. He pulled her under him, and a deep rumble resonated from his throat.

The tensely bunched muscles of his arms surrounded her. It might be a mistake or only her wild imagination, but his embrace provided a deep sense of security. The crush of his hard chest against her breasts sent waves of heat and wetness between her legs. He pushed down the top of her bodice, ran a thumb over a hardened nipple, and pressed his thickened member against her abdomen. She rocked against him, urging more.

He sucked and nipped her nipple. "Ahh, my sweet, you're as ripe and ready as a plump berry.

Her aureoles puckered with arousal. The throbbing at her apex intensified exponentially when his hand slid along her thigh and pushed up her skirts. *What in God's name am I doing?* But she quickly slammed the door on further questions of that nature.

Of their own volition, her legs parted, granting him access, and he took it. The palm of his hand pressed onto her mons, his thumb rubbed heated circles against the nub of her arousal. Her hips thrust against his hand as his fingers invaded her warmth.

He pressed his forehead against hers. "You're beautiful. You make me forget myself. I ache for you, mo stór. I'm near bursting to enter you. Will you have me freely, Andra?"

He started to say more when she stopped him. "Say not another word, Kendrick. Let's not ruin this moment. You want me. I want you. Let that be enough." She pressed her mouth to his and suckled his full, lower lip then plunged her tongue into his mouth as he lifted above her and gently nudged the tip of his shaft against her entrance.

After a few, quick thrusts, a form of madness possessed her. She ignored all thoughts and the clanging bells urging caution. She fed their passion with full abandon. When she climaxed, she threw back her head, cried out her pleasure, and clutched him to her as he found his own release.

Sated and resting languidly in his arms, Andra's thoughts wrestled with concern over her recklessness. She couldn't seem to rein in her passion for this man, and he seemed less inclined than she did to proceed cautiously. Of course, he was a man and a laird; what did bedding one more woman matter to him. Yet the thought that she was most likely just another conquest hurt deeply, even though she chose to ignore those feelings. Besides, she suspected he would not pursue her if she rejected his advances, and right now, no matter how insane the idea, she definitely craved his pursuit.

Kendrick leaned over her and brushed his thumb along the worry lines creasing her forehead. "What troubles you, lass?"

"I...I don't know what to make of us, Kendrick. I think we are both behaving completely out of character. Well, perhaps not you, but I can certainly speak to my own behavior. This passion overrules my good sense and is more than a little unsettling."

Her eyes filled with tears and she lowered her lids hiding from his gaze, bewildered at her behavior. "I don't want to earn a poor opinion from you. I don't...I mean, I'm not...a loose woman. I have not been with a man since...." She paused, why did she suddenly feel the need to explain herself to him?

"Let me just say it's been many long and empty years." She

took a deep breath, "I am embarrassed at how easily you have breached my defenses."

Chuckling, he kissed her temple and gently pulled her into an embrace. "Do not fash yourself, Andra. 'Tis I who should apologize for taking inappropriate liberties. It is out of the norm for me as well, you ken." He held her away from him and studied her intently then stood and extended his hand to her.

Raising her to her feet, he draped his arm around her shoulders. "You are right, I am not behaving properly, and I should not press demands on you and take advantage of your vulnerability. Let us take our time, get to know each other better."

Andra could barely look at his lovely face. She didn't know how to handle this passionate reaction. Considering the situation, her behavior shocked and embarrassed her, especially in the glaring light of day. Everything she'd read about this time period suggested she'd be condemned for her forward behavior. Then again, sexual congress outside of marriage had been going on since the dawn of man. Maybe the societal mores often alluded to in books were overly presumptuous about women's chastity throughout time. Still, she couldn't argue that she seemed to be doing everything wrong and failed miserably at corralling her suddenly liberated libido. This passion, though magnificent, would most likely hurt her in the end.

As though he recognized her discomfort, he adroitly changed the subject. "The storm is moving in, we'd best return before the rain starts."

Chapter Twenty-One

For the next week or so, Andra lost track of time as one day morphed into the next with easy routine. Awake before dawn, she repeated the exercises she'd begun on the day she determined to get back in shape. She offered her services wherever she could around the keep. Working with Jane making salves and herbal-scented creams and soaps became her favorite job. In the evenings, she joined the family at the dais engaging those around her in congenial conversation. The children often talked her into telling stories or singing a goodnight lullaby.

Kendrick's duties took him away during the day and sometimes overnight. They had not spoken of their last outing and nor had he engaged her again. She longed for him to come to her, but at least they were on cordial terms. *That was good, wasn't it?*

When in the keep, she could feel Kendrick's presence and knew he tracked her movements as well. In all probability, no one missed his or her frequent furtive glances. Every night his footsteps halted outside her door, and every night he moved on to his own room and left her undisturbed. Then he would suddenly disappear for a few days.

Some days later, Andra walked beyond the castle walls for the first time, apart from her ride with Kendrick. She went with Jane and Isabel in search of the wild herbs that Jane said grew in a field adjacent the village.

A sudden ruckus near one of the cottages drew Andra's attention to a man knocking a young woman to the ground. The woman, a girl really, perhaps only sixteen or seventeen, her lip already swollen and bleeding cowered with her arms wrapped over her head. A brute of a man continued to lash blows on her even after she'd fallen. Andra sprinted ahead and stood in front of the woman. Arms up, hands tilted in front of her, she yelled, "Back off, mister. What do you think you are doing?"

A shocked expression flashed over his face as he took a momentary step back. Fury quickly replaced his astonishment. He spit at her feet. "How dare ye speak to me, ye whoring Sassenach. I'll treat my woman as I see fit, and ye'll stay out of me way, or I'll smack ye as well."

Isabel and Jane collectively gasped and called for Andra to return to them. Ignoring their pleas, she stood firm. She also ignored his slur. The derogatory term didn't surprise her. It didn't please her either. Unfortunately, rumormongers here would not differ from anywhere else; but it did heighten her indignation. "I don't think so, buster. She's just a girl, and that is no way to treat a woman of any age. What could she have possibly done to deserve such a brutal beating?"

"That's none of your concern," he snarled, puffing out his chest and stepping forward in a threatening manner.

She could smell the whisky on him. He was drunk. She spoke to the woman while keeping her eyes on the man. "Get up and go to the healer."

He pointed his finger at the woman. "If ye get up, ye'll nae be returning to this house."

Visibly shaken the woman seemed unable to respond. "Get up and go to Jane!" Andra commanded more forcefully.

"Ye'll nae be ordering my woman aboot, ye filthy Sassenach." He swung his arm to punch her. She effectively blocked the punch, though the block would result in a hefty bruise on her arm, and managed to flip him on his back. He kicked out and knocked her off her feet. By then, the guard who had been following the women at a discreet distance arrived, unsheathing his sword with a whistling hiss, which he pressed to the man's throat.

"Dinnae move or you'll taste my sword, you bastard. You'll answer to the laird when he returns."

That brought their outing to a swift, immediate conclusion.

Andra refused to leave the woman with the man and dragged her back to the keep with them.

Vera, who had witnessed the fracas on her return to the castle, had obviously run ahead and informed Beatrice, because the laird's mother and Lorne were standing on the steps when they came into the bailey.

By the time they reached the entrance, Andra had learned that the woman's name was Sile, and the man was her betrothed. The girl was barely sixteen, as she suspected. She went directly to Lorne and Beatrice and dipped into an awkward curtsy. "I witnessed this young girl being accosted and intervened on her behalf. My apologies for bringing her here without your permission, but I could not leave her under the circumstances."

* * *

Lorne shook his head, struggling to suppress a smile. Then he noticed Andra's clothing, dirty with leaves and sticks stuck to her gown, and a large tear along the hem and one sleeve. Her hair looked like she'd rolled in the dirt, and it tumbled around her shoulders in disarray. The smile left his face immediately. When Kendrick returned and learned of this altercation, all hell would break loose. "Come into the keep, and we will discuss the matter." He ordered everyone inside.

Isabel, Jane, and Sile were visibly upset. Beatrice turned to her son. "I'll take them to my rooms and learn what they have to say about the matter. They should not stay here under everyone's scrutiny."

"Nae, let us all go to Kendrick's solar to discuss the matter. Have one of the servants bring warm cider and wine."

They had barely disclosed details of the event when thundering footsteps slammed down the hall. The door banged against the wall, and Kendrick entered with Rabbie and Struan close on his heels, still dirty, and sweaty from their activities of the day.

"News here travels faster than on YouTube," Andra groaned. Lorne glanced at her quizzically, but did not remark on her strange words because all eyes were riveted on their laird. A scowl covered Kendrick's face and tension flew off him in heated waves.

"Join us, Kendrick." Lorne said to his brother, keeping his voice calm. "It seems there has been an altercation with this young lady and her intended," he waved his hand toward Sile, "and Andra saw fit to intervene for her safety."

* * *

"So I have heard." He crossed his thick arms over his chest and scowled at everyone in the room, noting the young girl's swollen face covered with bruises and her lip crusted with blood.

His mother, always calm and cool during times of distress, rose gracefully to greet him. "Won't you take refreshment, son? Wine or whisky?"

"Whisky, thank you, Mother." Glaring at the group he continued, "Someone better start explaining the situation."

Before anyone could utter a sound, Isabel ran into her brother's arms. "It was terrible, Kendrick. We found this poor lass being sorely mistreated by her drunken, crazed betrothed. Andra stepped in to save her. She was magnificent. You would've been verra proud."

He raised his eyebrows at his sister, and patted her back. "Shush Isabel, you are safe now." With a smoldering glare, he turned his face to Andra.

"Mother, I think the young ladies have had enough excitement for one day. Please escort them to their quarters. Sile will stay in the women's solar for the night."

Beatrice handed a cup of whisky to Kendrick then ushered the girls from the room. Isabel dipped a shy glance at Rabbie as they exited. When Andra rose to leave, he pointed at her, "You, stay."

Lorne and the guard reiterated the story. "Shall we put the man in the dungeon for a day to dry out, brother?"

"Aye, that would be best. Struan will see to it. We'll discuss what to do with the man once he sobers up. Meanwhile, I'd like to speak with Andra privately."

When Lorne passed his brother, he placed a hand on his shoulder, "She was only trying to help. She's been away from the Highlands for a verra long time. Besides, you ken you have said repeatedly that no man should raise a hand in anger to a woman. Any one of us would have done as she did."

Kendrick grunted in response as his men left the room.

With a hard edge to his voice, he addressed Andra, "With a guard nearby why did ye not wait for his assistance?"

"He did assist me. Initially however, he was too far away from us for me to wait. The brute was huge and beating that poor girl. I couldn't stand by and allow that to continue. And I would step in again if I came upon it tomorrow." She stubbornly lifted her chin, making it clear she would not apologize for her action.

He took three wide steps across the room and pulled her into his embrace, cradling her head in one large hand the other one splayed across the small of her back. "You're going to be the death of me. You could have been seriously injured or killed. What possessed you to step between a drunken man and his woman? Come to me first, or to Lorne, Rabbie, Struan, or one of the other men. You mustn't put yourself at such risk, do you understand me?"

She laid her head on his shoulder. A bone-weary sigh escaped her throat. "I think I'm very tired and need a bath. We can discuss this later, can we not?"

He held her away from his chest and she winced at the pressure of his hand over her arm. When he pushed up her torn sleeve and saw a bruise already purpling, he stepped back and noticed the other damage to her gown. His nostrils flared and a battle roar shook the rafters. "I will kill the man myself."

She laid a calming hand to his chest. "No, Kendrick, I'm fine. It's just a bruise. He inflicted no serious damage, he was drunk, and he's a brute. But you needn't kill him."

How had this slip of a woman managed to unleash his protective and possessive nature to a finely honed lance he'd gladly wield against anyone intending her harm? "You must promise me you'll never do that again, Andra."

"I am capable of protecting myself, but I'll come to one of you first, if that's possible."

"Nae Andra, not if. You must always come to one of us. That is nonnegotiable. Our ways may not be what you're accustomed to. A man has the right to do with his wife as he sees fit, but I will not abide brutality toward women and bairns in my clan. Still, you must not interfere. Do you understand me?"

She hugged him tightly, then stepped away, placing a cool hand to his cheek. "My honorable, fierce Highlander," she smiled up at him and with a sweet, tired voice said, "I think I need to rest now."

He recognized the avoidance tactic, but she did look exhausted so he dropped the subject for now. He offered her his arm and escorted her to her room. "Shall I stay with you, Andra?"

"No, I think I need some time to myself. I'd like to retire early."

He had hoped she would invite him into her room, but he would not force himself on her. When she closed the door, he placed his hand on the hard surface, trying to quell the equally hard shaft between his legs. Just smelling her lemon-mint scent was enough to unhinge him. It took all his restraint to keep from going to the dungeon to rip apart, with his bare hands, the man who had injured Andra. How dare any man in his clan touch her with violence? He truly felt murderous at the thought. Staying with her would be a far more preferable and enjoyable release from his frustration.

Chapter Twenty-Two

Every night he found himself outside her door, hard and throbbing, wanting to enter her room and her body. Every night he left her undisturbed. He woke early every day and walked the parapets to observe her exercises. He engaged in fierce practice sessions with his men and took even harder rides, punishing every horse in the stables. He wanted her, more than he wished to admit. But his father and the elders would resist his marriage to an unknown with no clan ties. Her Cameron surname would also raise suspicion in many minds.

Almost a week had passed since the incident outside the village, and they had not been together for more than a few brief moments each day he was at the keep. Though always courteous, even flirtatious at times, their encounters never progressed to anything more. He'd tell himself it was best to stay away from her; the relationship shouldn't progress further. However, that was a lie, and he knew it. He intentionally avoided her despite a throbbing urgency that robbed him of his sleep and interfered with nearly every waking moment.

He felt like a foolish, green lad courting his first lass. That feeling was beyond bizarre considering the passion they had already shared. What did this desire mean exactly? Most of the time, he craved her with unreserved lust. Yet when he thought about them together, he longed to have the spitfire as a permanent part of his life. What did she want from him? Not permanence it seemed. He often caught her staring into the distance with a sad, yearning expression on her face. And as yet, she had failed to disclose anything to help him understand the dilemma and mystery of her presence.

The next morning when Andra entered the bailey just before dawn, Kendrick watched as one of his young warriors approached her. They engaged in an easy banter. He could tell she attempted to cajole the lad into something. The crystal peal of her laughter drifted on the morning air as clear as a chime even from the distance he stood. A jolt of jealousy gripped him so savagely he nearly fell over the wall.

To his amazement, she engaged the man in hand-to-hand combat. "God's teeth! What possesses the lass to be so brazen?" Then he had to cover a laugh as he watched her flip the man over her thrust out hip. "So that's how she did it."

Struan harrumphed coming to stand beside him. "Mayhap we should engage your wee banshee in our training practices. Her skills continue to improve and they were impressive to begin with." Kendrick's focus was so riveted on her activities that he hadn't heard his friend's approach.

"I think not." Kendrick's temper ratcheted up. "It seems I must stop her morning activities. It's not good to have the lads too focused on her, especially if she can drop them with so little effort. 'Twould cause no end of problems managing the men." Why did Struan's comment irritate him so much?

Struan laughed, "Seems to me it either speaks poorly of the lad's skills, or quite highly of hers."

The fact that Struan found the situation amusing provoked Kendrick. "Our men are the best-trained warriors in the Highlands and you ken it."

"Mayhap you're right though," Struan continued, ignoring him, his usual scowl plastered over his face. "Next thing you ken other women will be in the bailey with their wee fists flailing aboot, challenging the men to duels." Then he laughed again—a deep, rumbling sound. Kendrick could only stare at his friend in the throes of inexplicable humor.

Few people gained Struan's praise, much less a woman. It surprised Kendrick to find the man champion Andra's activities, even though he attempted to hide it under his bushy scowling brows.

Kendrick knew the guards also keenly followed her morning routine. Every day more guards walked the parapet to watch her target practice and exercise, and he found himself agitated and short tempered with all of them. However, to directly engage one of his men in her practices was unacceptable; the last straw. He shouldn't have tolerated her unladylike behavior, but he had enjoyed watching her. He found her endlessly fascinating.

"I should have stopped this at the beginning," he snarled. Racing down the stairs, he entered the lower bailey with purposeful strides. Unaware of his approach, she continued to parry and block blows with the lad.

"What de you think you are doing?" he growled. The lad, Michael, immediately dropped his arms and Andra landed a sharp blow to the young man's midsection, bowling him over.

"What does it look like? We're sparring," she answered, with more than a little irritation in her voice.

"Our men dinnae spar with women. Leave the bailey, Michael," he commanded with a growl. "Go polish and sharpen the blades." He dismissed the lad with a wave of his hand while glaring at Andra.

"I've allowed this to go on long enough. I've made allowances for your behavior because you're not a proper Highland lady, but you are not behaving like any lady I have ever known, from the Highlands or elsewhere. You will refrain from this undignified display henceforth."

He raked his eyes over her lithe form and noted the skirt knotted to one side hiked above one knee. Even though she wore her tight trews underneath, this was not proper garb. So why did he find her attire so fetching, even a bit amusing? Even worse, why did he want to strangle every man who watched her?

He knew why. He had taken her body and that meant she was his and his alone. Yet that wasn't true either. He had not taken her; she had presented herself to him. The first time, she had served herself up like a ripe, dewy peach on a platter of moonlight and pine scent. The second time was an equally satisfying, mutual coupling. She gave, he took. He gave, she took.

A snappish retort brought his focus back to the present moment. "Oh, that's rich. I stand here in the wild Highlands where men are brutes who treat women with less regard than their horses, and you dare to tell me that it's improper for a woman to strengthen her body or learn basic self-defense techniques because it's not ladylike!"

A sheen of sweat covered her brow, her hands fisted at her hips; she near vibrated with a need to vent her anger and frustration. Moreover, she'd selected him as her target. "You think to chastise me and dictate whether I have the right to defend myself, yet you can't even give me a proper greeting for days at a time. Well, think again, sir."

"I'll have you know, I am quite skilled in the art of self-defense. If I were you, I'd see that every woman and lass in this castle knew at least a few rudimentary techniques of self-defense, not to mention skill with a bow or at least with a dirk." Her voice continued to rise precipitously. "What if one of your fine warriors or one of your enemies sets upon an unsuspecting woman wishing to do her harm? Should she not have the right to defend herself?" Of course, she referred to the incident with Sile.

"Hold your wheesht." He grabbed her arm, his fingers biting into her flesh, "You are not me, now are you? The women of my clan dinnae need to fear for their safety because my men ken their duties and protect the clan and dinnae abuse women in their care."

She smacked his hand away, "No, I will not quiet. I am my own person, more than capable of making a few decisions as to what I should do to improve my health and strength in order to survive in this—"

She stopped herself mid-speech, and he wondered what else she'd almost revealed. In her anger, she had disclosed much that made no sense to him. On the other hand, her father had probably taught her methods of self-defense for her safety as they traveled the world.

"You could hardly call what happened to Sile protection." she hissed and jerked away stomping off toward the weapons shack.

Kendrick caught her in a few strides. "From this moment on

you will confine yourself to the castle and duties of a proper lady."

She raised her chin at him, "Maybe I'm not a lady. Maybe I don't want to sit demurely sewing or tending to your every whim or the needs of your barbaric men. What then? You'll cast me out—deem me unacceptable or damaged goods? Why can't you just leave me alone if I don't meet your high and mighty criteria of a proper lady? My workouts don't interfere with other duties I have assumed in the keep. I have not heard any complaints."

"There is much talk about you, lass, and some of it is not to your benefit." Kendrick's hand tightened on her arm. The speculation about her caused many raised eyebrows. After the confrontation over Sile, and everyone's awareness of her morning exercises, the gossip had spun in every direction imaginable. Fortunately, she had charmed many clan members with her thoughtful interactions and quick willingness to lend a hand. Besides, a number of women had already expressed a dislike of Sile's intended, so plenty of them praised her reaction in that matter. Still, he intended to squash further confrontations like this morning's display and the gossip that would surely follow.

Tears welled in her eyes, but she blinked to prevent them from spilling over her lashes and pelted him with a determined glare. "You're hurting my arm—which proves my point. Please release me, and I'll return to my room."

He loosened his hold but did not release her completely. "You try my patience, Andra. Why must you constantly be obstinate and flaunt your differences? Dinnae you realize the harm it could cause you?"

She turned away from him, adopting that quiet stare that took her a million miles away. "Talk to me, Andra. Tell me what troubles you. Why do you feel the need to work yourself like a man training for battle?"

"That's just it. It seems to me living—," she paused, then heaved a heavy sigh dropping her shoulders as though defeat weighed them down. He felt her retract the words about to slip from her lips. When she spoke again, her voice barely lifted above a whisper. "Living in a world where every day you are faced with constant danger means everyone must be prepared for battle at all times, wouldn't you agree?"

"Are you daft? Do you really think you could protect yourself against the likes of my men? Nae, you cannae. 'Tis why you must do as I say. No woman could stand against a trained Highland warrior no matter how great her skill."

Frustration creased her brow, "Never mind. It is clear you tire of your pledge to protect me. Since I do not fit snugly into your definition of a lady, I release you from any further obligation on my behalf. You needn't concern yourself about my welfare."

A flash of heated determination smoldered in her eyes. "However, listen well to me Kendrick; I will *not* cease my practice or workouts. If it is too distressing to you and your men, please advise where I might continue away from everyone's observation."

God's teeth, she was pushing his last fiber of control. "You won't defy me on this, Andra. You won't go outside the keep unaccompanied, and you will desist with this uncomely display."

"Then perhaps it is time I seek sanctuary elsewhere." Andra broke from his grip and flew across the bailey and into the keep.

He watched her go, a war raging in him. He would not let her leave; of that, he was certain. He looked up to the parapet. Only Struan and Rabbie stood in view, the other men had wisely moved to the far corners and out of sight.

* * *

Later that day, as Andra approached the women's solar, the earlier exchange between herself and Kendrick kept replaying in her mind. Why had she behaved like an angry shrew? She could not settle her thoughts. She wanted him with a fierceness that disquieted her. Her chest wrenched with a desperate need for Kendrick to want her as well. There was also a seething urge to smack the man. He had remained courteous, but aloof since their last sexual encounter. What? He hadn't been satisfied? He certainly seemed more than satisfied at the time. By twenty-first century mores, many men would consider her behavior reserved, possibly even prudish. Yet here she didn't fit the typical mold of an eighteenth century lady; she never would. Now he'd reprimanded her attempts

146

to regain her full vigor. Of course, he could not understand her behavior; she barely understood it herself. More importantly, had her angry words this morning caused an irrevocable breach that would land her in far worse circumstances?

Once in the women's solar, she fidgeted and shifted in her seat. All effort to ply her hand at stitching failed miserably. Beatrice noticed her poor attempts at needlework.

"I imagine accompanying your da on his worldly travels dinnae provide many opportunities to perfect your stitching." Her voice was gentle, almost sad. It reminded Andra how imperfect and unqualified she must appear to the woman.

"I'll admit it is not my best talent." She smiled in spite of her discomfort.

"Aye, but she is an expert markswoman with a bow," mentioned Isabel.

"So I've been told," laughed Lady Beatrice. "Everyone brings their own gifts and talents to their family. Dinnae fash yourself, dear, I happen to agree that women should use every skill they possess, even if it be a bow and arrow. Many Highland lasses are quite skilled with the bow and even hunt to feed their families when the men are away."

Andra's face flushed with embarrassment. She had not been aware the women knew of her morning activities. She knew the guards observed her from the parapet, but no one attempted to curtail her activities until Kendrick so abruptly accosted her this morning. None of the women or the guards had made a comment to her about it. How stupid she was being. Gossip provided the main form of entertainment at the castle; of course everyone knew about her practices. The gossip mongers must be having a grand time at her expense.

Jane entered with an ancient, stooped woman holding her arm. Lady Beatrice rose to assist the woman shuffle to the chair beside her. "Alith, we have missed you these many days. 'Tis good to see you improved enough to join us today."

"Och, I am fine, my dear. Dinnae fash yourself over me. Sweet Jane tends to me needs."

Jane expertly fluffed a cushion and placed it behind the old woman's back.

"I keep hearing an angel singing. Her voice is as pure and clear as the deep, blue loch outside the castle walls. Would this be the lass?" The old woman looked at Andra through eyes milky with age.

"Lady Alith, let me introduce you to our guest, Lady Andra Cameron."

"Come sit beside me, these old eyes need you close to see."

Andra sat beside Alith and took the old woman's gnarled hand in hers. "It's my great pleasure to meet you, Lady Alith."

The old woman squinted in an effort to clear her vision, then touched Andra's cheeks with both hands. Her hands were cool and felt like light sandpaper. When her hand dropped over Andra's, her fingers slid over her rings. "These are verra fine rings on your fingers."

"Yes, they belonged to my parents."

"Ah," she seemed to drift for a moment. "And are they with you, lass?"

"No, my parents are both dead."

"Tsk tsk. And what of your other kin, do you seek to find them?"

"No, there is no one left, only me." Andra said, her chest so tight she could barely whisper the words.

"'Tis a sad thing to be the last of your line, to lose all those you love," Alith soothed. She squeezed Andra's hands with surprising strength. "Be comforted, the MacLean's are a fine clan and always welcoming. You will do well here, just give it time."

* * *

Vera sat quietly off to the side, attempting to appear as though she were not eavesdropping. She frequently joined the women when they gathered to mend clothing and ply their needlework. It presented the perfect opportunity to both start and gather gossip. Dispersing tidbits of information to interested parties provided a chance to earn extra coin or personal favors, always a value to her.

Andra's continued presence felt like a burr under Vera's skirts. She seethed with jealousy over the new woman in their midst.

What was all the fuss about anyway? Why did the men lose their focus when Andra entered a room or sang her stupid songs? *Simpering fools ruled by their cocks.*

The laird had not enjoyed Vera's favors in over a year, but she had consoled herself that it was because he'd spent much of that time away from the castle. Now he had this foolish woman distracting him from her attentions. He barely even acknowledged her presence anymore and that prevented her from obtaining knowledge that would add weight to her purse. All over a stinking Sassenach no less! Why was the laird so interested in the woman? Since Andra claimed to be a Cameron and a Sassenach, she knew just who would pay to know about her.

Chapter Twenty-Three

The following morning Andra went down to the bailey before the first gray streaks softened an inky sky. She carried the urn in her leather satchel. Kneeling in the dirt, she opened the smooth wooden container sifting its contents to test how much remained. "Enough for several more attempts," she whispered.

"Okay, Dad, let's try again shall we? I need to leave this place. Please, Dad, send me home." She touched the cross at her neck reverently and let a few ashes drift on the wind. Without realizing it, she started to sing and rock back and forth. Nothing happened, but more than a few eyes watched her in the dark.

After several minutes, tears trickled down her face. Perhaps she needed to be in the exact place where she had first come through to this time in order for her efforts to weave their spell and send her back to the twenty-first century. She would need to devise a plan to return to that place. First, she must resume her workouts. No matter what Kendrick dictated, she refused to relinquish her fitness and strength building efforts.

A bare sliver of moon did not provide sufficient light to see the far targets. Only the two closest to her were somewhat visible. No matter, she would take a few practice shots based on her memory and the dim outline of the stacks. She'd learned to shoot at night when you relied on the sounds around you and the movement of shadow over shadow rather than clear vision. She hit the targets several times, then dropped her bow and started her run around the bailey.

Trailing along the outside wall of the keep, she sprinted full out. The air was clean from a midnight rainstorm. The pliant ground leaned to muddy but she never let a bit of rain or mud stop her before, and she certainly wouldn't let it happen in this new place. When she turned at the lower end, her foot caught on a tree root that had crept under the wall. Falling face first into the dirt the air knocked from her lungs, she paused only long enough to brush off, commit the location of that root to memory, and sprint away again. Another few minutes passed before a strong arm lifted her off her feet.

"What do you think you are doing? Did I not command you to cease these activities?" Kendrick's words hissed in her ear.

Andra squirmed against him and pummeled the arm wound tightly around her waist. "Release me, you brute. You may have commanded me, but I told you I had no intention of stopping my workouts."

Kendrick flipped her over his shoulder with no effort. She continued to struggle, flailing her arms against his back, and attempting to kick him with her feet. He tightened his hold on her legs and soundly smacked her ass. "I warned you, Andra, you will not defy me."

When they reached her room, he kicked the door open then slammed it shut with the heel of his boot. Planting her firmly in front of him while pinning her arms to her sides, he gave her his most intimidating scowl and growled deep in his throat.

A raging defiance tensed her stance, and then she suddenly drooped, feeling a bone-deep weariness. "Don't you tire of this, Kendrick? Can't we call a truce? Can't you let me do as I wish while you go about your own business?"

"Nae, you will not do as you wish. I am laird, this is my castle, these are my people, and no wee lass will be usurping my authority. Sitting in the dirt keening into the night will make people think you are a witch or mad or both. Moreover, I've already told you to stop your training. Mayhap a few days in the dungeon will cool your continued belligerence."

A tight muscle ticked in his jaw, his lips were a grim line, and his eyes flared with febrile heat. Every muscle in his shoulders and arms tensed. He was serious and very angry, and she had no desire to spend any time in a dungeon. This was not good.

She let her shoulders slump and tried to relax under his grip, but kept his gaze. "I am truly sorry, Kendrick. Let us not argue, please. Can't we find a compromise so you are satisfied and I can continue to improve in strength and skills? It really is in my best interest. I enjoy the invigorating challenge of archery and running. I used to run long distances every day."

* * *

"In your best interest!" he roared. "Why do you think that what you consider in your best interest would overrule my direct orders?" How could it possibly be in her best interest to train like a warrior? His fingers tightened on her arm. Moreover, where had she lived that she could run long distances every day without risk of attack, unless guards had accompanied her?

His expression would have stopped any of his men in their tracks, but not Andra; she refused to look away or back down.

This would not do. He could not have her countermanding him in front of his men, a fair number of whom walked along the parapet yesterday and again this morning. Clearly, this brazen lass and her pre-dawn activities titillated everyone's curiosity.

"Lass, you must desist. I am not a brute, but you drive me to behave like one. Surely you ken my men would lose respect for me if I failed to punish your rash behavior." He could only think of one form of punishment he wanted to deliver. His burgeoning cock surged and thrust for release in her.

"I would have lashed any man who dared disobey me in such a manner to within an inch of his life." Fear flashed in her green eyes, and they brimmed with tears. She fought valiantly against them, but a few escaped, leaving white tracks through the dirt smudged on her cheeks.

Damn, if she didn't tug at every emotion he kept buried and under tight control. He leaned toward her. When she did not turn away, his mouth crushed over hers, his tongue demanded entrance to her hot depths. Andra relented and opened her lips to his invasion. When he released her arms, they slipped around his neck and desperately clung to him. Their heated passion flared, as undeniable as the rising sun.

A sort of madness consumed him. Although still angry with her, he also admired her obstinacy, and he desired every ounce of her fire. He deftly removed her shift and sucked at the spot under her jaw where her pulse pounded wildly, then nipped and kissed her throat and her beautiful, full breasts. His tongue flicked over the chemise covering her tight buds and drew a firm mound into his mouth suckling deeply.

Her head flew back; she groaned loudly, nails scraping through his hair, over his shoulders. She unpinned his plaid and it dropped in a puddle on the floor, then tugged his leine over his head.

He pressed his hard member against her pubic bone. Rather than pull away, she pressed the entire lean length of her body tightly to his. He swung her into his arms and moved to deposit her on the bed. His hands slid down her sides and pushed her leggings down smooth, firm flesh. She kicked the clothing away with her feet.

Kendrick rose above her, resting on his elbows. His thumbs swiped the tears and dirt from her face. God's teeth, he wanted this woman in his bed every night, he wanted her fierce defiance and lush passions. Though certain he didn't wish to stop, he paused, granting her a moment to change her mind.

She lifted her legs around his thighs and rolled her hips so her wet slit moved over the tip of his shaft. His coiled muscles tensed under her touch. She urged him on. "Kendrick, please."

He nudged against her mound and slowly dipped into her heat. Their tongues tangled and in one swift stroke, he plunged into her depths. She shifted slightly, adjusting to his length, then clenched her muscles tightly around him and everything exploded. Crazed with need their mouths devoured each other's cries and moans. When his fingers reached between them and he rolled his thumb over her nub, she cried out with an intense orgasm. She sucked his shoulder and bucked against him, urging him to find his own release simultaneously as he roared his completion.

When he finally rolled away sated and exhausted, he took her with him until she draped across his chest. It took several minutes before they regained their voices.

Kendrick kissed the top of her head and chuckled. "*Mo chuisle*, I think I could grow accustomed to punishing you this way."

Her fingers danced over his skin with a feather light touch. "Please don't put me in the dungeon."

He stiffened, then rolled to face her. "You dinnae need to bed me to ask that boon, m'lady." He didn't find her comment amusing. Did she capitulate in an attempt to bargain against his not truly serious threat?

Andra pushed against him and jumped from the bed. "This..." she waved her hand over the bed, "I—this—you think I made love with you to cajole you out of—what! It was a joke, you buffoon. You think I bedded you out of fear?" Her mouth opened and closed with sputtering gasps. She grabbed the bed clothes and covered her nakedness. "How dare you cheapen what just happened with such an accusation. Get out!" she screamed at him, pointing to the door. "Get out you-you, monster!" She turned away from him, struggling to contain a sob that still managed to escape her throat.

Kendrick wrapped his kilt around him with amazing speed. He studied her back, rigid with anger. He knew that the boon comment was the wrong thing to say, and for the life of him, he did not understand why he'd said it. Did he really think she had bedded him out of fear that he would lock her in the dungeon? Yes, no, perhaps. Many women would have done just that, hoping to escape punishment for misbehavior. Yet her passion flared like a shooting star, she desired him as much as he desired her, and not because she feared any threat of retribution.

He couldn't bring back the words and he needed space from her to think about this growing attachment. "As you request, m'lady, but you will spend a few days in your room and not leave until we speak again. That is an order, and I warn you not to test my patience further." Kendrick firmly closed the door, slipped a bolt, and locked her in. His mind was a muddled mess.

When Kendrick stormed into the bailey, the first rosy streaks of day splashed across the sky and several men had begun sparring. Andra's leather satchel containing the funeral urn lay where she'd left it on the ground next to the bow and arrows she'd used in her practice. He snatched them up and set them aside to return to her later. He called to one of the squires for his practice claymore. Weapon in hand, he entered the arena. The men, clearly aware of his sour mood, occupied themselves in heated mock battles, pretending not to notice his presence.

He approached Struan, Rabbie, and Alec. "Prepare to test your skills men!"

No matter how hard he punished himself, he could not wipe from his mind the expression of hurt he'd brought to Andra's face. It was obvious that neither one of them possessed one ounce of control when their desires surged. He wanted to trust her, yet after all they had been through and all they had shared, she still refused to be completely honest. *Why? Why?* No feasible explanation came to him. Women were damned confusing creatures. For now, this vigorous exertion provided the only means available to vent his exasperation.

Thirty minutes later, bent over and struggling to gather their breath, all four men dripped with sweat. Alec excused himself to tend to some of the younger boys.

"Have you punished us enough yet, cousin?" Rabbie asked.

He snarled. "What are you blathering aboot!"

"Seems to me he's got the right of it" Struan huffed. "You do seem to be in a more punishing frame of mind than usual. We all ken what this is aboot. We both saw you sling Andra over your shoulder like a sack of grain. Dae you need one of us to handle the lass for you, then?"

A swift cuff to the jaw knocked Struan to the ground. Kendrick stood over him hands on his hips, fury in his eyes. "Dinnae push me on this, Struan. Furthermore, none of you will handle the lass," he thundered and then stormed out of the bailey.

Rabbie lent a hand to pull Struan to his feet. "That went well, wouldn't you say?"

Chapter Twenty-Four

Never before had Andra felt so desired or so eager to take a man to her bed. Their passion for each other unmoored her senses. Every time they argued, they seemed unable to control the explosion of desire that surfaced alongside their anger. And when faced with the option to turn him away, she had pushed the small voice of caution to the furthest reaches of her mind and embraced the want and need that swept every other thought away like yesterday's dust.

Andra dropped on the bed and buried her face in the pillows to smother the wrenching sound of her sobs. *You are so stupid.* Why had she jumped into bed with him again? Why did she even mention that damn dungeon? It was a passing thought, a joke. Okay, maybe not, but she didn't think he was serious about that anyway—or did she? He seemed to enjoy messing with her mind and likewise, she knew she got under his skin with her constant obstinacy and defiance. Why did she do that?

Andra could see the men engaged in mock battles in the corner of the lower bailey. After a few hours, a faint knock tapped at her door. It sounded too soft to be Kendrick and she couldn't open the door anyway, as he had locked it from the outside. She heard the lock click then the door swung open. A kitchen maid entered, head bowed, carrying a tray with cheese, bread, fruit, and ale. Kendrick must have posted a guard outside the door. The man waited at the threshold, watching the maid, but never looking at Andra. Once the girl scurried down the hall, the guard closed and relocked the door without comment.

Andra sipped the ale, but took only a bite or two of the food.

Perhaps she could get the guard to allow her to go to the women's solar. She knocked at the door. "Are you out there?"

"Do you need something m'lady?" the man asked.

"You may have my tray returned to the kitchen." He opened the door. "May I go to the women's solar? I believe Lady Beatrice expects me."

He accepted the tray, but did not make eye contact. "Sorry, m'lady, but the laird has ordered you're to rest, and no one is to disturb you." He closed and locked the door without further comment.

Hours later, faint sounds filtered into her room as the clan gathered for the evening meal. Still, no one came to her door and no additional food arrived. Hours passed, but she couldn't gauge the time. She regretted sending the noon meal back to the kitchen with barely a mouthful eaten as hunger now rumbled like a snarling dog in her stomach.

The sun had long ago dipped over the horizon, and the last streaks of amber color at the rim between earth and sky had faded to a bruised blush. She watched the darkening sky fill with the splendor of a thousand dazzling stars, and barely felt the chill in the air. Bereft and achingly empty she watched a sliver of moon crest the distant hills as they darkened to black. Rather than stuck in a dank dungeon, she at least looked out at the world from her window.

"What am I to do now, Dad? I can't get back. I'm falling hard for a mad Highland warrior who is not interested in me for any purpose other than to slack his lust. To tell the truth, I'm not complaining too much on that accord, he is quite thrilling actually. Okay, I'm sure you don't want to hear about that anyway." She missed her father with a bone-grinding ache. He had been her constant champion. Their relationship exemplified much more than mere parent and child. He had always been her best friend.

"Ahh, Dad, none of what I'm experiencing fits your romantic tales about chivalry and honor. I do everything wrong, say the stupidest things, irritate the people I must rely on for my sustenance and safety. I want to go home, and then again, I don't. I'm lost, Dad. Can you hear me?" she implored the heavens as silent tears slipped down her cheeks.

* * *

When his mother and the bairns asked after Andra at the evening meal, Kendrick told them she felt unwell and should not be disturbed.

Lorne raised an eyebrow and cocked his head when he heard his brother lie to their mother. Kendrick knew Lorne had seen him physically remove Andra from the bailey that morning, as had several other men. Lorne had asked after her when Kendrick passed him on his way to the bailey that morning, commenting on how long their discussion had taken, but Kendrick decided to keep their issues to himself and just grumbled.

Lorne called Kendrick aside. "What happened between you and Andra? Did she spurn your advances, brother?"

"'Tis none of your business, leave it for now, Lorne."

Lorne was not about to drop the issue. "Dinnae you think it's a bit harsh to deny her food and separate her from the bairns? Mother will not be pleased to hear you are keeping her locked up."

"Are you questioning me, Lorne?" Kendrick seethed. He had been right; her behavior disrupted his authority. Everyone seemed to champion the lass despite her outrageous exploits. "You forget yourself, brother. She will not leave her room until I release her. And you ken I'd never deny her sustenance."

Lorne shrugged his shoulders and with some asperity said, "As you command, *Laird.*" His brother did not conceal his annoyance.

When Kendrick approached Andra's door carrying a tray of food, he could hear Andra speaking. "I told you to admit no one to her room." He admonished the guard.

"I swear, the lady is alone. She has been humming and singing and mumbling for hours, but no one has entered the room." Kendrick dismissed the man with a wave of his hand.

He listened outside her door for several minutes. Soon she started to sing a song he had not yet heard. Pressing his ear closer, he strained to catch the words. Her voice strummed a deep, inner chord that always made him want to fold her in his arms. As she sang words he'd not previously heard, the hairs rose across his neck and arms. The haunting melody told about lovers finding each other, merging into one. The words slipped into his head and heart like quicksilver. He knew he'd never expel them from his mind. The room grew quiet when she finished. He unlocked the bolt and entered.

"I have brought your evening meal, lass." He set the tray on the table by the fire, now reduced to a few dying embers. He added a log and peat and stoked the blaze. She did not turn from her position by the window.

"Come, sit, and eat, Andra. You barely touched your noon meal. As you say, it is in your best interest to regain your strength."

"It seems I've no appetite, Laird MacLean. And by your own admission, you have little interest in my vitality."

He wanted to shake some sense into her. He wanted to brush the russet waves of hair away from her nape, lick, and kiss every inch of her neck and all regions above and below. "You are wrong there, Andra. I care verra much for your welfare. Is that so difficult for you to comprehend? Have I not brought you into the fold of my clan, fed you, clothed you?"

"Yes, you have done all of that, and I must seem exceedingly difficult and ungrateful. I cannot thank you enough for your kindnesses. I—what are you doing?"

She stopped abruptly when he strolled toward the wardrobe and rooted through her things. She studied him with an unabated panic that made him want to smother her with kisses and cosset her in his embrace, but he intended to end her constant prevarication.

Kendrick turned to Andra holding her carpetbag and her leather satchel in his hands. He scrutinized her response, wondering at the terror on her face, then emptied the contents of her bags onto the bed.

"It is time to answer my questions, Andra. I have no desire to distress you. I ken you've been through an ordeal. I've been patient, now you need to trust me. I give you my word; no harm will come to you no matter what you disclose." He hoped he could honor that promise.

She stood there; arms wrapped tightly across her chest, a slight breeze blowing strands of hair around her face. Shoulders squared, back straight, teeth nibbling her lower lip, chin tilted up, she unflinchingly returned his stare with her typical false bravado.

He picked up the clear plastic cosmetics bag containing the bottles of pills, a small brush on a handle, which he'd seen Andra use to clean her teeth, and other sundries he could not identify. "Let's start simply. What are these medicinals and where did you get them?"

"You can read. They are what they say, medicine to reduce fever, chills, aches and pains. The brush is to clean one's teeth and the tube contains tooth cleaner."

"Aye, I have seen the results of the tablets with both you and Lorne. But the containers are made of material with peculiar fasteners I have never seen before." He slowly unzipped the bag watching her expression turn from bravado to fear, and dumped the contents on top of the table in front of her.

Picking up the toothpaste he tugged at the top, squeezed the tube, pulled out his dirk to cut into it. She grabbed it from his hand and slumped onto the chair. "What do you want from me, Kendrick?"

"That's simple. The truth. All of it." He replied.

Unscrewing the tube, she squeezed a small dab of white paste onto her finger. "Taste it." She put her finger to his lips and he sucked her finger into his mouth. An erotic image popped into his head. Her shocked expression and widened green eyes suggested she might be thinking the same thing. She quickly pulled her hand back to her lap.

"So this is why you always taste so sweet." He smiled, hoping to grant her comfort and ease. But he couldn't suppress his soaring arousal.

"It's akin to the mint leaves you're always chewing." she answered, grazing his crotch with her gaze, then averting her attention from the bulge under his sporran by studying the rug in front of the fire.

Laying the tube on the table, Andra dropped her head into

her hands. "The truth! You want the truth. The truth is I want to go home. Yet when we're together, I can't think of being anywhere else."

His visceral reaction to her comment shook him. He didn't want her to leave. Her expressed conflict about leaving helped, but not enough.

"When I tell you all of the truth, you will not believe me and then you'll toss me in your damn dungeon and throw away the key. Or worse, you'll tie me to a stake and light the fire under my feet. That's the truth."

Kendrick knelt on one knee in front of her and took her hands in his. "Your hands are cold," he said, rubbing warmth into them. His strong, calloused fingers gentled on her incredibly soft skin. He loved touching her skin, smelling her sweetness, watching her move through the keep, the gardens. Suddenly, he wanted her to find her home with him, to choose to stay with him. "I promise, Andra, I will believe you, and I will not punish you in any manner."

Exhaling she rose and picked up the carpetbag. She removed a false bottom and retrieved several items. Andra studied the items in her hands as she came slowly back to the table and dropped into the chair.

"Kendrick, I give you my word that I am going to tell you the absolute truth and explain everything I can remember that led to the moment when I first encountered you." Piercing him with searching eyes she paused then, resolved, pushed on. "Will you promise me, please, that you will listen to my entire story and set aside your initial reaction and judgment until I am finished?" Her deep green eyes pleaded for his compliance.

He nodded, but a strange sense of dread swam though his veins.

"Set the food aside, please. I have things to show you." He set the tray on the floor and took the chair opposite her. Finally, the moment of truth was upon them. He noticed her tight body strained like a bowstring, and Kendrick knew she was about to impart some terrible tale.

After his younger years spent in courts all over Europe, he'd developed excellent skills at detecting liars and uncovering falsehoods. Tension emanated off her like a tangible living thing. It coiled and slithered until he felt as tense as she looked. He kept his face neutral and watched her closely. She laid a few items on the table and covered them with trembling hands.

Lifting her face to his she said, "I am from the future. To be exact, I am from the year 2013. From a place called San Francisco, which is on the far western coast of the North American continent at the edge of the Pacific Ocean. The land you call the colonies."

She did not turn away or even blink, steadily holding his gaze. What was she saying? Kendrick stood abruptly, knocking his chair backward and crossed his arms over his chest. "Andra, please, dinnae do this. Dinnae weave fantastic tales in an attempt to mollify me. You promised me the truth. What you say is not possible and you ken it. Yet her face displayed no hint of deceit."

"It obviously is possible as I am here, though I do not know why or exactly how it happened." Waving her hand toward his chair she urged, "Please, you promised to listen with an open mind. Please sit, and let me prove to you that what I am telling you is true."

"You cannae prove what is impossible." His voice thundered with his growing anger. The muscle in his jaw ached from grinding his teeth. What game did she play? Perhaps she was insane. He rubbed his hands through his hair until he could feel its complete disarray, and then rubbed his hands over his face. He grabbed the wine he had brought and paced the floor swigging large gulps. After a few minutes of pacing, he handed the bottle to her. She took a long swig, keeping her eyes on his face.

"Please sit down, you are frightening me. Let me show you a few things that may help you understand."

She turned her hand over exposing a leather pouch, and handed it to him. "This is my wallet also known as a billfold. It's a bit like your sporran but carries only items of identification and currency." She nodded, "Open it. You will find photographs. Umm...excuse me; photographs are akin to miniature portraits.

I'll explain more about them in a minute. The first one shows me with my father. It was taken several years ago—in my time." A tear slid down her cheek and she swiped it with the back of her hand.

He looked upon an extraordinary image of Andra standing by an older man. He'd never seen the like before. Kendrick closely examined the image encased in the same clear shiny material as the container from her bag. He looked at her and back at the portrait several times. "'Tis a verra good likeness, astonishingly real." He studied the older man closely and felt a shiver down his spine. He couldn't place why, but the man looked familiar.

"The next one is my mother. My father took that image more than twenty years ago in my time. My mother died when I was seven years old. There is also dated currency. Pull out the paper bills and read them. Printed on the bills you'll see their issue date. Some of them are newer so they do not all display the same dates, but they are all from the future. There are also English pounds, England's currency from my time."

He concentrated on the photos first. "Och, you resemble your mother. You have her face and smile and the same hair color." None of this could be possible, could it?

"Yes, my father always said I am like her in many ways. Except for that picture, I can barely remember her." A wistful expression crossed her brow.

"Do you have an image of your son?" He had no idea why he raised that question. His mind screamed that none of this could be true. The urge to run out of the room and lock her away fought with his need to hear everything she had to say, no matter how fantastic.

"Yes, I do."

She removed another slip of paper, yellowed and worn around the edges and handed it to him. A picture she had obviously held in her hands thousands of times. A tiny babe rested across her chest, her hair was plastered to her face creased with deep weariness and pain. The image of her and this precious baby she had lost overwhelmed his senses.

She assumed that far away stare, her eyes damp with memories.

With a hand pressed against her abdomen, she continued. "The scar on my stomach that you asked about…is a surgical scar. There was an accident in my ninth month of pregnancy resulting in an emergency C-section."

"C-section?" His questioning expression urged her to continue.

"It's an operation to remove the baby if they won't come. He lived for a very short time. I only had him for a few hours." Her voice hitched, suppressing a sob.

He set the wallet down and took her face in his hands, leaning his forehead against hers. "I am so sorry for your loss, a stór. I ken how it still pains you deeply." A loud thrum hummed in his ears as he considered her nightmarish tale. Nevertheless, she clearly struggled with this disclosure and with her loss. He kissed her lips gently.

She sighed and pushed him back. Patiently, she continued to describe and explain the remaining items in her bag. He asked dozens of questions, and she answered them all without hesitation. Finally, she recounted the events that lead to the portal opening and her abrupt entry into his time and onto their path that day. She quieted and waited for his response.

Kendrick blew all the air from his lungs and took a deep, replenishing breath. Leaning forward in his chair, he ran his big hands through his hair, and allowed the silence to envelop them. Was any of this possible? On one hand, he struggled to believe it; on the other, she clearly believed everything she told him, and the evidence presented in her defense deserved his consideration.

"Kendrick?" A silent plea etched Andra's face. She seemed to hold her breath, fingers touching the cross at her neck. "Please believe me. I promise, every word is the truth, and I will answer any other questions you ask to the best of my ability." The silence in the room suffocated him.

He stood and paced around the room. Her eyes trailed his agitated movements, but she didn't press him. She waited for a response, but he could not find words adequate to speak rationally. "I need some time to digest what you have told me, Andra." He cupped her cheek, then turned and left without another word, bolting the door behind him.

Chapter Twenty-Five

Kendrick didn't know what to do with the incredible images and information swirling in his mind. He had locked her in her room again because he feared she might decide to run away in the night. Exhaustion, incredulity, and fear, emotions he struggled to suppress swamped his thoughts.

He paced the parapet in an effort to gather his composure. With whom could he discuss this information without jeopardizing Andra's safety? And without them thinking he too had lost his mind. What could he do to help her? Was it even remotely possible she told the truth? If so, could he help her return to her own time if that is what she truly wanted? More importantly, could he let her go? As much as she exasperated him, he had never felt such strong desire for any woman. No matter how hard he tried to deny those emotions, they shook his reserve every time he drew near her, every time he heard her voice.

He looked out over the hills where a pale shimmer of light filtered through the trees. What would he do if he suddenly found himself in another time and all of this, everyone and everything familiar was lost?

"Unimaginable," he said, shaking his head. Yet, if she told the truth, this feisty woman, who had burrowed under his skin and anchored in his chest, had faced it all with amazing grace and tenacity.

Rabbie walked onto the parapet. "Good morrow, cousin. You look a bit raw and agitated for so early in the day. What has the lass done to upset you now?"

"Aye. I spent most of the night talking with her."

"Och, talking was it? More explosions, then? Is the lass still locked in her room?" Rabbie needled in a good-natured manner, trying to lighten Kendrick's mood, but he could find nothing humorous in his recent discoveries.

Kendrick didn't take the intended bate. "Rabbie, I wish to take you into my confidence on a matter of great importance that must remain between the two of us."

Rabbie looked at him curiously, "Aye, you ken I am trustworthy and able to mind my tongue. What troubles you?"

"Come to my library, there are too many ears here."

When Kendrick finished his tale, Rabbie walked to the table and poured them both a dram of whisky. Handing his cousin a cup, he tossed the burning liquid down his throat. "Well now, that tale definitely needs a bit of the *uisge beatha* to swallow it down. What are your thoughts on the matter?"

"The woman drives me to the edge of madness, that she does, but she no doubt believes her story. Then there are the strange things she showed me—currency from her time and pictures that defy the imagination. She defended her claims with calm certainty and precise explanations. She did not equivocate. Bloody hell! Am I as crazy as she is if I say I'm inclined to believe her?"

Rabbie had always helped calm and center Kendrick's mind. They were opposites in many ways. Rabbie, slow to anger, took an inordinate amount of time to come to a decision, yet unfailingly reached an accurate conclusion. Furthermore, Rabbie was not a superstitious man. Kendrick trusted him, as much or more than he trusted his brother and never needed his steadying influence more.

"To tell the truth, Kendrick, I dinnae believe she has ever outright lied to us. She avoided answering our questions at first, but if what she tells you is possible, you cannae blame her. From the beginning, Struan called her a witch. That must have frightened the poor lass. Look how she charged after him following the incident at the river when he accused her of witchcraft again. Verra brave, dinnae you agree."

"You dinnae believe all the nonsense about witchery do you, Rabbie?"

Rabbie tilted his head, appraising his cousin and mulling over the question. "If they had the power people claimed, then why are they always among the poor and wretched, or those gifted with the healing arts? If they possessed such powers, why wouldn't they be able to escape punishment?" He paused, then shook his head, "Nae, it makes no sense."

They stood in thoughtful silence, looking out the long, mullioned windows facing the back of the keep. In the distance, the ocean appeared as a gray, heaving beast in the silver light. "You ken, Rabbie, for generations stories have persisted about the stone circles and magic surrounding them. People still firmly believe in the fairy folk, though I dinnae. Still, with all my travels and university education I ken more exists in this world than the sages can explain. She presents the most fantastic story I've ever heard. Yet, I cannae find another explanation for what I've seen with my own eyes."

"Mayhap you could use some distraction while you consider the lass's story. A guard from the northern borders rode in less than an hour ago. He spotted Camerons reiving our livestock again. Should we take a few men to ride out and investigate?"

The suggestion offered the perfect excuse to gain space and perspective. "Aye, a day or two away from the keep would be good. Perhaps on the way back we could shoot a few deer to add to the winter stores. The exertion and fresh air will help clear my thoughts. Ready the men. I'll speak with Andra before I meet you at the stables."

When Kendrick returned to Andra's room, her disheveled state flattened him. The sight of her lying on the bed crying into her pillow, pounding her wee fists against the bed, smashed any remaining reluctance he felt about accepting her story as truth, however unbelievable.

Sitting on the side of the bed, he rubbed his hand across her back. "Dinnae fash yourself so, lass, you'll become ill if you go on like this." She didn't respond at first, then rolled over and looked at him with puffy, red eyes, and a drippy nose. He scooped her into his arms. A powerful urge to protect and possess her swept through him. As much as he needed his next breath, he needed this woman. He would never let her go.

"Och, you'll be the death of me, you ken. I needed time to digest the information you showed me." She curled into his embrace like a wee bairn.

"Please tell me you believe me. I swear on my families' souls, I am telling the truth. Don't leave me locked up and alone," she whispered.

He took her chin between his thumb and finger and lifted her face. "What you've told me is beyond anything I could imagine, and I want us to take our time and talk about it further." He kissed the top of her head and wrapped his arms tightly around her. "But first, I must leave for a while. I will not lock you in your room. Try to mind yourself and dinnae cause any trouble until I return. Just for a few days, please refrain from your morning exercises."

His lips lightly brushed hers and he laid her back on the bed. "You're exhausted, rest a while, Andra. Keep what you've told me to yourself until I return. We'll sort this out, I give you my word." He wanted to stretch out beside her and eliminate these thoughts from both of their minds with a frantic, bracing coupling, a heated passion that would relieve her fears and calm them both, but it must wait until later.

She clung to his fingers, looking up at him, then slowly rolled to her side. "You're right. I'm exhausted."

* * *

When the noon hour arrived without Andra coming to the great hall, Beatrice went to her room to investigate. No one responded to her knock so she gingerly opened the door. Andra rolled over and rubbed her face. Sleep had not caused the red blotches that spotted her cheeks and rimmed her swollen eyes.

"Och, are you not well, dear? Should I call Jane to tend you?" her voice rippled over Andra like a cool wind.

"No, I will be fine." She looked out the window at a sun high in the sky. "My apologies for sleeping so long into the day."

Already aware of the previous morning's events in the bailey, Beatrice suspected Andra and Kendrick had not yet resolved their conflict, or at least not to the lass' satisfaction. Anyone could see the desire that flamed between her son and this woman. As their mother, Beatrice knew her sons well and though generally kind and thoughtful in dealings with members of his clan, Kendrick's temper could be quick and fierce if challenged.

She admired the woman. Andra appeared to be of solid character, fortitude, and intelligence. Her son's strength would not subjugate this woman's character into oblivion. Kendrick needed a partner capable of standing beside him as he provided for and protected their clan, and Andra could be that woman. Beatrice did not fret over the young woman's lack of family or dowry.

As a mother, she might not directly interfere with her son's lives, but a gentle shove here or there would not be amiss. Beatrice sat beside her and smoothed the hair from her forehead. "Tell me what troubles you? Has Kendrick upset you?"

"Yes. No. Yes, but I probably upset him far more. I'm sorry. I shouldn't be discussing the laird." A sheepish expression flitted over her face and revealed her discomfort speaking about Kendrick with his mother. There was very little Beatrice missed or failed to hear about, but she'd keep her counsel for now.

"Let us get you up and dressed for the day. A little food in your stomach would do you good. A walk in the gardens always helps me sort my thoughts and 'tis a lovely day to be out of the keep."

The children bounded into the room, followed by Isabel. "Andra," Kyle cried, jumping on the bed. "Why are ye still abed? Dae ye feel poorly?"

"No, I'm fine. I think I've turned into a bed bug and don't want to leave my covers,"

He made a face and a retching sound.

"You better watch out or the bed bug will get you." She tickled him and his laughter peeled into the air. Beatrice noticed Andra's mood lighten when the boy's little hand sought hers, as he always did when in her presence.

Chapter Twenty-Six

Strolling into the kitchen's vegetable and herb gardens, Andra came to an area where Alith and Jane busied themselves harvesting plants.

"Greetings, m'lady, how fare you this lovely day?" Jane stood and wiped the dirt from her hands before reaching to assist Alith to her feet.

After exchanging a few pleasantries, Jane took her basket of clippings to tie up and hang from the kitchen rafters for drying.

"Will you lend your arm to an old woman and help me to yon bench. I enjoy warming these tired bones in the sun," Alith said. Taking Andra's arm, she led her out of the herb section, around a large tree to a bench on the west side of the keep. They sat in pleasant silence, soaking up the restfulness of the garden and the sun's warmth. Alith patted her weathered hand over Andra's, "You sorely miss your home and kin, even these dimming eyes can see that 'tis so."

"My father's passing was recent. I do miss him greatly." Glancing over the gardens and to the hills beyond tears filled her eyes.

"He was a good man, your father?" Alith asked, hesitantly.

"Oh yes, he was the best of men, strong, intelligent, and thoughtful. He always put my needs and concerns above his own. No woman could ever hope for a kinder father. He taught me all I know."

"And your mother, did she teach you as well?"

"My mother died when I was seven years of age. It is sometimes difficult to remember her. Those memories that remain are of a beautiful, gentle woman." Andra sighed and dropped her chin.

Alith's withered hand patted hers comfortingly, rubbing across her father's ring. "'Tis a heavy weight you carry. I am here for you, dear one. I hope you'll sit with me when your losses feel too heavy. I'm a verra good listener and would wish to lift your sorrows if you'll allow it."

"That is so kind, Alith. You were correct about the MacLeans. They have been very considerate to my plight while taking me into their home." She swiped at the tears on her cheeks.

"Och, 'tis true. They are verra inviting to those who have lost their way in the world."

"Have you always lived with the MacLeans, Alith?"

"To be sure, it seems as though I have. As a young woman, I had me own home and family, but 'twas verra long ago. They're all gone now. I first came to Ruadhstone Castle as a young widow who had recently lost both husband and son in a war. The laird's grandmother was a new bride at the time. We were inseparable as bairns, you ken, as she had fostered with my family. We grew verra close, dear as any family, though not of the same blood. When I arrived, late in the last months of her first, difficult pregnancy, it seemed the natural choice to stay and assist her. My presence aided her and she provided the sanctuary and solace I so desperately needed." Alith's milky eyes misted over as she slipped into memories of long ago. Andra and Alith sat in quiet companionship, the soft breeze ruffling leaves and bending down the grassy hills. Andra had fallen in love with this rough, wild place and the people who lived here.

Eventually, Alith excused herself to take her rest while Andra remained in the back garden. How quickly she had filled every aspect of her life with assumed duties where she found herself constantly in the presence of others. This brief moment of solitude felt deliciously revitalizing.

Suddenly, Vera ran through the postern door in the lower wall and Andra's quiet retreat abruptly ended. "Help, oh please, you must come right away, Kyle has had an accident down by the loch."

Andra jumped and ran to her, "Should we not call for help?"

"Nae, there is no time. You must come quickly, please." Vera clutched at her hand and dragged her to the gate she had just entered.

The hairs on Andra's arms prickled, and a shiver ran down her spine. She set aside the concern that niggled at the back of her mind, dismissing it as fear for Kyle. She ran as quickly as possible. She hated the way the excessive clothing and long skirts hindered her speed.

They ran along a dirt path, through a circle of trees and behind the back of a low mounding hill that led to the loch. They seemed to take the long way around, but she didn't raise a question as they rushed ahead. Suddenly, there were horses speeding toward them. Andra couldn't tell where they'd come from, but released a sigh of relief that help had arrived. Then she saw Senga and Isabel gagged and tied, held captive on two of the horses. Andra opened her mouth to scream when someone threw a blanket over her head and cruel hands tossed her over a horse knocking the breath from her lungs.

She struggled against her captor. Arms like steel bands gripped her tightly and an unfamiliar voice snarled, "Settle yourself, wench, and I won't knock you out. I'll order those young lasses' throats cut where we stand unless you cooperate and remain quiet."

She kicked and twisted and tried to scream, but the blanket covering her face muffled her voice. The man bent over her and bit her shoulder so hard she was certain he'd drawn blood, even through the blanket and her clothing. As though that wasn't enough to subdue her, he punched the side of her head. "I said to hold your wheesht, bitch. Dinnae push me to further injury. I prefer you alive, but dead would work as well."

Bile rose in the back of Andra's throat. Attempting to calm herself, she drew gulps of much needed air into her lungs. That caused her to hyperventilate, and she feared she might faint until Vera's panicked voice penetrated her terror. She slowed her breath as she concentrated on the woman's words.

"Why did you grab the other girls? They weren't part of the plan. They are no use to you. You need to take me with you."

Vera did not mention Isabel's relationship with Kendrick. If their captives didn't recognize her, that information might save the girls. Then again, it might not. Who could reason out the thoughts of a man willing to kidnap, gag, and bind innocent women and girls?

He barked his reply, "My plans don't concern you. Go back to the castle. Make excuses for their absence. When Kendrick returns and you ken how many men are forming for the search, go to the meeting place in the grove outside the village. A man will wait there for your information."

Vera's voice squeaked anxiously. "Nae, nae, you mustn't leave me here. Lorne may send out men tonight when the girls don't return, especially if Kendrick is not back. They will suspect me if I try to leave the castle at night. I cannae stay. You promised to take me if I brought the woman to you."

"You make certain they don't know of the young'ens absence. If you dinnae do as I tell you, Vera, you'll have more to fear from me than from them, and you ken it. Now go, do as I command, or I'll kill you here."

"Ride fast men," the brute commanded. The horse under Andra spun in a circle and sprinted ahead. They rode for a long time at breakneck speeds. She had no idea the direction in which they headed or who had captured her. Why had Vera done this? She could not possibly think to get away with it. Kendrick would throw her in the dungeon or hang her, not necessarily because she had lured Andra away, but because these brutes had taken his sister.

Think Andra, think, and stay calm. The words her judo instructor had drummed into her head entered her jumbled thoughts. *If you are ever taken, stay calm, pay attention to your direction, smells, sounds, the direction of the sun beating down, they all provide clues that will help you escape. Remember the imperative: stay alive.*

How could she think clearly or identify her surroundings trussed up and blinded? The image of the girls gagged and bound helped focus her mind. She must at least appear composed. Grappling with the situation she realized one shoe was missing.

She didn't know where the shoe had dropped, but used her foot to knock the other off. Her captor either didn't notice or didn't care. She hoped someone would find them and they would mark their passing. Kendrick would come. He would find them. She had no doubt.

Andra tried to discern their direction by what little light penetrated the blanket over her head. But could only determine that the light had dimmed. She also realized the air had cooled significantly, but that could mean anything from a sudden shift in Highland weather to them entering a dense forest. Every part of her ached miserably, especially the bite on her shoulder. Terrible infections resulted from a human bite and this man smelled none too clean.

"Sir, can we stop for a respite?" she mumbled through the fabric. He didn't respond. "I must relieve myself and I'm certain the younger girls need to as well."

"We'll rest when I say. And if you soil me, I swear I'll beat you senseless." He sounded as though he would enjoy beating her.

A while later the odor of cook fires and men talking entered her awareness. The horse stopped and her captor threw her roughly to the ground. She scrambled to her feet at the same time a hand yanked the blanket off her head.

"Let's have a look at the creature that has captured the interest of the great Laird MacLean," his tone hostile and acerbic. He walked around her like a wolf stalking its prey.

"Interesting," he said, rubbing his chin with a huge, thick hand. Long nails caked with black debris scratched at a few days' growth of whiskers. "You aren't what one would expect, not the laird's type if you get me meaning."

She didn't. The specimen in front of her lacked every manner of decency, from the filth about his person to his rude and cruel behavior.

"A bit long in the tooth mayhap. Still, you are a comely enough wench. What's your name?"

Andra stood straight and did her best to quell the trembling in her limbs. Behind her, a chorus of bawdy catcalls, whistles, and crude comments let her know the girls were somewhere to her left.

She heard one of them whimper and turned in their direction. A rough hand snatched her hair and pulled her head back.

"I asked you a question, woman. The lassies are none of your concern." The man stood a little over six feet, leanly muscled with long, greasy, black hair and eyes so dark she could not discern a pupil. He reeked of whisky, sweat, and horse. She didn't think he had bathed in months. Thin lips opened in a snarl as he rolled his tongue over yellowed teeth.

When he released her hair, she stood straight and squared her shoulders. "My name is Lady Andra. Who are you and why did you take us?"

"Well now, aren't you the demanding one. Did I give you leave to question me, bitch?"

Assuming that was a rhetorical question, she chose not to respond. Before she could blink, he smacked her across the face.

"Why did you hit me?" Andra rubbed the red welt already swelling on her cheek.

"Hmmm. You speak English with a most peculiar accent. Hear tell you claim to be a Cameron." He pinched her chin between his thumb and finger. "You dinnae look familiar to me. Who are your kin? You dinnae resemble any Cameron clans I'm familiar with—a bit too much polish," he hissed as the back of his hand trailed across her cheek and down her throat. His eyes undressed her with a downward sweep.

She stepped back, "I have no kin," she responded, breaking through his vile revelry. "I am not from here. What is your name, and what do you want with us?"

He puffed out his chest, and flicked her chin from his hand. "I am Laird Cormag Cameron, and you, my pretty, are me bait. I hear that The MacLean has taken a special interest in you. Though why he'd be interested in a woman with no kin to swell his ranks is a curious question."

He stepped closer, his face inches from hers, and his repulsive breath filled her nose. "Dae you warm his bed, lave his cock with your tongue?" he flicked his tongue against her cheek.

She barely repressed a gag. God, she prayed this beast didn't hark back to some distant, black sheep relative. He repulsed her in every way. There was certainly no thread of resemblance, and Cameron was a common enough name, even in the eighteenth century. They couldn't all be related.

Suddenly he gripped her breast and squeezed hard. The feel of his hand on her shocked her into action. She fisted both hands and slammed them with all the force she could muster into the crook of the arm clutching her breast. Jamming her foot into the side of his knee, she managed to knock him off balance and darted toward the trees. She knew she couldn't escape, but reacted instinctively. He caught her before she took more than a few steps. "So you like it rough, m'lady. Well now, as it happens I prefer it as rough as you can take and more. It will be me great pleasure to accommodate you on that count," he said, as he spun her around and punched her in the stomach.

All the air left her lungs in a gasp. Andra doubled over, retching and gagging. Then he backhanded her and knocked her to the ground.

"Cormag!" someone yelled. "Don't damage the goods until I've decided her value to my plans." Black boots strode forward and stopped between where she lay in the dirt and the swine who'd accosted her.

"The bitch smacked me. She needed a bit of discipline." Cormag snarled.

"I witnessed the interaction. Seems to me she simply responded to your brutish behavior. For now, I want her to manage the other girls you decided to bring along—without my permission, I might add. I wasn't looking to start a war, you know. It's much easier to dispatch small contingents of primary warriors than an entire army."

She wondered if the officer, clearly unhappy about the presence of Isabel and Senga, might release the younger girls.

A gloved hand extended to her. Andra looked up to see an officer from the English army. He was about the same height as Cormag but clean-shaven with sandy hair and piercing, pale eyes. She did not take the proffered hand, but shakily gained her feet without assistance. She could taste blood at the side of her mouth.

She nodded her head, "Sir." Questions formed on her tongue, but she swallowed them down.

"My lady, I'm Colonel Richardson of Her Majesty's Dragoons." He wore boots spit-polished to a high shine; surprising since they stood in the middle of a forest, and every other man's clothing displayed a heavy coating of dust and sweat from traveling. His coat and pants were impeccably clean as though he had just put them on, not a crease or fleck of dirt marred the material. She noticed he kept one side of his face turned slightly away from her.

When he faced her fully, a hawkish stare scoured down her body. She noticed a thick pink scar along the side of an otherwise beautiful face; it ran from his mouth to his ear. "If you behave, and do as you're told, no further harm will come to you or the young ladies."

His voice was gruff, threatening. She didn't believe him for one minute. "Why have you taken us? What do you want?"

"That is none of your business, madam. The more interesting question is why would an English lady be in the company of the likes of the MacLeans? Did this miscreant Cormag plant you as his spy? You don't resemble any of the Camerons I know."

It seemed he didn't trust Cormag. When he spoke, the scar limited the movement of his mouth so that he appeared to grimace. Cormag grumbled something she didn't understand, his hot breath on the back of her neck as he moved behind her.

"I do not know this man Cormag. I am certainly not related to the vile creature."

"That was not an answer to my questions, my lady. Perhaps you need a moment to collect yourself and reconsider your situation, hmmm. You *will* answer all of my questions, I assure you." He kept his eyes on Andra and called to one of his men.

"Harold, take the women to tend their personal needs." His gaze challenged her to turn away from his face, but she kept her expression blank and latched onto his chilling, gray eyes.

"Do not be foolish enough to attempt escape. The punishment would be severely uncomfortable for you and for them." He nodded toward the girls where the man called Harold dragged them toward a group of trees beside a creek.

He barked at Cormag. "Come to my tent, we have things to discuss." The colonel tipped a long, beaked nose down at her as if she was no more than an annoying gnat. With long strides, he stepped away, taking caution to avoid mud patches and animal droppings.

* * *

Cormag dug his nails into her arm, cackling in satisfaction. Finally, all his schemes to best Kendrick MacLean stood right here in front of him. And she was a looker to boot. She had lovely unflawed skin except for the split lip and bruised cheek he had delivered. Her curvaceous body would soon carry more of his personal branding. Using and abusing her for bed sport to satisfy his dark cravings would prove most intoxicating. To do so with Kendrick's wench excited him beyond measure. He'd hated and despised the man all through their youth.

No matter what he did, Kendrick had always bested him, won all physical contests, found favor with their elders, and always charmed the ladies. Then he had the audacity to marry the woman who should have been his. Kirsten had eyes for no one but Kendrick; she wouldn't even look at Cormag or dance with him when he attended gatherings. She rebuked his advances because Kendrick had bewitched her. Oh yes, he'd relish his revenge while defiling Kendrick's wench.

"The colonel will give you to me eventually, me pet. He knows how to reward his men." Licking his lips, he shoved her toward the man holding the girls.

She glowered back at him. "Ahh, yes, keep that fire stoked wench, I do like 'em wild. 'Twill be more enjoyable to break you, and I will break you in every way you can imagine and ways you cannae. And your little maids will provide a bit of fun for me men, after I've warmed them up a bit."

Chapter Twenty-Seven

Harold, their guard, removed their bindings and followed the women to a place deeper in the trees. When Andra asked him to turn his back, he refused. Each girl took a turn behind a tree while Andra attempted to shield her from the man's leering eyes.

On their return to the camp, Andra made a quick assessment of their surroundings. A creek about five-feet wide trickled over a rocky bed and wound through deep woods. Tethered near the stream, two-dozen horses grazed, and there were as many or more on the far side of the clearing. A hill a couple hundred-feet high rose behind the spot where they'd staked several tents.

Clumps of men sat in front of another cluster of tents nearby drinking and playing dice or cards. Several small fires and one larger one crackled near two supply wagons several yards from the men's tents. One group of men sat opposite and further away from the English soldiers. They wore brown-plaid kilts or were dressed in dirty trews with sweat-stained shirts. It seemed the English and the Scots aiding them in terrorizing the locals stayed separate in camp. In fact, all the men, English as well as Scots wore dirty, stained clothing, except for the colonel.

Their guard escorted them to a tent pressed against a steep hill mounded with large boulders and scrubby growth. The colonel's baritone voice emanated from a tent several feet from theirs and positioned farther away from the hill behind.

As they walked past the men made lewd comments and gestures toward them. The guard roughly pushed them through the tent flap and called to the Colonial, "Do you want me to bind them again?"

"Give them food and refreshment first," was his brief, nonchalant response.

Andra pulled the girls away from the entrance. The tent measured about seven-by-seven feet. Someone had thrown a few blankets on the ground. A small table with one candle and no chairs sat to the side of the center pole. She walked to the sides and back, listening for movement. Kneeling in the dirt, she slipped a finger under an edge at the back and discovered no guard posted there. Only a large boulder pressed close to the rear canvas. She could hear Colonel Richardson arguing with Cormag about whether they should keep or kill the girls.

Kneeling next to the girls on the blankets, she took their trembling hands and whispered, "We will make an escape plan as soon as they settle for the night. Isabel, I don't think they know your identity. Give them a false name if they ask you. Do not claim to be related to Kendrick."

"I did not tell them our names, and I don't think they ken who we are, so why did they take us?" Isabel whispered, clutching tightly to Andra's hand.

Andra cupped her cheek, "I don't know why exactly. It seems the colonel only wanted me. Perhaps they took you to gain my cooperation."

Isabel nodded and put on a brave face. "My brothers will come for us, I ken they will, and they'll kill them all." She reached her other hand to clasp onto Senga.

Andra squeezed their hands. "Do not fash yourselves. We will survive this," she assured them. But her gut twisted with uncertainty.

A young soldier, perhaps a few years older than Isabel, wearing an English uniform brought their meager rations of bread, cheese, and watered wine. Stealing repeated glances at Isabel, he noticed her holding her blistered wrists where the rope had rubbed them raw.

"When I return I'll bring you salve and bandages to wrap them," he nodded toward her hands.

Not missing the chance to gain an ally, Isabel dipped her chin and batted her eyes, "Thank you kindly, sir, that would be greatly appreciated. I dinnae catch your name."

"Lucas, my name is Lucas Temple." The guard outside yelled for him, and he quickly left.

Lucas returned later with ointment and strips of linen. Andra drew the girls closer to her and reached for the supplies. He might be helpful, or he might get it into his head that he could claim Isabel for himself. "I'll do that. It would not be proper for you to handle the ladies, but we do sincerely appreciate your kindness."

"When you are finished, I must bind you again, m'lady." He spoke to Andra, but his eyes never left Isabel, who kept her head demurely turned from his gaze, watching him from under her dark lashes.

After tending to Isabel, Andra dropped the clothing off her shoulder to apply ointment to the bite there.

Lucas hissed, "Who bit you?"

"Who do you think? Could you bring hot water for me to clean this first?" If he complied, she thought he might possibly become their only ally in the camp.

"I don't think that is possible. The ointment will help. Use the watered wine to wash it first. Stay away from that bastard if you value your life." He obviously didn't care for Cormag Cameron either.

"We wish we'd never made his acquaintance in the first place. Unfortunately, we were not given that option." She watched him carefully. Would he help them? "Do you know why we have been taken?"

He stared at her for several seconds as though carefully weighing his next comment. Before he answered, another guard yelled for him to leave the lasses unless he planned to loosen them up for the rest of the men.

"I'm binding their hands," he yelled back. "The colonel has ordered all men stay away from this tent." Taking the ropes, he tied their hands in front of them and then lashed them together preventing them from moving independently and latched the rope to the pole supporting the tent. Andra noticed he did not tie the binds too tightly across Isabel's wrists. When finished, he tipped his chin to her, "I'll be on late-night duty outside this tent," and then he left.

Chapter Twenty-Eight

Vera returned to the castle, angry that Cormag had not taken her with him. He had promised to take her to his keep if she helped him take his revenge against Kendrick. In the beginning, Cormag's plots and schemes amused her. Eventually, she decided she wanted Kendrick for herself, and over a year ago, she'd managed to bed him on a few occasions. Now that he'd spurned her for an annoying English chit, she knew how to exact her revenge. She needed to keep everyone from discovering her involvement until she could gather some useful tidbit of information and escape.

She didn't really want to consort with Cormag but he had rewarded her well enough over the past few years. His lust for her knew no bounds. She convinced herself that she could tolerate him if it meant she'd become lady of his keep or at least his mistress. Providing him with a son would cement her position and she'd never need to do menial work again.

After a short while, Vera found Kyle looking for his sister. "Lady Isabel and Senga have retired to Isabel's rooms and dinnae want to be disturbed," she informed him.

When he started to whine in protest, she knew just how to stop him. "A lad who is a babe in need of his sister's coddling probably can't be trusted to help with the puppies born in the stables a few days ago."

He squealed and grew very serious, "Oh no, I am a verra grown-up lad. I'm verra good with puppies." His face darkened a moment. "I use to have one of me own."

"Ah, I see. Mayhap the stable master will allow a grown-up lad such as you to tend the pups. If you're verra good, mayhap he'll allow you to keep one." The boy's eyes gleamed hopefully and he did as she bid without further discussion.

Next, she encountered Beatrice. "Beggin' your pardon, m'lady," she dipped a perfect curtsey, "Isabel asked to be excused from the evening's meal."

"Is she unwell?" Beatrice asked, concerned.

"Oh no, m'lady, she is well. Senga has finally spoken, and she thought it would be best for them to have quiet time to encourage her further."

"When did this happen? What did she say?"

A smooth liar, Vera didn't blink. Her life depended on convincing Lady Beatrice. "We went to the village earlier with Andra. She asked I join them to gather wild flowers and herbs for her soaps. On the way home, we stopped to check on old widow MacAllis. The widow was feeling poorly, so Andra decided to stay to help put her croft in order and prepare an evening meal. I'll fetch her back in the morning, m'lady." She bobbed prettily. "When we returned to the keep, Senga whispered something to Isabel. I nearly fainted from the shock as I dinnae think the girl could speak. Isabel asked me to bring them food and see they not be disturbed this evening."

"Of course, I understand. It gladdens my heart that the girl is finally speaking. Thank you for alerting me."

"Aye, m'lady, 'tis me pleasure to be of service. I'll check on them later if you wish."

"No, I think Isabel is right to request an evening for them. You go on about your duties."

Watching Beatrice enter the great hall, Vera breathed a sigh of relief for the few hours' time that exchange brought her. She needed to get away from the keep soon, but also needed information that would provide a good reason to go to Cormag.

Unable to sleep, Vera roamed through the shadowed corridors of the castle in the pre-dawn hours looking for things of value to steal; things she could easily hawk for coin. As she neared the old laird's rooms, a sudden commotion had her dipping into a sheltered alcove.

Lady Beatrice rushed to her personal guard, "Bring Lorne to me immediately." She looked stricken and disheveled.

"Och, finally, something of interest." she said to herself. She waited several minutes before the guard returned with Lorne. They entered the old laird's rooms together. It seemed an eternity before the guard exited alone. She sidled up to him coyly.

"Padrick, a commotion woke me, and I saw you and Lorne rush up the stairs. Can I be of service?" He swiped his hand through his hair not saying anything at first.

She suspected it was the old laird, as he'd been ill for years. In a subdued voice she asked, "Has something happened to Monroe MacLean? Should I fetch the healer?"

He shook his head dropping his gaze to the floor. "Nae, 'tis too late. Old Laird MacLean has gone to his maker, God rest his soul. Mayhap you should wake cook and have her prepare a meal for the family to break their fast. Send me one of the lower guards for instructions as well."

She dipped her knee in a mock curtsey, "Aye sir, you can count on me to handle things."

Within half an hour, Lorne had dispatched men to locate Kendrick and his warriors. He also sent messengers to alert allied lairds. All the commotion provided a perfect cover for Vera to slip out of the castle. She stole some provisions from the kitchen, a small dagger, and several pewter mugs, which she rolled into her plaid. Despite her meager cache, she had no time to delay. At the stables, she waited for the first messengers to depart, then went to the stable-hand.

"Lorne has instructed me to take old Bessie and retrieve Lady Andra from the widow's croft." She smiled sweetly. "She's been such a comfort to Lady Beatrice since she arrived, she will be want'n her here as quickly as possible."

The lad looked at her curiously, but did not ask questions as he saddled the old horse. Vera wanted to ask for one of the better mounts, but knew that would raise too many questions, and the lad might seek authorization from the stable master. No sense inviting trouble. She rode out behind several other messengers. As soon as she entered the trees and the messengers turned in another direction, she pushed the old mare to a hard gallop. About a mile past the village, she reached the old, deserted hut where Cormag's man supposedly waited for word from her. Smoke trickled from the chimney rising over the thatch. Someone was inside. Pulling behind the building, she saw a horse tethered nearby.

"Hello, are you awake?" she called. She slid off the horse and approached the door hanging lopsided on old leather hinges. "Hello, 'tis me, Vera, are you awake."

A gruff looking man came out scrubbing his face with large, callused hands. She recognized him. He had been with Cormag during one of their previous meetings. "Say what you have to report?"

She would not let him leave her here. "You must take me to Cormag immediately. 'Tis urgent business I have with him."

"Nae, you report to me, and I deliver the information." His black, bushy eyebrows drew into a straight line across his scowling forehead.

Vera drew herself up to her full height and fisted her hands on her hips. "What I have tae tell The Cameron is nae to be disclosed. He told me himself that he would kill me if I told certain information to anyone other than him."

"'Tis not what he told me." The man folded his arms over his burly chest, clearly not intimidated by her.

"If you ride over yon hill, you will see men rushing in all directions from the MacLean's castle. Much is afoot and I cannae trust the information with anyone but Cormag. If you must blindfold me first, then do so, but hurry up about it and take me to him directly if you value your sorry, worthless life." Brash intimidation was her only hope.

He scrubbed his bristly chin with a fist then turned into the hut. She waited impatiently tapping her foot and watching for riders who might have followed her. Shortly, the man came out dressed and hauling his bedroll and saddle.

"If Cormag is displeased with me taking you to him, you'll suffer sorely for your deceit." He pulled out a strip of linen from his saddle pack and ordered her to turn so he could bind her sight.

"You should ha' taken a better mount, this old nag won't make it to our destination."

"Let's take her as far as possible. When she collapses, we'll continue on your horse." Vera was anxious to get moving.

"Nae, you'll have to ride with me; we can't have someone find a MacLean nag along our trail. 'Twould be too easy for them to figure our direction. I'll nae tolerate any scheming from you, or I'll rip out your lovely locks." He twisted her braid in his fist and pulled hard. "Dae we understand each other?"

Vera wanted to spit in his face, but curbed her response. It would have to wait until later, but she would exact her revenge; she always did. "Aye, let's hurry before someone comes this way."

Chapter Twenty-Nine

A commotion outside the colonel's tent woke Andra. Every part of her stiff, sore body rebelled. It took a minute to gather her thoughts. It was still dark outside, and she could hear a man's urgent voice in discussion with the colonel.

"Damnation," the colonel hissed. "The complete annihilation of this accursed race of mongrel brutes and half-wits can't come soon enough." He called to his men to join him in his tent.

A few minutes later, she heard Cormag as well as the burrs of other Scotsmen's voices mingling with the English. They argued and shouted, but none of it made sense.

"No!" the colonel commanded in a tone demanding immediate compliance. "You and your men will stay at this camp with some of my men until I send word about your next move. Do not mess with the women, Cormag, or I'll relieve you of your bullocks and a few other loathsome parts of your anatomy. Am I understood?"

Andra could not hear Cormag's reply, but the idea that he would be in charge of them in the colonel's absence terrified her. She wondered which of the English would remain, though she didn't trust them any further than Cormag and his miscreants. Somehow, she must get the girls away from here soon, especially with this change in circumstances. Now that the camp might be under Cormag's authority, would the young Englishman help them? She needed to find out quickly and make their escape.

"Sir," she called to the guard outside their tent. "We need to attend to our personal needs." The girls woke at her nudging and Isabel wanted to know what had happened.

"I don't know, Isabel, but it can't be good. We must make an effort to get away as soon as possible. A rider advised the colonel of a problem that requires he leave with some of the soldiers. Cormag and his men will be staying in the camp. Do you think you would recognize landmarks to find our way home if we could escape?"

Isabel straightened her spine, a determined look in her eyes. "Aye, I've been to a number of the clan holdings adjoining our land and to the Cameron's lands. Some are allies, some are not, but I think I could find our way."

Andra wondered whether she should risk their lives with an attempted escape. Convinced they would risk something far worse if they stayed, she set her thoughts to how they might sneak away.

"When the guard takes us to attend our business pay attention to how many men leave and how many remain. We'll take our chance as soon as possible. You know your brothers must have discovered our absence by now. They'll have search parties scouring the land. Perhaps that's why they've called the colonel away."

She prayed for an imminent rescue, but would no longer wait for it to happen. The very thought that Kendrick and his men might be riding to their aid gave both comfort and concern. Images of him swooping in on his great, gray charger, as he had the night she had found Senga and Kyle, filled her with dread. Yes, they were warriors and accustomed to confrontation, but even warriors suffered injuries or death in battle. Now that she suspected their present captors had perpetrated the atrocity she'd discovered before, fear clawed at her gut. Why had they attacked those people and put them to the sword? Everything in this brutal era confused her.

"I won't crumble, Dad," she whispered to herself, rubbing the ring on her left hand, urging confidence she didn't feel. "I'll play my part and make you proud."

Isabel placed her bound hands over Andra's, as did Senga. The young girls looked so vulnerable, so small, and so innocent. "We're not afraid, if you're with us." Isabel said.

Two earnest, young faces looked to Andra for guidance. Their willingness to follow her lead steeled her resolve. She would see them to safety somehow. They would survive.

An English guard took them to a large oak just past the clearing. "Why has the colonel left?" She knew he wouldn't disclose anything but asked anyway.

The man shoved and almost knocked her off her feet, which hurt terribly since she did not have her shoes. Then he grabbed her and pulled her against his chest, breathing into her ear. "The colonel's business is no concern of yours. Keep your mouth shut and tend to your business before I forget my orders and tend to my own needs, if you know what I mean." A large strong hand groped her backside.

She shuddered and pulled away. It was a bleak night. One could barely discern shadows the dark was so complete. A heavy mist swirled across the ground, softening the sounds of their movement. Even the rippling stream seemed blanketed. Faint sounds of thunder rumbled far in the distance, promising the possibility of a storm, despite the clusters of stars still visible between mounding clouds. The colonel and a contingent of his men had departed, leaving several soldiers and Cormag's men at the camp. The soldiers seemed to be on heightened alert, strapping on mail, swords, and pistols at their hips. Andra thought she saw Lucas beside the horses, but couldn't be certain. Cormag's men huddled near a fire on the other side of camp, no doubt plotting their own vile strategies.

Their guard returned them to the tent and re-tied their hands. Andra remembered she still had her *sgian dubh* inside her vest pocket. She decided not to have the girls try to retrieve it until they managed an escape. No viable plan had yet come to mind and she didn't want a guard to discover she possessed a hidden weapon.

Tense hours passed while nothing occurred. She stayed alert even though the girls had drifted asleep and now slumped against her. Soft gray bled into a shimmering silver sky when a rider pounded into camp.

She heard the English call out, "Who goes there?"

"Dugal MacDonald. I have urgent business with Laird

Cameron and the colonel."

"What the hell! Why did you bring her here?" she heard Cormag snarl.

"I had to come, Cormag. Tell this brute to unhand me and remove the binding. I have urgent news." Andra recognized Vera's voice and perked up.

"Take her to my tent." Cormag bellowed.

Perhaps ten minutes passed until one of Cormag's men told the guards that he'd come to take the women to his laird. An intense argument ensued until Cormag commanded. "Release Andra! You can keep the girls until I'm finished with the wench."

The guards hesitated for a moment. "We are English soldiers, and do not answer to you, Cormag. Remember what the colonel said. You are not to touch the women in his absence."

"I heard him, but things have changed. I needn't remind you that I am Laird Cameron, and your colonel would not have managed success in half of his recent skirmishes and other endeavors without me and mine. Send the woman to my tent immediately."

When one of the guards ushered Andra into Cormag's tent she spotted Vera leaning against a table drinking wine. "Why do you need her? I've just given you all the information you need." She stretched out a naked foot and rubbed it seductively up Cormag's leg while glaring at Andra. "We have business of our own to attend to," she purred.

Andra stared at the woman with undisguised loathing. "Why are you involved with this scum?"

Cormag backhanded her, re-splitting her lip. "Shut your mouth unless I ask you a question. The old laird has died." He sneered then laughed. "That means your rescuers will probably be delayed. And I hear that Kendrick and his men have not returned to the keep. Perhaps a fight resulted from the diversion we used to steal you. Mayhap your precious Laird MacLean died in the skirmish. What I want to ken is how many men went with MacLean to the borders?"

"I wouldn't know." Andra stiffened her back and glared at

him. Her heart ached for the grief that Lorne, Kendrick, Beatrice, and the rest of the clan would suffer. She decided not to tell Isabel until they reached safety.

The bastard circled, smelled her hair, then flicked his tongue along the side of her neck. She wanted to vomit. "I hear tell Kendrick found you after their last battle with the colonel and me men. They were hidden in the hills somewhere around here, and you are going to tell me where their hiding place is."

Andra didn't answer.

Vera rolled her eyes. "What is it about this woman that makes men slobber all over themselves? Cormag, let's go to your keep where we can mount a proper defense."

Cormag spun on Vera like a viper. "Dae you dare dictate to me?" he hissed.

"Nae, Cormag, but this wench is useless, and we should take shelter and plan a proper defense."

"Dae you think you are a military commander now?" He grabbed Vera by her throat. "Nae, you are a nuisance, and now that you have left the MacLean's keep, you're of no value to me."

Fear crossed her reddening face for a second. Then she placed a hand on his shoulder and one on his crotch. Gasping, she purred, "Cormag, you dinnae mean that. You ken I make you shudder with desire. We are two of a kind, meant to be together."

He spun her behind the table and bent her across the top; his thick hand pressed her face onto the rough wood. "You are a hot, little minx. Mayhap you're still of use to me." He continued to hold her down while the other hand pushed up her skirts; his eyes never moved from Andra's face.

Vera's involvement with this beast appalled Andra. The girl had been the catalyst for their abduction. Still, she didn't want to watch him rape the girl either. "Do you smell something?" she asked, lifting her nose in the air while keeping her eyes on Cormag.

He cackled and snarled baring his yellow teeth. "Oh, aye, that's the smell of the wench's hot cunny burning for me, just like yours will when I'm finished with her."

"No Cormag, the stink in my nostrils is the stench of fear, of death and the clawing hands of the dead that hover around you." She lifted her finger pointing over his shoulder as though a horde of apparitions floated behind him.

Fear flashed across his face, which he quickly suppressed with an arrogant façade of rage and lust. Nevertheless, Andra hadn't missed it.

"She's a witch, Cormag. Throw her out. I've heard she keens and casts spells in the pre-dawn hours." Vera cried, her wide-eyed fear plastered across her brow, both from Cormag's ministrations, and because she apparently believed Andra might actually be a witch. "Have the men burn her at a stake, and I'll tend you like you've never experienced. You ken I satisfy your lusts."

"Shut your mouth, wench. I'm going to give you what you deserve." Banging Vera's head against the table again, he fumbled with the laces at the front of his trews. "Pay attention, bitch." He snarled at Andra. "You're next, and I promise, you'll be beggin' me for release before I'm finished with you." He shoved into Vera and thrust hard against her several times. The veins bulged in his forehead and his face turned crimson.

Vera tried to talk to him again. "Cormag, I ken what you want and how tae give it tae you. Let me up, Cormag, and I'll help you." Ignoring the girl's plea, he kept thrusting, licking his dry chapped lips, glaring at Andra.

Disgusted, fear charging every nerve fiber, Andra turned away for a split second. She willed away the fear and revulsion swamping her, and turned to face her nemesis. Black eyes, darker than the gates of hell, bore into her. Perhaps if he feared her, he would stop. Then again, maybe he would rape her next, followed by a burn at the stake.

She didn't know whether to scream for help or attempt to attack the man herself. If she called out, would the men who responded experience the same lust that now consumed the devil in front of her? The girls counted on her to return to them. That had to remain her primary concern.

Steeling her voice, she attempted a deep growl and tried again, "You have much to answer for Cormag Cameron, both in this life and the next. I see dark hands grabbing at you. All the women you have defiled, all the innocents you have murdered. Their loss will not go unpunished, and they will not leave until your body and soul are torn to shreds and sent to hell where you belong."

He grunted and snarled, continuing to slam against an oddly subdued Vera. "I have no soul. That was lost to me long ago. I—fear—nothing!" he grunted with each thrust. Then he lifted Vera's head off the table, pulled his dagger from his hip, and slit her throat without a flicker of remorse.

Chapter Thirty

Someone screamed and screamed. Andra couldn't tell if the screams issued from her own lungs, or from the recesses of hell itself.

Two English guards, one of them Lucas, entered Cormag's tent with pistols drawn. Lucas yelled at Andra, but she couldn't hear him. Other men shouted and shoved, to get in or out of the tent, she didn't know which.

Lucas dragged Andra across the clearing toward the tent where the girls were. "My lady, take deep breaths. The girls will be frightened enough over your screams. You must calm yourself."

As they approached the tent, he told the other two guards what had happened and directed them to get the ensuing melee at Cormag's tent under control. "I'll take care of the women," he assured them.

Once inside, he turned her to face him. "Lady Andra, I did not join Her Majesty's Dragoons to harm innocent women and children."

She couldn't respond to anything Lucas said. All attempts to calm herself failed as the image she had just witnessed lashed her mind.

Finally, Lucas slapped her cheek and shook her shoulders. "Andra, collect yourself! My apologies for the rough treatment, but you must come to your senses and move quickly. Cormag has gone mad, and I don't know when the colonel will return. You and the young ladies are in grave danger."

He went to the girls and cut through their ropes. "I moved one of the horses behind the colonel's tent. I could not move more than one for fear of detection, so you will need to ride together. As soon as I leave, slip under the back, grab the horse, and go over the hill behind us. Circle down through the woods, and then enter the stream below so your trail will be lost. When you leave the stream, stay concealed in the trees as much as possible. The fog is thickening and may provide additional cover as you make your escape."

Andra came to her senses and moved into action. Action always helped her focus. "Do you have any weapons we can take with us? A bow and arrows perhaps?"

"Yes, I put one on the saddle. Don't stop to use it unless you have no other choice. Once they discover you've gone, there's no telling how things will go should they catch you."

Isabel touched his cheek with her slender hand. "Our thanks to you, Lucas Temple. May the good Lord bless you with better companions in your future."

He held Isabel's gaze for a moment, as if memorizing her face, and then swiftly departed.

A brawl involving several of Cormag's men and English soldiers distracted the guards when the women made their escape. Bent forward they crawled out of the back of their tent. Dark clouds and thickening fog blanketed them in a muffled gauzy cloak. As soon as possible, Andra helped the girls mount and prayed the men would kill each other before they noticed them gone.

Once they crested and dropped behind the hill, she looked around. "Do you recognize any landmarks, Isabel?"

"Nae, the fog obscures too much of the landscape, but I don't think Lucas would help us escape then give us false directions."

"No, you're right."

They followed along the base of the hill, through the woods and entered the stream some distance from camp. Andra walked the horse through the water for quite a while. Their pace was too slow. It wouldn't be long before the men discovered their absence and began a search to recapture them. They had to pick up their speed or find a place to hide; she could not allow those beasts to take the girls again. Kicking the horse to a canter, she rode out of the stream. Twisting through thick bramble and dense clusters of trees, never positive of their location, but certain they headed away from the camp, Andra taxed their horse to its limits.

They had only traveled a few hours before they heard a sound like far off thunder. Andra knew that thunderous sound. The pounding of horses' hooves approached them from behind. She moved deeper into the woods and maneuvered their mount under a grove of trees with low hanging branches thick with autumn foliage.

Urging the girls onto a sturdy lower branch she hastened them up, "Climb as high as you can. Cling low against the branches. I'll lead the men away from your hiding place. Don't come down unless I come back for you, or members of your clan or allies you recognize arrive."

Isabel kissed Andra's cheek, and then climbed up without a word of protest. Andra handed her the bow and quiver of arrows. "Don't shoot unless you are sure they have discovered your hiding spot. Then shoot to kill. But do nothing to draw their attention."

Senga squeezed Andra's shoulder, let a whimper pass her lips, and took Isabel's extended hand. They climbed high into the tree as Andra took off at a full gallop bent on keeping their pursuers away from the girls. The thick blanket of debris on the forest floor might provide sufficient coverage to hide her trail. An urgent refrain, whispered like a mantra, beat against her brain. "*The girls must not be found; the girls must not be found.*"

A loud clap of thunder rumbled, then another. The heavens opened a deluge over her head. Andra prayed to every deity she could name, including the spirit of the horse under her, who sped through the forest like a wild demon.

"There they are!" A man called out. He had spotted her darting through the trees.

She glimpsed a road ahead on her right, bent tight against the horse's withers, and galloped forth. The open road would allow her greater speed than skirting through trees, especially since her pursuers rapidly closed the distance between them. The men screamed their war calls, and she screamed one of her own, calling upon ancestors known and unknown to give wings to her frantic flight.

A man on a huge, brown charger tried to cut off her slathering horse. Skirting his attempt to stop her, Andra kicked hard on the sides of the poor animal giving his all to aid her escape. She had managed to ride a good distance from where she'd hidden the girls. She prayed it was far enough. Eventually, Lucas pulled up to her right side and grabbed the reins out of her hands.

Captured. She cried in her heart, but released no tears to reveal her emotions to the men.

Lucas reached over and pulled Andra onto his horse. For a young man he possessed surprising strength. "I'll take the woman," he shouted. "Stay between Cormag and me. I don't want him anywhere near us until the colonel returns," he ordered the soldier beside them.

Cormag pulled up behind, screaming. "Where are the other whores? She kens the MacLean's hiding place and hid the women there. Give her to me. I'll get the location out of her one way or another." He was slathering and foaming at the mouth worse than the exhausted horse under him.

"You're not in charge here, Cormag. You'll not touch the woman. I follow the colonel's orders. Take it up with him when he returns." Lucas turned his horse and headed back to their camp at a trot.

As soon as they rode away, he leaned against her ear and whispered, "I apologize, my lady, but don't fear. I won't turn you over to Cormag for any reason. At least you hid the girls."

Chapter Thirty-One

Kendrick and his men reached the MacLean borders a few hours after leaving the keep. They chased the thieving Camerons into the hills. The reivers left most of the cattle behind in their flight. A few men took charge and moved them back to their grazing grounds on MacLean lands. Kendrick and the remaining men spotted a herd of deer and killed three, which they dressed in the field. They roasted some of the meat over an open fire and strung up the rest to dry. Their stomachs full, satisfied with their day's work, the men bedded down for the night.

Kendrick and Rabbie took the first watch, walking through the tree line. They hadn't spoken about Andra again since she'd revealed her secrets earlier that morning.

"Have you given further thought to Andra's story, cousin?"

"Aye, 'tis all I can think about." He rubbed his hands through his thick hair and across the back of his neck. "It staggers the imagination, but regardless of how incredible her confession sounds, I believe she tells the truth"

"Aye, I concur," Rabbie whistled through his teeth. "Now that she's trusted us with these burdensome secrets, we must protect her from those who might use or injure her for that information. Dinnae you agree?"

Kendrick leaned against the trunk of a large beech tree, shaking his head as he spoke. "The questions that remain are: what do we do with this information? How does it affect our clan? Why did providence send her to us? And what do we do about the lass now?"

He couldn't imagine her with anyone else, nor could he

fathom not having her in his life. He had claimed her with his body. He desired her with an unquenchable fire that burned his loins. It was lust. It was passion. She was maddening, obstinate, alluring, and no matter how much he tried to deny it, he wanted her as his own.

"Well, if you'll forgive the intrusion, cousin, it seems pretty clear to me what you want to do with the lass. Yet, dinnae you think she deserves a proper commitment and a home where she'll be protected?"

Kendrick glared at Rabbie, but acknowledged the sentiment, "Aye, that she does."

"Sooo…" Rabbie drew out the word before launching into dangerous territory. "You plan to find her a husband within the clan, then? 'Tis not my plan to wed yet, but I'd take her off your hands if you wish. You ken I'd protect her with my life."

Kendrick repressed an urge to smash his cousin's face. "Stop provoking me, Rabbie. You'll not be wedding the lass and neither will anyone else." He responded with more vehemence than he'd intended. "'Tis too dangerous to trust anyone with her secrets, and you ken it."

"Umm, that's true. I think you're in serious danger." Rabbie turned away, but Kendrick didn't miss the smirk on his cousin's face.

"What? What are you blathering about?" Rabbie was like a dog with a bone. He would not relent now.

"I think she has captured your interest more than you wish to reveal, even to yourself." Rabbie chuckled and stepped away, putting his hands up in a defensive gesture.

"She's been accepted by most of the clan. A few dissenters remain, but none of consequence and they'll come around eventually. Mayhap you should marry the lass. She's spirited, strong, and fearless as any warrior, you ken. What more could a laird need or want in a mate? And her lovely wee voice could make angels rejoice, and sooth your frayed nerves. Besides, marrying her would certainly provide the protection she needs."

Rabbie's eyebrows rose precipitously, and he took a step back from Kendrick. "I'm just saying what you're think'n, and you ken it. Now it's up to you, *Laird,* to do the right thing."

"Mayhap she's been accepted. But…" Kendrick couldn't finish his train of thought because it spun into the universe with too many possibilities, none of which he was ready to consider, much less discuss with Rabbie.

"She wants to return to her home, to the life she knew and understood. I keep trying to conceive how I would react and manage if I were in her place. It boggles the mind to think on it."

The cousins stared into the woods, sheltering their own thoughts on the situation. "I think I'll turn in. I want to leave before first light on the morrow. I'll get John to join you on watch." Kendrick went to his bedroll knowing sleep would desert him this night.

After only a few hours' rest, the men packed up the meat and headed for home. They rode out long before the first light of dawn and proceeded at a leisurely pace. When they reached a point a little over an hour's ride from the castle, a fast rider approached them. It was Struan, who had stayed at the castle with Lorne.

"MacLean, I have grave news for you. I'm sorely sorry to tell you that your father passed early this morn. Men have been disbursed to find you, and also to inform your allies."

The news didn't surprise Kendrick but the grievous loss pained him just the same. The men passed the news along the line.

"Davey," he called to one of them, "pick a few lads to help you with the meat, travel as fast as you can, but take care to not lose any in your haste." To the rest of the men he yelled, "We ride hard lads, keep up as you can." He spurred his horse to a hard gallop flanked by Rabbie and Struan.

* * *

There was considerable commotion in the bailey as they rode over the barbican and through the gatehouse. Lorne sat astride a big, dapple-gray warhorse in the center of the bailey barking orders. A contingent of men dressed for battle steadied their mounts.

"Brother," Lorne called to Kendrick over the clamor. "Jesus, praise the saints you have arrived."

"Och, what are you preparing for?" This level of activity was not in response to his father's death.

"Isabel, Senga, and Andra are missing."

He hissed, his nostrils flaring and his mouth flattening into a hard grimace. "Are you certain? When did you discover their absence?" This news ripped through Kendrick as swiftly and harshly as if struck by an enemy's claymore. He knew his brother would have combed every inch of the castle, outbuildings, even the village before he'd make such a claim.

Lorne directed the stable lads to saddle fresh horses for Kendrick, Rabbie, and Struan. "Aye, we're certain they're gone. You were correct to distrust that bitch, Vera. One of the stable lads said she took old Bessie out before dawn, when we sent messengers about Da to our allies. Last night she told mother that Andra had stayed at widow MacAllis' and that Isabel and Senga had asked for a night alone in Isabel's chambers. Yet no one ever saw the girls return to the castle from their foray to the loch. And Alith said she last saw Andra when they sat together in the herb garden yesterday afternoon. Therefore, she was not with the lasses."

"Widow MacAllis never saw anyone yesterday. An hour ago, we found the body of the lad who had accompanied the girls as their guard. Someone had cut his throat and evidence of at least five riders trampled the ground near his body. There was no sign of the girls. We found the guard at the edge of the meadow on the north side of the loch." 'Tis one of their favorite spots to gather wildflowers and herbals. Unfortunately, that location brings them verra close to the forest and is not visible to the tower guards."

"Has anyone found Vera?" Kendrick asked as he jumped from his horse.

"Nae, but we found old Bessie wondering near the abandoned hut outside the northeast side of the village. The hut showed signs of recent occupation. A lone horse rode out from there. We sent a few men to follow each path. One returned a short while ago with this." He pulled a woman's shoe from under his plaid. "Mother says it belonged to Andra."

Lorne handed him the soft, leather slipper his mother had

given Andra during her first days at the castle. "Aye, 'tis hers. Damnation! Lorne, this could be another trap. Mayhap the reivers at the northern border were a ruse to pull a contingent of our warriors away from the castle. Those miscreants left in a hurry, and we recaptured most of the cattle far too easily, without any man injured. I kenned something about that felt wrong."

He wanted to scream. His battle cry would reverberate through the hills when he rode out of the bailey. Everyone would know Laird MacLean rode to battle, and he would take no prisoners. If those whoresons had harmed one hair on his sister's or Andra's head, he would flay them alive and rip out their still beating hearts.

"I'll take your horse, Lorne. We cannae all leave. This could be another ruse to weaken our security and attempt to capture the castle. I'll take Rabbie, Struan, and your fresh men and leave you with my men, who will arrive shortly with fresh kill we dressed in the field. Have you sent riders to the Keiths and McDuffs yet?"

"Aye, men have been dispatched. Riders left before dawn to notify the clans about father. We expect allied lairds should arrive within the next few days to pay their respects. They will have men at arms with them. We can count on those men to help reclaim our women and protect the castle if an attack is imminent. I understand your request that I stay, Kendrick, but I don't like it at all. I'd much prefer to accompany you and the men." Lorne's horse skittered under him.

"Aye, I ken you want to join this fight, but I need you here, Lorne."

As the men mounted fresh horses, Beatrice came out of the keep with Alith clinging to her arm. Their eyes were red and moist with unshed tears and Beatrice's voice hitched as she tried to speak. "My sons, you must bring our ladies home. My heart cannae lose our daughters too."

"Aye mother, we will bring them back. For now, Lorne will stay behind to direct messengers and secure the castle. We'll send word back as we discover information." Kendrick did not miss that his mother referred to all the women as her daughters. He blinked a moment at how right her words sounded to his ears.

"Has Father been placed in the chapel?"

"Aye. If you're delayed for more than two days, we'll inter him. Do you wish to join me and pay your last respects before you depart?"

Hesitating but a moment, Kendrick turned and sped to the chapel. After uttering words of prayer and pleading for his sire's guidance, he kissed his mother's cheek then ran back to the bailey. Alith waited beside his horse. She laid her hand across Kendrick's shoulder. "Andra is ours, lad, I feel it in me bones. We must get all of them back."

"I will not fail them or you. Take care of mother." He kissed the old woman's forehead and leaped on his brother's mount. In a cloud of dust and gravel, he and the men sped from the bailey, the air reverberating with their war cries.

Chapter Thirty-Two

Andra felt as though she'd been riding through a nightmare for weeks, and it culminated in this horrid camp she had escaped only hours ago, though it seemed like days. Lucas dismounted and pulled her down with him. He returned her to the tent she had previously occupied, bound her hands, and attached the rope to the tent pole again. "I'm sorry, my lady. I cannot do else for you right now. The best I can do is to keep Cormag and his men away from you until the colonel returns. Then it will be up to him to decide what will happen next."

"He's not likely to be very kind toward me, but I thank you for your earlier help getting the girls away from this cursed place." There was no sense antagonizing the man. She understood he simply performed his duty and had put his head on the line attempting to help them earlier.

"Do they know you helped me?" she whispered.

"No, and if you tell them, they will shoot me as a traitor." He looked beseechingly at her, his head tilted to the side. "I told them you must have snatched a knife and cut your rope during the melee that occurred at Cormag's tent when he killed the girl. Their men's subsequent fight provided a plausible distraction for that to occur." He hesitated for a moment. "Since I value my neck I will deny any other story."

"Of course. I understand." The likelihood that he could aid her in another attempted escape was slim to non-existent.

"Do you know why they want me? I am no one. I have no family who can ransom me, no one who will come to my rescue. Although kind enough to give me shelter, I mean nothing to the MacLeans. I am of no value to anyone." Her voice sounded desperate, whiny. She could feel a trickle of sweat sluice down her back and under her breasts.

"Obviously the colonel and Cormag believe The MacLean will come for you. They both have long-standing grudges against the man and his brother, each for his own reasons. I don't know much else. I'll bring you something to eat in a while." He left and stood outside the tent with another guard.

Cormag tried to obtain her release to him, but the guards and other soldiers pulled their weapons insisting they wait for the colonel. Andra wanted to stay alert, but a deep weariness settled over her. The rush of adrenaline that had served in their earlier escape abated, and all remaining reserves floated away like a puff of smoke. A fitful sleep took her into the depths of dark and disjointed nightmares.

Awareness of firm hands lifting her to a standing position worked through the fog of her exhaustion. She snapped her eyes open and tried to pull away. Her hands were still bound to the pole and every part of her body rebelled toward collapse.

"Stand up, woman! The colonel wants to speak with you." One of the men who had been on guard outside the tent forced her to her feet.

"I need to tend to my personal needs first."

"Fine, but don't try anything. You'll not escape from me." Other than Lucas, these soldiers were of the same ilk as Cormag's men. With the least provocation, any one of them would cause her serious harm. She seethed and felt an overwhelming urge to kick him in the nuts. Unfortunately, that would accomplish nothing but a punch or smack, or worse.

The guard pushed her inside the colonel's tent. Though he must have recently returned, someone had polished his boots and his jacket was spotless. The scarf at his neck and his breeches revealed a few stains that marred his otherwise pristine attire. She suspected it annoyed him greatly. He brushed at some non-existent debris on his sleeves and stared at her, the scar pulling his mouth into a twisted, leering scowl.

He turned, angling the scarred side of his face in shadow, "I hear you've had an adventurous day, Lady Andra."

A wicked dagger appeared in his ungloved hand as he strutted across the space between them.

This is it.

He moved until she could feel his breath on her face, and struggled to maintain a calm veneer while she held her breath. She flinched, surprised when he slit the ropes binding her wrists. The sudden release caused a sharp pain in her stiff shoulders, but she refused to rub the pain away. He moved to stand a few feet in front of her.

"Where did you leave the girls?"

"I don't know." She vowed not to give him any information about their escape.

"Who aided your escape?"

Lifting her chin, refusing to look away, she kept her voice firm and low. "You don't think women are clever enough to act on their own behalf when threatened by ruthless cutthroats and rapists?"

He moved the dagger under her throat so swiftly she had no time to step away.

"Don't antagonize me, Lady Andra, or you will see just how ruthless I can be. I've had a tiring day, and my patience wears thin."

Her heart thudded in her chest. She watched his eyes drop to the vein that pulsed blood through her neck. No doubt, the vein he planned to slice with his wicked knife. "Surely your men have filled you in on what transpired in your absence. There is little I can add to that." She hated the strangled hitch in her voice.

"Did you take the girls to the MacLean's hiding place in the hills?"

"I don't know of any hiding place."

"Cormag says differently."

"And you would rely on the word of that worthless whoreson, piece of shit?" she brashly retorted. Fear drove her anger to the surface.

He raised his brows. "That's hardly appropriate language for a lady."

"Even you won't deny my rude assessment of Cormag Cameron. Besides, I doubt many *ladies* would address you with flowery speech while you held a knife to their throat."

"There you are wrong. Most ladies would weep, beg, and attempt to ply their womanly wiles. I can see why a warrior might be intrigued by you."

"No one is intrigued by me." She kept her eyes glued to his and exerted every effort to prevent her lips from quivering and her hands from shaking.

He stepped back, re-sheathing the knife. Waving a dismissive hand, his voice softened. "The girls are of little importance. Sit. Perhaps you would care for some wine. It's most unfortunate you had to witness that distressing bit of violence earlier today. Cormag is a barbarian."

He offered her wine, while slandering Cormag after holding a knife at her throat. This was a good re-enactment of Dr. Jekyll and Mr. Hide. Nevertheless, she sat on the stool offered.

"Why do you associate with him if you hold him in such disregard?" Conversation about his motives was the last thing she should pursue, but she couldn't help herself.

"He serves my purposes. Sometimes we must meet with the devil to accomplish our greater goals.

"My men are scouring the woods and I have sent scouts to learn how many will be coming to your rescue. Then I will set my trap and finally put an end to those worthless MacLean brothers."

"What is your complaint with the MacLeans?"

He abruptly turned and slammed his fists on the table, his face a twisted mask of fury. His erratic mood swings suggested a mind as unhinged as Cormag's. He simply possessed a bit more spit and polish around the edges.

"My complaint is that they breathe air into their lungs. My complaint is that they are Highlanders, the worst scum God ever placed on this earth."

Something in his posturing suggested his complaint had to

do with the ugly scar that marred his otherwise flawless features. Even though she should not voice an observation, her tongue rattled on anyway. "He has bested you in some fashion and you seethe with the need for retribution, even to the point of aligning with the likes of Cormag."

He snapped his spine straight, squared his shoulders. Andra could see his fight to rein in a volatile temper. Waving his hand at the expensive rings on her fingers, the diamond studs in her ears and the exquisite cross at her neck, he barked, "No ordinary woman would possess such riches. Are you of noble blood, my lady? What is the great secret of your heritage and family that you so vigorously withhold the information? From what Cameron clan do you descend, and from whom are you hiding?"

Here we go again. The endless questions for which she had no answers anyone would believe. She could see the hatred in his eyes, and this time it did not soften. Maybe she should tell the truth and let him think what he would.

"My family is dead, I am from far away, and only recently came to be at the MacLean's castle as they offered me protection and shelter while I am in Scotland."

He reached his hand forward and attempted to touch the cross at her neck. She slapped his hand away and covered it with her own. Strong fingers twisted into the front of her gown and pulled her to her feet, he yanked her against his hard chest. The other hand squeezed her upper arm like a vise.

"You dare strike at me! What brash behavior. You forget yourself, my lady. You are my captive, and I will take or touch what I please."

Andra lifted her chin boldly. The shock of her defiant manner registered briefly on the colonel's face, and as quickly, he shuttered his emotions.

"You hold yourself with considerable boldness and condescension for a captive. What could possibly engender such arrogance under the circumstances? Perhaps you mistakenly believe some relation or protector able to exact retribution on your behalf will arrive shortly. Or some errant knight will charge in to secure your rescue. If so, let me disabuse you of that notion. After I have dispatched the MacLean brothers and that miscreant carrying your same surname, you will be mine to handle in any fashion I choose."

His scrutiny, while he delivered this speech in a calm, superior tone, filled her with an urge to scream and rail against his smug self-assurance. Instead, she repressed the rage that floated under a veneer of serene complacency and refused to flinch at his marred countenance, which he now presented full-faced daring her to recoil.

Unfortunately, she could not control the slight tremor in her hand gripping the cross under the pressure of his hold. She gripped it so tightly it punctured her skin and a trickle of blood slipped between her fingers, but she would not release it to this man. She wanted to spit in his face, but knew he would kill her on the spot. Steadily, she held her focus on his face while clamping her mouth shut, grinding her teeth to hold in a sharp retort. From this moment on, she vowed to keep her wits, her emotions, and her tongue firmly under control.

The trickle of blood seeping between their joined fists diverted the challenging scrutiny of his eyes. "Ah, I see now why so many seem to hold you in considerable regard." He released her hand and appeared uncertain what to do with the blood that marred his palm. He withdrew a pristine handkerchief from his jacket pocket while continuing in that annoyingly confident tone. "You do not cower when most would or certainly should. You do not flinch away from my countenance."

Now he'd shocked her at his casual mention of a scar that he hid with posturing or blatantly displayed to garner a response. A response he would no doubt find loathsome and worthy of reprisal.

"You are clearly a woman in need of a strong man, one capable of curbing your willful behavior." He released her arm, likely sprouting bruises from his tight grip, and slid the back of his hand along her cheek. His voice became soft yet full of venom, "I will enjoy taking you from Kendrick. Perhaps I'll let him live long enough to watch me claim your body. It would sweeten my revenge."

How could it be possible that she'd arrived in this desolate place and now had two vile cretins vying to claim and destroy her for revenge on the man she'd fallen for like a lovesick teenager? Andra wanted to curse this lunatic to his face, but for the moment, he was the lesser of two very evil men she needed to escape.

A loud commotion outside the colonel's tent announced Cormag's approach. "I'll have that woman now, Colonel. You gave me your word that she'd be mine. I deserve my revenge, and I'll pry the information from her you seek. Kendrick stole from me and murdered the woman who should have been mine. Upon your word, we agreed I'd have that fancy piece you dally with in exchange for my allegiance and in compensation for what MacLean took from me."

"Leave my tent, Cormag. I'll let you know when you can have the woman. Right now she is entertaining me." He gave Andra a lopsided, grimacing smile, his voice lowered to a snarl. "You see how I protect you from that filth. Be assured you would not find that mongrel's attentions satisfying, and I fully expect your compliant behavior in exchange for my continued protection."

He hissed out a very frustrated breath and continued as though she had faded away and he was ruminating to himself. "The man plagues my patience. He holds such a festering hatred over his thwarted desire to claim Kendrick's dead wife, already gone many years, as his own. Foolishly, he believes his hatred and revenge takes precedence over mine. Eventually his usefulness will wane, and he'll come to an unpleasant end."

Andra suspected Cormag grew close to that end because he knew far too much about the colonel's questionable tactics and ongoing plunder of the area for his own gain. She couldn't think of an appropriate response and dreaded to think what *entertainment* the colonel expected from her so she held her tongue.

"Lucas," he called. When the young man entered the tent, he threw her toward him. "Take her to her tent and be certain she is securely bound. Keep two guards on her, with strict orders to let no one else in, especially Cormag."

* * *

Ushering her into the tent—her prison, he apologized. "I'm sorry you find yourself in the middle of this mess. If I could help you further, I would."

"Why? Any aid you give me puts you at great risk. Why do you help me?" His kindness baffled her when every other man had treated her with open distain or lechery.

A twinkle glinted in his eye, "I don't know. Perhaps you remind me of my older sister." He leaned in conspiratorially. "Her mum was a Scot too, God rest their souls."

"I'm sorry for your loss." Surprisingly, she truly did feel sorrow, as much for herself as for him.

He observed her as though he'd just discovered an odd zoo specimen. "Can I trust you, my lady?"

"If you think to ask me to promise that I will not attempt escape at every opportunity, don't bother. For your previous kindness, I won't lie to you."

He tilted his head in observation of her. "You are a most remarkable woman. If I leave these bindings loose would you give me your word not to try an escape until I tell you the moment is right?" She started to respond negatively when he held up his hand.

"It's anyone's guess how things might turn in the next few hours or days. I would recommend you wait for your rescuers. Another botched attempt at escape would probably result in serious injury, torture, or death to you. If something should happen to me, then certainly take every opportunity to escape. Otherwise, if you can wait, I am certain your friends will come. If you were mine, I'd move heaven and earth to reach you."

His words surprised her. "How old are you, Lucas?"

"I am soon one and twenty, my lady." He smiled sheepishly.

"Are you married yet?" She didn't know why she asked such a personal question, but his kindness spurred her on. Talking seemed to calm the potent fear that bubbled through her veins.

"Not yet. I must earn my position in her majesty's army first. When I can provide a proper home for my family I shall seek a wife. I hope she possesses your strength of character."

A sad smile lit her face. *Chivalry still exists, Dad.* "I hope you are successful in your efforts, Lucas. You are a gentleman and deserve to find a good woman for your wife. Don't let the likes of these men twist you into the ugliness that possesses and distorts them. They will poison your soul. You must seek some other position as soon as you are able."

"Thank you for those thoughtful words," he smiled sheepishly. "I'll bind your hands in front so you can reach that *dirk* stuck in the side of your vest should you find the need to thwart the less savory men in camp."

A shocked expression crossed her face.

"Don't fear. I won't take it from you. Wait, as I've said. You'll know when the time is right to make a move. In the meantime, I'll do my best to protect you."

Chapter Thirty-Three

Kendrick came across a place where, despite the recent downpour, a number of horses had recently churned the mud. "Rabbie, Struan, let's spread out through these trees. These hoof marks indicate a recent skirmish happened here. Keep your eyes on the canopy as well; they may have spotters or archers hidden in the branches."

Maintaining the point position Kendrick moved cautiously, Rabbie and Struan pulled wide to either side of him. The rest of the men spread out in an inverted v-formation behind them, weaving carefully through the trees.

Another half-hour had passed when Kendrick spotted a lone rider on a hill to their left. With a flick of his wrist, he directed one of his men to pursue the man. Unfortunately, the man escaped, lost in the forest before Kendrick's man could apprehend him.

He signaled to Rabbie and Struan. "They are waiting for us. I have a bad feeling about the trap being set. 'Tis certain they ken we are coming."

One of their fore-guard sentries returned to report that he had spotted suspicious movement in the trees not far ahead. Rabbie pulled out and headed in that direction with Struan flanking him. Kendrick kept moving forward with the rest of the men. "Watch for arrows." He called after them.

"Rabbie! Rabbie! Oh, thank God you have come." Isabel dropped out of the tree branches, and Senga followed behind her.

Rabbie couldn't believe his eyes. How had the girls managed to get here, in a tree in the middle of the forest? He gave a sharp whistle, calling Kendrick and the rest of the men to their location.

Rabbie had never felt such relief in his life as he reached up and pulled the quaking girl into his arms. He held her face and kissed her forehead. "Thank the saints, we've found you, sweet Isabel. Are you injured?" He rubbed his hands down her shivering arms.

Struan reached to Senga and pulled her onto his lap just as Kendrick charged out of the trees.

"Isabel! Thank God, we've found you. How did you get in that tree? Where is Andra?" Relief over his sister's return to the safety of her family's embrace warred with his anxiety that Andra was not with the girls.

"Oh Kendrick, my eyes have never been so happy to see me brother. Andra saved us. One of the Sassenach guards set a horse aside for us and Andra managed our escape. When the men came close to catching us she put us here, gave me her bow and rode away to distract them from our hiding place." Isabel sobbed and clung to his hand while refusing to release her hold on Rabbie.

Kendrick dismounted. "Hold your wheesht, Isabel. You are safe now. We have you, but you must tell us everything you can about your captors and their location."

The men conferred over various strategies to confront their nemesis and retrieve Andra. They had placed the girls under an oiled tarp by the tree, given them ale and dried meat to revive their strength, and placed two men to guard them.

"Saints alive, that woman will surely be the death of me." Kendrick clenched and unclenched his fists while pacing a path through the forest's carpet of debris. "If any of those bastards have harmed her, they will suffer in ways they cannae imagine."

"The lass is as brave as any of our warriors. She'll survive and we'll get her back, cousin." Rabbie offered assurances to Kendrick. How he wished his cousin's veiled optimism would come to fruition. Knowing the men who held her, unimaginable images filtered through his thoughts even as he strategized over the best course of action to pursue.

Rabbie's fleeting, worried expression conveyed he shared his concerns. Despite an urgent desire to surge ahead, a show of control directed Kendrick's actions as they planned for the coming battle. This was why his men trusted him completely; he would not allow his emotions to interfere in battle. He presented them with a cool, self-possessed leader, fierce in the face of adversity. His men would follow him into any skirmish without reservation.

Struan had remained quiet, his bulky arms clamped across his chest. "We need to send the lasses back to the castle first. They cannae be put in further danger."

"Aye, Struan, you will stay with me. Rabbie, I want you to escort the girls. Take six men with you. If you encounter any allies who you would trust with your life, release the lasses to their protection for the remainder of their journey to the castle, and then return here with whomever they can spare. Once a scout returns with information on the enemy's camp, I'll leave one man at this point who can direct you to our location. I ken we are in for quite a battle, and I do not want to go in blind." Unfortunately, Kendrick could barely restrain the urge to rush headlong into the trap he knew awaited them.

"One of the scouts should be returning shortly with information. You have the right of it. Those bastards are laying a trap." Struan looked toward the road expectantly.

Kendrick nodded, "That is the way of both Richardson and Cormag—set the trap, reel them in, and then slaughter everyone. They are ruthless to the core, and they both bear me a grudge, however unfounded their grievances. We cannot expect any quarter from them, and I'll give them none in return."

Pacing across the clearing while carefully observing the surrounding hills and trees, Kendrick continued. "Cormag grows increasingly unstable in his hatred after Kirstin's death, and Richardson will never forgive the scar I dealt him, even if I gave it in battle, and he would have done the same to me if he'd had the chance. Besides, I am certain they are the men who burned out those crofters where Andra found the bairns."

Rabbie interjected, "No doubt they had hoped those poor souls could provide information about our cave. That hidden refuge would provide one more shelter for their incursions into the Highlands. You ken that Cormag has long coveted Ruadhstone castle, and Richardson probably imagines he'll claim it for an army outpost. Its strategic location in the Highlands would provide a boon from which to engage in their nefarious activities."

"Aye," Kendrick nodded, "but our allies are strong, and we will not allow them to take our lands under any circumstances."

Struan rubbed at his scruffy jaw and paced about, his usual posture while sorting through all possible battle contingencies. "They ken where we are positioned, and it will be full dark soon. Will we bed here for the night?"

"No, a heavy fog is settling that will muffle our movement. As soon as we know their location, we will advance to them. I'll not leave Andra in their grasp for a moment longer than necessary. We ken this land as well as they do, perhaps better, and Highlanders are not afraid of a bit of fog and dark. Before morning I plan to be in their midst and will take back what is mine."

The words were out of his mouth before he considered their significance. He had just verbally claimed Andra as his. Of course, he suspected it came as no surprise to his closest friends and family. Nevertheless, he did not miss the smirk on Rabbie's face, nor Struan's sham of a scowl.

Shortly after Rabbie departed with the girls, one of the scouts returned with information on the location of the enemy's camp. He reported their numbers at perhaps a dozen or more than the number of men currently with Kendrick.

"No doubt Richardson will set a score of men along the ridge above the camp. They can easily shoot down warriors approaching from almost any direction. If we can get a few archers behind the men on that ridge, it will be to our advantage."

He called to several of his archers giving them instructions. "Once you reach the edge of the forest, flank the ridge. Don't head in on the main path. Leave the horses under the cover of trees and climb the remaining distance on foot, staying close to the boulders that are scattered over the hillside. If possible, do not announce your arrival until you hear us engage them in battle in the camp. Then move swiftly, and take out as many as you can. We'll give you a half-hour advance to get into position."

"Aye, my laird, we will nae fail you or your lady." It was Michael, the lad who had sparred with Andra in the bailey, who addressed him. He was one of their finest archers and Kendrick knew the man's skill would provide an advantage in this skirmish.

As he walked away, Struan could not hide his chuckle, a rare sound from his lips. "They are all besotted with your lass. 'Tis a good thing you've decided to claim her properly. That is your plan?"

He could not take back the words he'd spoken, nor did he wish to. Still, Kendrick could hardly believe his ears to hear Struan once again championing her. "What are you blathering aboot? I'm just getting the lass out of the clutches of two of the worst whoresons this land has ever seen."

"Och, to be sure of that." Struan scowled. "Yet, did you not just say you were claiming what belongs to you? And if not, well then, it seems more than one of the men may have aspirations toward claiming the lass." Struan grumbled and tugged on the straps securing his weapons. "Though if you ask me, she's a bit too feisty for most of them, don't you ken?"

"If you keep needling me, Struan, I'll knock you on your arse again." He could not deny the fact that Andra had charmed her way into the hearts of many of his clan, despite being a Cameron. Moreover, the crushing fury he felt at the thought of her in the hands of his enemies, or any other man for that matter convinced him he must reach her swiftly.

Kendrick's men busied themselves checking their weapons, strapping on claymores, mace, dirks, and *sgian dubhs*. Some had donned mail under their plaids; others donned hardened-leather jerkins. As they readied for the coming battle, they grunted encouraging banter to each other. His men were outspoken against the Camerons' continued reiving, plundering, raping, stealing of women, and the murder of their clansmen and allies. This latest kidnapping was the final insult. Settling the score should be swift and final, and to a man, they agreed with him that the coming battle was long overdue.

Chapter Thirty-Four

Though Andra had fought against falling asleep again, tension and exhaustion won out, and she drifted into nightmare realms while leaning against the pole to which she was tethered. The clash of metal on metal, warrior cries, and the harsh neighing and screeching of horses in battle drifted into her nightmare.

Only it wasn't a nightmare. She woke to the sounds of battle emanating from everywhere at once. Grabbing hold of the pole, she sprang to her feet, shaking the last vestiges of sleep from her brain. She pressed her body against her bound hands, and managed to retrieve her *sgian dubh*. Holding the hilt with her teeth, she furiously worked the blade against the ropes. She nicked her wrist several times, but ignored the pain and trickles of blood. A few more scratches under the present circumstances held no significance. The blade was quite sharp and quickly severed the binding.

Clutching the dirk in her hand, she entered the fray. Fog swirled under her feet and through the trees where the first shimmers of light created a ghostly scene of horror. The noise was deafening, yet strangely muffled. Fear froze her to stone as bile rose in her throat.

Then, Kendrick charged through the trees on a huge, dapple-gray horse, rushing the enemy like an avenging angel. The beast reared and instantly killed the man charging them. Her eyes locked on his for a brief moment, his mouth opened in a scream or command, but she could not make out his words.

Suddenly, Cormag's filthy breath filled her nose and he twisted the *sgian dubh* held in her hand, deftly turning it against her throat. "I've got you now, m'lady, and your hero will not be taking you from me. You're my retribution, and I intend for Kendrick to witness your degradation and demise. It is me due for all he took from me."

Sliding the blade along her collarbone and under her shift at the shoulder, he slit the fabric cutting her in the process. She felt a sharp sting and the warm rush of blood but the pain didn't fully register in her mind. The material of her gown slipped down her arm and exposed one breast.

Had he cut her throat?

All feeling had fled, replaced with a scalding fury. Her thoughts drifted, and she seemed to separate from her body, barely cognizant of the heinous, clutching bastard dragging her across the compacted dirt.

She looked to where she'd last seen Kendrick, but he was no longer on his charger, and the animal had moved from the center of the melee. Then she saw him—engaged in violent battle with the colonel some yards away from where she stood. Their swords slashed and clanged, sparking the misted air. The smell of churned mud and blood mingled to become a coppery tang that permeated everything. The whoosh of arrows whizzed through the air from the ridge above, finding their targets on occasion, but just as often hitting a horse causing the beast to rear and scream in agony, or hitting a tree with a dull thud. Shouts of Gaelic rose as a group of warriors accosted the men on the ridge from behind.

Cormag mumbled something incoherent in her ear while attempting to push her toward the heart of the battling men. Then he screamed in frustration trying to gain Kendrick's attention. "Look at me, ye bastard, I have your woman, and she'll be mine for the rest of her days, however long I decide to allow her to service me. Think on that as you breathe your last." The colonel reacted to Kendrick's momentary distraction to the taunt and managed a slice against Kendrick's thigh. The wound did not stop him.

The colonel, quick footed, maneuvered away from Kendrick's thrusts while still brandishing his sword, and yelled, "Dammit,

Cormag, draw your sword, and enter this battle. Leave the woman for now."

In her peripheral vision a flurry of motion moved swiftly toward them. Lucas slammed into Cormag knocking all three of them off their feet. She hit her head on a rock about the size of a football, briefly knocking her senseless. When she looked up, Lucas and Cormag engaged in hand-to-hand combat with long dirks. She couldn't find her dirk in the dirt around her. Attempting to stand, she became woozy and lost her balance, falling and rolling from beneath the men's scrabbling feet and through the front of the colonel's tent.

Her head pounded, and she found it difficult to catch her breath, but she would not let them take her unarmed again. Rolling to her side, she rose to her knees and reached a hand to touch the warm wetness on her face.

"Damn and double damn, if this keeps up, I'll end up addlebrained for life," she hissed. Her hand came away covered in blood. She wiped it across her bodice and pressed against the knot on her head in an attempt to staunch the flow.

After a moment, she looked around for weapons. A bow and quiver leaned against the side of the tent wall. Rising on shaky legs, she gulped in air and steadied herself as she lifted the weapon. Though larger than the ones she'd recently practiced with, she could manage it; she had often used her father's bow.

"Dad, if ever you are with me, be here now, I need your strength." Andra strapped on the quiver, notched an arrow, and slipped out of the tent. Lucas lay in the dirt not far away, bleeding profusely from a wound on his side; Cormag was gone. The young man's wide eyes took in her appearance.

"Oh my God, you are bleeding, my lady. I am so sorry I did not get to you sooner," he rasped. "Run to the horses by the river; get away from here."

"Lay still, Lucas. My thanks once again for your aid, but do not worry. I believe I shall live." Why she thought that she could not say.

While searching the battle scene for Kendrick, she moved

quickly toward the stream to provide enough distance for accuracy with her shots. Finally, she located him. He and the colonel were still engaged in combat. Each man managed to match the other's thrusts, blocks, and lunges with a corresponding move. Sweat coursed over their faces. Then she saw Cormag rushing forward behind Kendrick. He raised his sword to deliver a fatal blow.

"Bastard!" she spit through gritted teeth. A hot rage tore through her; she would not allow him to kill her man.

Without hesitation, she raised the bow, aimed, and released. The arrow flew true and thudded into Cormag's chest, throwing him back against a tree where his sword slid from his hand. She turned to her side and vomited, whether because she had just killed a man or because of another head injury, she had no clue, and didn't take a second to examine that thought.

The colonel saw Andra shoot Cormag, and failed to repress his shocked expression. The momentary distraction allowed Kendrick to lunge a fatal thrust and twist it into the man's belly. The colonel fell, dead before his face hit the ground. Unfortunately, two of Cormag's men moved in to challenge Kendrick just when Struan maneuvered to his side.

She notched another arrow and looked up. Following Kendrick and Struan as they fought back to back against three men, she waited for her shot. The battle began to slow as men succumbed to their wounds. Blood soaked Struan's left arm slowing his sword swings in that direction.

One of the men moved to his injured side. Andra took aim and managed to bring down that dragoon. This time she held down the bile and firmed her resolve. If they survived, she could contemplate her actions later; meanwhile, she must fight. She couldn't get another clean shot because their battle had moved too close to her position, and she feared hitting one of her own men.

"One of my own? My man?"

She absorbed these thoughts through the haze of her brain. Yes! They were her own fierce Highlanders; whether or not they claimed her, she claimed them.

Several of MacLean's men battled around her. Her woozy

head caused difficulty concentrating. Her arms ached and her ears rang. She felt as though she stood outside of herself watching the skirmish and her own movements in slow motion.

Notching another arrow, she looked to the ridge from where a clash of weapons cracked above her and saw Michael engaged in hand-to-hand combat with one of the colonel's archers. Brushing the blood and muck out of her eyes with her forearm, she raised her bow, took aim, and held her breath. Michael fell and she loosed her final arrow along with her breath, striking the other man under his arm as he raised his sword. She didn't know whether her shot struck too late to save young Michael, but she prayed it was not. Turning back toward Kendrick, her arrows spent, she could no longer hold onto the bow and dropped it at her bloodied feet.

* * *

Kendrick, with Struan's help, dispatched the last of the men they were fighting. He turned toward Andra, who stood several yards away. Her hair hung in damp tangles, tears streaked white tracks down her cheeks. Blood covered her face and one shoulder, streaks of dirt and blood lashed across her bodice. One shoulder and breast was exposed, also covered in blood, but saints be praised, she was standing. To him, she looked like the most glorious warrior goddess ever regaled in myth or legend. It was as if he had come out of the pouring rain and darkness for the first time in his life, and she was the sun that warmed him, body and soul.

The battle near over, shouts of "MacLean" filled the morning air. Kendrick moved purposefully toward her, this bloodied, wild version of the Huntress Diana. Nothing else filtered through his vision. He burned to hold her in his arms, to claim her as his. She took a tentative step toward him, then another, then sprinted forward with her arms flung wide.

He swung her into his arms and crushed her against his chest. His lips touched her hair, her ear, and he whispered breathlessly, "Andra, *a chuisle mo chroi.*" "*Pulse of my heart.*" "*Mo chuisle, mo muirnin,* Andra," he continued while kissing her damp cheek, lips, and neck. "*My love, my darling Andra.*"

Andra lifted her face to his, gripped his thickly muscled arms tight, and pushed away, "*Mo chuisle*," she said in response. She opened her mouth to say more when a movement at their side caught her attention. One of the warriors stood above Lucas, about to deliver a final deathblow.

She wrenched out of Kendrick's embrace. "Nooo," she screamed, dashing forward, "Hold!" Her hand splayed in the air as if she could thrust it across the distance and stop his action with her force of will.

"Do not strike that man!" It was not a subtle plea, but a full-throated ferocious command, issued like the warrior she had become.

Her vehemence startled Kendrick and a flash of jealousy tore through him. What did she know of this man? What was he to her that she should rush to save his life? A Sassenach lover? No, it occurred to him this might be the Sassenach Isabel had mentioned, the one who had assisted in their escape. He raised his hand, "Step back John, we will see to this dragoon."

She dropped into the dirt beside Lucas and took his cold hand in hers. "Please," she cried, "please, don't die." Brushing damp hair off his forehead her fingers slid down below his jaw searching for a pulse. A whisper escaped her lips. "He lives."

Kendrick knelt beside her and moved the lad's hand from his side. The blood still flowed, albeit slowly. Cutting away the jacket, he saw a puncture wound between two ribs. He called to one of the men for a wad of linen to staunch the wound.

"Will he survive?" Andra pleaded, her eyes brimming with tears.

"I don't know. He is young. If the lung wasn't punctured and there is no damage to his organs, he might survive. Is he the one who helped you, lass?"

"Yes." She swiped at the tears streaming down her face. "Yes, and at great risk to himself, he managed to keep me safe from that miscreant, Cormag." The mention of that name made her shake and gasp with great heaving sobs. She turned her face into Kendrick's neck, desperately clinging to his shoulders.

"Shush, *mo chroi*, 'tis over now, you were verra braw, *mo chuisle*, verra brave." He ran his fingers through the tangles of her hair, pressing her to him, aware that his own heart thudded in his

225

chest like a *bodhrán*. She had captured him, mind, heart, and soul; she was everything he'd never known he needed. Lifting her into his arms, he ordered John to tend the young soldier as if he were one of their own.

The sound of thundering hooves drew their attention to the trees and ridge above. He quickly set her down, pushing her behind and removed his sword in one swift motion. A contingent of men led by Rabbie tore into the center of the camp and another led by The McDuff rode over the ridge above them dispatching the last of their enemies.

"'Tis aboot time you showed your ugly face, now that we've won the battle." Struan rumbled loudly. Another warrior was tending the wound on his arm.

"I didn't want to spoil your sport, you old mangy dog," Rabbie laughed and swung off his horse to check Struan's arm.

"'Tis but a scratch. Check on your cousin and Lady Andra, she's looking sorely injured if you judge by the mire covering her." His eyes gleamed with respect as he nodded toward the couple.

A gust of air and a soft thud sounded on the ground behind Kendrick. When he turned, Andra was sprawled unconscious in the dirt. He had a half-second of panic before he swooped down and lifted her against his chest. Calling for whisky, water, and bandages, he carried her into the tent behind them and laid her on the table.

"Andra! Andra, open your eyes." Gently tapping her cheeks, he kept calling to her, but she didn't respond. Dousing some strips of linen with water and whisky, he started to clean away the debris while checking the many wounds marring her delicate flesh. Rabbie did the same standing on the opposite side of the table. They spoke no words for a few moments while they attempted to assess the damage.

"Her head and shoulder wounds need stitching." Kendrick cursed a blue streak at every wound attended. "The wrist cuts and foot wounds appear minor. The head wound is my biggest concern. She is barely recovered from her last ordeal and illness."

"God, they sorely treated our lass." Rabbie washed the

numerous nicks at her wrists, which had clotted over. He also found deep bruises, rope burns from the bindings she had cut away, and finger bruises on her neck and upper arms.

"Those bastards," Kendrick hissed.

"I assume you finally killed those rotten excuses for men—miserable good-for-nothing whoresons?"

Before he responded, John and Struan entered the tent. "The dragoon lad is fair agitated aboot the lady's condition," said Struan approaching the table. "Keeps mumbling he was too late, and it was entirely his fault; which makes me question why we are not killing the man?"

"The lady commanded it," John whispered, his awe apparent.

Another of MacLean's trusted knights, Alec, entered alongside The McDuff. "How fares the lady?" McDuff inquired.

The man beside him spoke up then. "Beggin' your pardon, MacLean, but she was the bravest lass I've ever witnessed; as true and fierce as any warrior on the battlefield today. I've never seen the like of it."

Struan grumbled, "What are you blathering on aboot, Alec, and why are ye standing here ogling the lass's injuries?"

The man lowered his gaze, "Forgive me sir, but you should have seen her when she exited this tent. I could see both her and Cormag as he rushed, hell-bent, to strike a death blow to you, MacLean." Nodding in the direction of the woman lying prone on the table he continued, "She amazed me!" He spoke with unrestrained admiration.

"Blood streamed down her face. Dirt and blood covered her bodice, and yet she raised a man's bow, took aim, and shot that whoreson Cormag in the chest before he reached you. Nailed him to yon tree like a target. Then she turned and shot one of the men who fought against you, Struan.

"Our men ran to protect her, and formed a wide arch fighting against men who tried to attack her position. I don't think she even noticed them. Another of Cormag's men engaged me then and as I struck him down, I turned to aid Kendrick and saw her raise that bow a final time and shoot a man on the ridge who had just struck Michael. A truer shot I've never seen, under the arm at his weakest point."

He took a knee and reverently bent his head. "I have long since pledged my life and sword to you, Laird MacLean, and now I pledge the same to Lady Andra. If you dinnae claim her to wife, then I beg you to allow my humble request to court her."

"Damn, this is not good," Rabbie, whispered to Struan.

"Foolish pup," Struan responded. "Next we'll have to intervene to save the man's life. The MacLean is still in berserker mode, you ken"

Murder fumed in Kendrick's eyes, but as he was about to turn and detach the man's head Andra mumbled his name. "Out," he commanded. "All of you, get out."

"We need to stitch those wounds without delay." Rabbie reminded his cousin as he ushered the others from the tent.

"Aye, in a moment, Rabbie."

Andra called to him in her delirium, but did not awaken. Kendrick could barely control his anguish. He didn't know what he wanted to do first. Kill that foolish knight vying for his woman's hand, slash to bits the already dead Cormag and Colonel Richardson, injure himself for failing her so completely, or take her to wife this instant, whether awake or no, with or without her consent. A muddled mess! His mind was always a muddled mess when trying to discern what to do with his brave, beautiful woman. His!

"Yes," he said softly, gliding the back of his hand across the smooth skin of her cheek. "Yes, Andra, you are mine and always will be, as I am yours."

Her eyelids fluttered for a moment, then stilled.

Chapter Thirty-Five

Marginally aware that some sort of conveyance transported her over bumpy ground, Andra sensed the presence of at least one other person resting beside her.

Dreams of her life in San Francisco flitted through her brain then morphed into images of bloodied warriors, the wretched screams of both men and animals; even her own screaming voice erupted through the dense, dark place where she floated. The smell of damp hay, sweaty men and horses, blood, and rain-dampened earth all took residence in memories she continued to shun. She could feel herself almost reaching the surface, and then willfully pushing back against it. She did not want to wake; even the nightmares were preferable to waking. Sleep, she clung to sleep, to a nether world of swirling images, sounds, and scents, to a place where she sought rest and escape.

* * *

"How many of the dragoons do you think escaped?" McDuff asked Struan, as they led the contingent of men returning to MacLean's castle.

"I cannae say for certain. The lad, Lucas, said he saw at least two escaping on horseback."

"If they return with others, it won't take them long to discover where we buried the bodies. Perhaps yon threatening storm clouds will cover our tracks and cloak the graves." Though concerned, McDuff offered no further observations.

"You ken the English will retaliate swiftly and with force even though the battle occurred because the Sassenachs and the Camerons had absconded with Laird MacLean's sister, the other child, and his woman."

229

"Aye, mayhap. Mayhap the men we sent after them will kill the bastards before they escape across the border." Struan looked over his shoulder seeking his friend and the wagon he guarded.

McDuff followed his gaze. "She's an amazing woman. It seems Kendrick finally met his match." he chuckled. "Alec is near crazed with his admiration of her. From the tales told by your men, it seems she is a warrior in her own right."

"Aye, that and much more." Struan grumbled, but could not hide the respect that near glowed from him when others praised her.

Kendrick and Rabbie rode in the middle of the caravan, one on either side of the wagon carrying Andra. Michael, though wounded, had survived thanks to Andra's arrow striking down his opponent. He and the young dragoon, Lucas, both lay unconscious in the wagon beside her.

"She stirs frequently, but does not wake." Kendrick's furrowed brow spoke plainly of his fears.

Andra had not woken since the battle ceased. The men had buried the dead, tended the wounded, slept fitfully that night, and headed out before noon the following day. Other than thrashing about in her nightmares, she did not respond to any attempt to wake her.

Rabbie offered words to assuage his laird's fears as well as his own. "We'll reach the castle before moon-set if we keep this pace. Mayhap Jane or Alith will provide treatment to wake her from this stupor. We've seen young, injured warriors, inexperienced with battle, fall into this type of sleep for several days following their first skirmish. A deep sleep is often necessary for their body and mind to heal."

Kendrick, though grateful for Rabbie's attempt to bolster him, was not reassured.

They entered the bailey in the depth of night to find the place brimming with people awaiting their arrival. They had interned the old laird earlier that day with numerous lairds from allied clans in attendance. As soon as word reached the keep that their warriors approached, a number of men rode out, torches ablaze, to escort the returning heroes. Lady Beatrice stood regally at the top of the castle's steps and greeted her son and his men with the joy only a mother can know on the return of her family from battle.

"Is she well?" she asked, reaching to touch Andra's face.

He clutched her against his chest. "I cannae say, Mother. She does not wake. Please send Jane and Alith to her room. I will come down directly to greet our neighbors and extend my appreciation to our supporters." He took the steps two at a time speaking softly, murmuring words of endearment to Andra while she drooped like a limp sheaf of wheat in his arms.

For another day, Andra slept like the dead with occasional moments of thrashing around in her bed. Alith had opposed the use of astringents to attempt to wake her. "She needs her sleep and will wake when her mind is once again settled," she insisted, after hearing the stories of the battle and Andra's ordeal. Alith sat by her bedside, rubbing her knurled fingers over the rings on Andra's hand as if they were a talisman against whatever evil pursued her in sleep.

On the second morning after their return, Kendrick walked the parapet in the pre-dawn quiet and noticed a movement in the bailey below. Andra came into view, her gaze fixed on the last stars in the sky, a bow in hand, quiver slung over her shoulder. A ghostly apparition, wearing only her night rail and a shawl with bandages wrapped around her bare feet. She stood like a statue, unmoving. The breeze blew her hair in unbound swirls across her back and over her shoulders. Uncertain whether she was real or a figment of his imagination, he couldn't move, the vision of her appeared so small, so fragile.

"Is she awake or does she sleepwalk?" Rabbie asked, as he approached Kendrick.

"'Tis hard to tell, her eyes are open but she walks as though in a dream. When I checked on her recently, she slept deeply. I tell you truly, Rabbie, she is a trial at times and muddles my brain as no lass has, but I cannot imagine letting her go or living without her."

Rabbie raised his brows at Kendrick. "You're besotted, cousin, no use denying what's evident to everyone. I don't mean to impose on your privacy, but she needs you, and you need her. Go to her, give her the comfort and courage only you can impart."

"I'll give her a moment to collect her bearings first." Kendrick couldn't explain his hesitance. Terrified, he watched as this ghostly specter of the woman he loved seemed to slip from his grasp. Nothing and no one could soothe that potential loss. They observed her for a few moments until Andra dropped her head. The bow and quiver slid away from her body and thumped softly to the ground. She slowly turned, her head still aimed at the dirt under her feet, and drifted back into the keep.

Without further preamble, Kendrick sprinted to find her. He rushed through the great hall, garnering a few curious glances from the waking men. Soon he stood outside her door listening for movement within.

He tapped lightly, "Andra, may I enter? Lass?" She instantly opened the door as if she had been standing there awaiting his arrival.

"Kendrick," she breathed his name like a prayer and threw her arms around his neck.

"Ahh, *mo chuisle*. You've had me verra worried." Brushing hair away from her forehead, he gently cupped her face in his hands. He searched her face for something he couldn't name.

"How long?" She looked up at him, tears blurring her eyes. "How long have I been unconscious, and how did we get back to the castle?"

He kissed her forehead as he closed the door with his foot. "We've been back two days and you were unconscious for nearly two days before that. How does your head feel?"

She touched the stitches at her hairline. "Fine, I think. I've been plagued with terrible nightmares until I'm not sure what is real and what is imagined."

"Aye, lass, 'tis the way with head injuries, you ken."

She leaned her head against his chest, "The beat of your heart is the most soothing sound to my ear." She started to slip from his embrace.

He lifted her and returned her to the bed, ever so gently settling her under the disheveled coverings.

"I'll call for some refreshment. You should rest a while longer." He attempted to pull away her hand that clutched at his wrist.

"Don't leave, Kendrick. Won't you lie beside me, please. I need to feel your strength and warmth."

He pulled off his boots and lay down beside her. The rope and feather mattress shifted as he added his weight to the bed. The faint scent of lemon- mint, and Andra filled his nose. The smell of the creams she made created a scent so uniquely her that even if someone else used them it would still not be the same.

She gazed into his eyes while long fingers trailed an outline along his hair, down his cheek, along his jaw, across his lips. Her touch sparked every nerve in his body. He gently sucked her fingers into his mouth, then kissed her palm. His organ sprang to attention, but he fought against the urge to take her. She didn't need his passion; she needed gentleness, compassion, soothing, and he would give her all of that and more. He would give whatever she wanted of him.

"I want to feel your skin against mine, but I don't think I'm ready for anything more. Can you do that, Kendrick? Can you just hold me in your arms, or am I asking too much?"

He stood and disrobed, dropping everything in a puddle on the floor, and she did the same without getting out of bed. When he slid under the covers, she turned her back against his chest and pressed her warm flesh into him. He near exploded when she pressed her buttock against his hard shaft, requiring him to take deep calming breaths. His arms bound her tightly to him, and he allowed her to drift to sleep without another word spoken. The sound of her even breathing eventually lulled him to sleep as well.

Before dawn the next day, Kendrick stole quietly from Andra's bed where she snored lightly, ensconced in deep slumber. He stood beside her for a quarter hour, watching the rise and fall of her breath, inhaling the sweet lemon-mint essence surrounding the bed sheets before he could tear himself from the room.

Worry plagued his thoughts. Worry about the mental and emotional effects of the recent battle on her gentle soul. Worry over what she'd revealed of her history, and concern about what her history would mean for her future. More significantly, what it would mean regarding a future they might share.

Chapter Thirty-Six

For two more days, Andra took her meals in her room, barely eating, and barring her door to everyone except Kendrick. He would sit with her for a while in the evening when they would take wine in front of the fire. She would ask after everyone but her voice lacked any sign of enthusiasm. Then the conversation would lull into an hour or more of silence. The woman he encountered at night was far more fragile than the woman he'd first met those many weeks ago. He feared that any wrong word or action would break her irrevocably, and he had no idea how to breach the shield she'd erected against the world.

They never discussed the revelation about her time travel or anything about her capture and the ensuing battle. And, to his everlasting disappointment, she never asked him to lay with her again. All the fire and spark that existed before, the spirit and joy that defined the woman he had grown to love, had burned to ashes and he didn't know how to rekindle the flame. No one heard her raise her voice in song, she never returned to the bailey for her morning workouts, she did not join the family for meals, and she did not engage with the children.

Three more days passed while Andra continued to withdraw rather than improve. Kendrick's thoughts and fears became an agony. He met Rabbie and Struan in the lower bailey to work with the men. Michael had come down for the first time since their return. His injuries were healing well, although he could not yet engage in mock combat; still, he wanted to be with the men.

"How is Lady Andra?" he inquired somewhat sheepishly. Alec had regaled every man, woman, and child who would listen with her heroics on the battlefield—numerous times, and Michael along with many others were beyond besotted. Everyone now accepted Andra as the laird's lady; even if he had not declared his intentions to his clan.

"She recovers, Michael, but her trials have exhausted her." Kendrick couldn't suppress his stiff grimace as he gave this lie to the young man whom Andra had saved.

"I owe her my life. Please tell her I am at her disposal to fulfill any task she might need of me." He dipped his chin respectfully then walked away to join a group of other young men.

"The lads are near tripping over themselves in adoration of your lass." Struan grumbled in his usual gruff manner. He fooled no one. "How is she, really? I have not seen her since our return. The bairns and young Kyle are driving everyone to distraction asking after her."

"Aye, that's true enough," said Rabbie. "Even Beatrice and Isabel have been desperate over Andra's refusal to admit them to her room. She has even refused Alith's entrance."

Kendrick stared up toward the shuttered window behind which she hid from the world. "To tell the truth, the woman who sits in that room is not the woman we all knew. She is broken, and I dinnae ken how to help her. The dragoon Lucas, who is recovering, has told me much of what he kens about her capture and the horrors she witnessed and survived at the hands of those…" He couldn't even mention their names without wanting to commit violence.

"Yet she won't talk about anything, and I'm afraid to press her too hard. The healers offer no suggestions, they only caution patience and time."

Rabbie shook his head in commiseration but Struan had other ideas. "What do you mean you dinnae ken how to talk to her? Caution! Patience! Bah! Turn her over your knee, bed her, tell her one of the bairns is ill, lie, cajole, just do somethin', man." He threw up his arms and stormed away grumbling that mayhap someone else should take the lass in hand.

Rabbie couldn't suppress a laugh. "Well, if that doesn't beat all. However, I agree with him. We need to think of something, Kendrick, before she's lost to us forever. By the way, have you told anyone else about her confession concerning her past? Mayhap you could get her to talk a bit about that."

"Nae, no one else has been told. I dinnae think it's a good idea to talk about it to anyone, especially her."

"Why? Are you afraid that's what troubles her so? Mayhap she wants to return to her time?"

Kendrick ran his large hands through his hair and shook his head. "You may be right, but I dinnae ken if that's even possible. Worse, I cannae imagine letting her go."

"Even if it's killing her to stay? I ken you love her, man, but you must consider what the future will be like for you both if she stays in this gloomy state." Rabbie grew still gazing at the distant hills. The cousins stood in quiet affinity, taking comfort in their shared silence. Rabbie spoke first, "I'm at a loss on what to suggest, and though I agree with the healers, like you, I want to find a solution."

These men were used to solving every problem with precise planning, brute strength, or grim determination. Sitting quietly, waiting for events to unfold taxed every element of patience, chafing against their need for action. "Well, I've got other duties to attend. Let me ken if there's anything I can do to help with Andra." Rabbie thumped his cousin's shoulder as he strolled away.

It was unusually warm for late autumn. An astonishingly blue sky with scattered puffy, white clouds lent a tranquil atmosphere to the day. Yet Kendrick felt no tranquility.

Beatrice approached Kendrick when he neared the keep's entrance. "Good day, son. 'Tis a bonny day to take Andra out for a ride." She lifted the large basket slung over her arm. "Sunshine and fresh air might set her to rights, and we won't have many more days like this. Winter will arrive soon enough. I had cook prepare a basket of foodstuffs and wine for a pleasant afternoon repast. It contains all of her favorites. Please, Kendrick, we are all worried for her. I've taken the liberty of having your horse saddled."

His brows peaked at the recommendation. "Not a horse for

her as well?" he queried. His mother didn't fool him for a minute. She had embraced Andra completely as one of their own, and her matchmaking machinations were on full display.

"Nae, she may not be able to handle a horse as yet. It would be safer for her to ride with you. Just hold her close and take it slowly."

Kendrick kissed his mother's cheek. "Have I told you lately that you are the wisest of women, Mother?"

"Pish, now. Get on with you. Take that bonny lass into the sunshine and see if you cannae coax a smile back onto her sweet face."

* * *

They rode in silence under a warm afternoon sun until they reached a high plateau dotted with pine trees overlooking the loch and rolling hills of gorse, heather, and fall grasses fading to shades of fawn and dusty greens. A large oak, still dressed in a glorious array of autumn foliage, dominated a hollow below them. Kendrick dismounted and lifted Andra down, holding her waist for a moment longer than necessary. "You've lost a bit of weight." He raised a finger and gently traced under her eye. "These dark circles do not add the right color to your flawless skin, which has grown too pale by far. I'm worried Andra, please help me understand what upsets you. I'll assist in any manner possible."

She stepped away from him, focused on a point beyond the horizon; he suspected her gaze sought a place beyond this time. He laid a plaid at the edge of the pines and set the basket down.

"Come, sit with me. Cook has provided a veritable feast for us and there's a verra good bottle of wine."

* * *

Andra didn't know how to begin talking again. If she discussed the jumbled feelings demanding release, she might start to cry, or scream, or both and would never be able to stop. She had indulged in far too much crying already.

With a withering shake she began. "I owe you an apology for my sullen behavior of late." Her tightly fisted hands pressed into her lap, and she couldn't look at Kendrick. "I am very sorry. I don't usually wallow in depression, but I am overwhelmed with recent events. It seems I can't get my groove back." Lifting her chin, she caught the raised eyebrows and comical expression on his face.

"You cannae get your groove back? What might your groove be, exactly? It sounds most painful." Small laugh lines etched around his mouth, even though he clearly had no idea what that phrase meant.

A small laugh slipped from her lips, followed by a choked sob that turned into hysterical laughter. She gripped her sides as tears streamed down her cheeks, sobbing and heaving for breath. This incessant crying frayed her nerves. Other than the grief following the deaths of her family members, she did not usually succumb to weeping. Although some saw her as reserved, she did not incline toward depression.

Kendrick pulled her into his embrace, rubbing her back and arms briskly with big, warm hands. "Och, now, Andra, if you dinnae stop, you'll have me bawling in a minute, and that won't do. Lairds are expressly forbidden to bawl."

He kept patting her back and running his hands over her hair and body. He kissed the top of her head, her forehead, her eyelids, cheeks, and when he hit her lips, he bestowed the gentlest of kisses. His full lips slanted over hers, his tongue nudged at her lips begging entrance. When her mouth opened to him, he delved into her warm depths with an eager hunger for more. Laying her back onto the plaid, he rolled over her resting on his forearms, cupped her face with his hands, and pressed his forehead to hers.

"*Mo chroi, A ghra*, I've missed you, Andra." his voice rasped with need.

My heart, my love. Had she heard him correctly? Then his words at the battle scene came back to her. When she'd first recalled those words on waking she thought they were a figment of her imagination, or words spoken from heightened emotions in the aftermath of battle.

She traced her fingers over his face and pushed him back so she could look into his dark-blue eyes. *Love?* Yes, she saw the love. They weren't empty words used to calm her. The sun, his warmth and professed love, slowly unburdened her heart. The heady feel of it mingled with the scent of pine to uncoil the tension and relax her, as she had not been in days.

"I love you too, Kendrick." And she did love him, undeniably and with an aching intensity. "Nevertheless, I cannot deny that this time petrifies me; I don't really fit in, do I? I don't think I can ever measure up to the expectations of a woman from this era. In addition, a constant fear assails me that this time issue will tear us apart. I know I could not bear that. Everything here is so alien to life in my world. It's definitely not like the fairytales my father used to spin. The violence and fighting—life is so very precious and yet so…precarious."

"Ah, lass, is it really so different? Are there no battles in your time, no sickness, no strife? Tell me more about where you are from."

He was correct, of course. Rife with more horrors of war than he could imagine, her era offered no respite from violence. But sound bites on the evening news dulled those events to no more significance than a movie watched with a certain detachment even though the loss of life was dear.

She talked and talked. All the while, he massaged her shoulders and rubbed her arms and back, as though his touch could anchor her in this new environment. Even though most of what she told him would be beyond his imagination, now that she'd started she couldn't seem to stop. She told him about great flying machines that could carry hundreds of people, about buildings as high as mountains that rose into the clouds. But when she spoke of men who walked on the moon, he pushed away, an incredulous expression on his face. "Now you tease, lass. What you describe is too fantastic to envision, even if you came from a thousand years in the future."

Her disclosures seemed too fantastic even to her own ears. "You must think I'm absolutely mad, but I promise you, Kendrick, every word I say is the truth, and there is so much more. Unfortunately, most of the scientific developments that led to these amazing inventions are beyond my knowledge to explain adequately."

"My love, what you describe is incomprehensible. 'Tis no wonder you want to return to your home. I have nothing to offer in comparison. But I am a selfish man and I dinnae want you to leave me." He pressed his lips to her forehead.

When she touched a finger to his mouth, he sucked it between his lips. "There is much in this time that appeals to me as well," she continued, suddenly shy. "You for one thing." She smiled. "And the peace of the countryside, the clean air and open spaces, and lack of crowds top of the list. I like the countryside, always did, even where I come from. Nevertheless, Kendrick, I worry that this time travel issue is bigger than we understand. I suspect something could occur in a flash that would hurtle me back to my home in San Francisco."

"And..." she coughed and dropped her eyes, "since the battle, I've been overwhelmed with guilt, I killed three men and they haunt my dreams. I'm terrified by the nightmares that wrench me from my sleep." She snuggled into his embrace curling against his chest, quieting for a while. The hushed rustle of wind through the trees calmed her, and the tension in his arms relaxed as well.

They lay together for some time before he responded to her admission regarding nightmares. "Lass, I can understand the nightmares. Many a warrior suffers the same and as a result, we embrace the joy of life even more fervently. You need to remember that you saved my life, you saved Michael, and even grumpy Struan, and possibly many more of our men. The enemy outnumbered us, though the superior training of our men made us well matched. Still, 'twas a miracle we only lost six of our own warriors. You saved Isabel, Senga—three times, and Kyle. You've been like an angel to me and mine and those bairns."

"Cannae you see that what you took, you've given back many times over? A warrior must always be mindful of the lives he saves if he is to stay sound of mind. And you, my braw lass, are as true a warrior as any one of my men."

"What awaits you in your time other than men on the moon and buildings like mountains?" She experienced no relief at his attempt to add a bit of levity.

"You've said all of your family is dead. I have a family here who already love you. I love you. You need family, a clan to embrace, a husband to protect and provide for you." His speech was rushed and it was obvious Kendrick would not relent. Since she'd known him, she'd watched him tenaciously pursue every goal. "Will you be my wife, Andra, and bear my bairns?"

"What! Your wife? You're asking me to be your wife?" Elation and shock rattled her, but he'd also asked her to bear his children and there lay the impediment.

"Oh Kendrick, if only—I—if only that were possible, but you see, I'm not certain I can have another child. After Daniel," she hesitated, moisture gathered in her eyes before she blinked them back. "The doctors said maybe I could conceive again, but further tests and possible surgery might be necessary to be sure. I never pursued the issue. So, you see, even if I can't return to my time, I don't think it's possible for us to marry. You must marry into a neighboring clan with a woman who can provide an heir, wealth, warriors, and filial connections. Isn't that what would be expected by the elders?"

Her heart squeezed in her chest. "You would not go against the urging of your clan, not if it caused dissension." She searched his beautiful face, "If they resented your choice you might eventually grow to resent your decision to take me to wife. And I could never agree to be your mistress nor watch you marry another should the clan not accept us as husband and wife."

Kendrick cradled her face with his hands. "Husband and wife is what I'm proposing, Andra. I will decide if and who shall fill that role, and I want you. Listen to me, please. Long ago, a tragedy hollowed out my heart. I gladly left it in the dust, dead and disposed of, a tattered, useless thing, then by a miraculous twist of fate or heavenly decree, who can say which, you fell in my path. A wild, brazen beauty from the future awakened my soul, something I am sore to relinquish again."

"'Tis true I've been lacking in gentlemanly behavior toward you on occasion, but I would never suggest you become my mistress. I'd never insult you in such a manner. Do you believe me so dishonorable that I'd suggest such a thing? You are mine. We belong together."

With heated fervor, he plastered ardent kisses over her face and neck. "I don't care aboot the heirs I might father. If you cannae conceive, then neither you nor a child could die in childbirth. That alone would be sufficient reason to rejoice, and I'll have no regrets. Lorne can provide an heir for the clan. I want you with me. I want you to be my wife."

As always, his passion pushed her fears aside. He rubbed his hands over the bodice of her shift, and pushed the top down. Licking a hardened nipple, he drew it into his mouth and sucked deeply. His rough, urgent hands pushed up her skirts and slid along her inner thighs to the wet depths at her apex.

Andra threw her head back and groaned as his fingers slipped inside preparing her tight walls for his invasion. She urged him to roll onto his back, and he readily complied. She lifted herself over his hips and pressed her slick folds against his shaft, yet denied him entry.

Her nails scratched his bronzed chest and through the hair that drifted down his belly. A smile creased her lips, the first in days. "You are a magnificent specimen, Kendrick MacLean, every woman's dream man. I cannot believe you love me."

"Believe it, *a chuisle mo chroi*. I love you, Andra. I swear I never thought to say those words, and ken I'll never say them to another."

What did he just say—*Pulse of my heart? Were those fireworks going off in her head?* The world spun out of control.

His voice rumbled, prickling over her skin. "When ye smile like that love, you're like a sparkling star, a summer breeze, everything fine and beautiful. I am yours for a smile,"

He pushed the hair away from her face. "I ache for you, lass." He lifted his hips pressing against her mons in an urgent plea. "If you're not ready, I'll wait, though it may kill me to stop." He moaned. "There's no denying my desire to join with you. Do not be afraid. Take the love I offer, be mine, accept me without reservation as I accept you."

"You win," she laughed. Tomorrow she'd worry over the time travel matter. Now, she wanted to make love to him, to immerse herself in the intensity of his touch, to release this plaguing melancholy with fierce passion. She wanted to block all other thoughts from her mind. He was a flashing beacon calling her home through the storm. Pulling her skirts to her waist, she lifted above him and guided his throbbing shaft into her heated core. Sliding down and lifting again, she reveled in the undeniable desire evident in his gaze as he watched them join. Clinching him tightly with her inner muscles, she threw her head back and soared.

* * *

Kendrick near exploded as soon as she slid over his hard erection. His hands gripped her hips and aided her movement until their rhythm beat hard and fast. Lifting her head, their eyes locked as he touched the nub where they joined and brought her to an explosive climax.

"You are beautiful," he whispered, watching her take him into her shuddering depths, clenching him with spasms of need. "I love to feel you writhe and pulse under my hands." This was his Andra, this magnificent, unguarded, wildly enthusiastic woman he adored. As he brought her to another climax, he joined the tumultuous explosion, releasing his seed deep in her womb. Her ability to give him children didn't matter; he wanted her, and she would be his.

Lying atop him, both of them panting, trying to slow their breath, a sense of peace settled over him. Their passion had pummeled the angst of the past few days into submission. Every fear singed by insatiable desire, consumed in this absolute moment, until everything else fell away except her flesh against his, and this urgent coupling that merged two souls into one.

Her eyes shining, she pushed against his chest and lifted her torso above his. "That was fantastic. You're always using sex to bring me back to my senses. Did you notice that?" she chuckled.

"I'm happy to oblige, my love. Lose your senses anytime. I'll gladly bring you back home."

Rolling onto her back, she flung her arm across her face. The air had chilled. He felt a shudder ran through her. He couldn't tell whether the sudden shiver resulted from a decision to forego attempts to return to her time, or due to the air wicking sweat from her skin. But she grew tense and still beside him. "What troubles you, Andra?"

"Kendrick, let us take a few days to think this over and discuss it further. As much as you honor me with your proposal, and as hard as it would be to leave you, I feel we must carefully consider all possible consequences."

When he started to protest, she shushed him. "Please, listen to me. Although scientists allude to time travel where I'm from, there is no scientific proof that I know of. Still, there are theories, and all of them suggest that changes caused by persons going to the past would result in devastating timeline changes for future generations, possibly resulting in my own demise in the future. According to those theories, no one should bring back information about the future, nor alter the past, as their interference could have devastating impact on the future. Perhaps I have already caused irrevocable damage to my own time."

"As you say, 'tis only theories, even in your time, and they may not be correct. Mayhap you fell through time to complete the things you've done here. Mayhap God ordains it either way. Even in your time this is not kenned."

A heartfelt sigh escaped her lips. "I cannot reason it out, but I do believe I should once again try to return to my time, if for no other reason than to assure us both that it's not possible and won't happen unexpectedly."

He abhorred the idea, yet her consideration to stay also encouraged him. That would suffice for now. Besides, he had absolutely no intention of releasing her.

"It grows cold, and the hour is late. We should return before Lorne dispatches a search party to find us."

* * *

Kyle scrambled around the stables in an effort to corral the puppies. "Lady Andra, ye are out of yer room." he exclaimed. "Are ye better then?" His voice was so hopeful.

He lifted the wriggly, little beast in his hands. "Look at my pup. Master says I can keep him if I behave, listen to me elders, and help take care of the litter. Isn't he grand?" His youthful exuberance soothed her soul.

Kendrick dismounted and helped her down, a smile on his lips. Kyle wrapped one hand into hers. His big eyes swallowed her up. "Will ye be joining the clan for the evening meal? Will ye sing tonight, Lady Andra? Everyone misses yer singing, even Struan." He scowled in an attempt to imitate Struan's gruff countenance.

Ruffling his auburn curls, she smiled. "Yes, I'm improving, but I think I'll take my meal in my room tonight. I'm not ready to sing yet. Perhaps I should teach you to sing a song of your own."

The boy's mouth dropped open and his eyes grew wide. "Oh? I dinnae ken if I can sing. Dae ye think I can?"

"Most assuredly. Perhaps we'll have all the children learn a song together."

"Tonight? Can we learn tonight?"

Kendrick stepped in, "Lady Andra is fatigued from her ride today and still needs her rest, Kyle. You can talk with her about singing tomorrow."

When they reached her chambers, Andra knew he wanted to join her. He'd been the only visitor she'd allowed for days, but she needed time alone. "We have much to think on tonight, and I'm exhausted." She lifted onto her toes and sweetly kissed his lips. "Until tomorrow, my love."

Chapter Thirty-Seven

Andra did not teach the children to sing the next morning. Before the sun rose, she sought Kendrick on his pre-dawn stroll along the parapet.

At the top of the stairs, she spied him. Even in shadow, his wide stance, broad shoulders, and flowing dark-blond hair was unmistakable. He exuded confidence and strength while watching over his lands for any untoward movement in the hills. His enjoyment of the morning's peace and quiet radiated from him. She thought to turn back, leave him to his reverie when he turned and reached out his hand.

"Come to me, lass."

"How did you know it was me?"

"I heard the rustle of your skirts as you climbed the stairs, but I would ken you in the blackest night even if you never spoke. Your sweet scent precedes you, Andra, and invades my senses on the slightest breeze."

The thick burr of his words made her tingle with desire. He made her want to toss up her skirts and behave like a simpering, love-struck idiot. However, she hadn't searched him out for a tryst. They had important matters to discuss. His hand, still extended to her, flicked ever so slightly, and she felt his pull straight to her center.

Neatly tucked under his shoulder, his arm wrapped tightly along her back and arm, she lay her head against him, realizing how sheltered and secure he made her feel.

"I didn't sleep well. My mind bursts with unanswered questions. The why and how this happened to me, and all that we discussed yesterday. I have come up with a plan."

He squeezed her shoulder. "Why do I feel as though this plan will not be to my liking?"

"Like it or not, I feel certain we must return to the spot where you first found me." She rushed the words to maintain her courage.

"Nae, Andra, I definitely dinnae like this idea."

She pried herself from under his hold and turned to face him. "Did you mean what you asked me yesterday?"

"If you mean my request that you become my wife, I did and still do mean every word. I want you with me, Andra. You make me feel whole in a way I have never known."

Her cool fingers sculpted the curve of his face, studying with their touch as if to memorize its contours even in shadow. "I have fallen madly in love with you. I want to stay with you yet am equally terrified of staying. Before we go any further, we must know if I am meant to return."

"Love, I can make certain that you are never in that spot again in your life. You simply have to decide that you want to be with me as much as I want you to stay."

She shook her head. "Despite the fact our time together has been relatively short, I have never loved nor wanted to be with anyone more in my life than with you, Kendrick." Yet every possible scenario of an abrupt catapult through time scattered through her mind like a swarm of annoying wasps.

"You confess your love, yet persist in this desire to explore something even you don't understand?" His clipped response, lacking any of the previous endearments, revealed his frustration. His expression hardened. "As you wish."

Yep. He was angry. Nevertheless, though she desperately wanted this man, she could not ignore her feelings. If she didn't do her best to find an answer, her fears would endlessly trouble her peace of mind.

"Please, don't be angry, my love. If I should be torn away, I don't want a moment of our time marred with bad feelings."

He pulled her hard against his chest and crushed his mouth to hers, invading and quarreling with his ravenous tongue, imploring, pleading with the prowess of his kiss.

Breaking the connection, he said, "This is what you will leave behind: a family and a man who will always love and protect you. Will you find that where you might go? How do you even ken you'll return to where you came from? Mayhap you'll land somewhere else."

She could barely concentrate when he broke away, "I—I do not minimize the significance of your love or offer of marriage. I simply must have this answered. Please try to understand."

His hands clamped ahold of her wrists. "Are you saying you will only stay with me if you have no other choice?" She could see him bite down on that last retort, holding other words at bay. Anger and disappointment flashed across his brow. "You wound a man's pride," he snapped.

She knew him to be a most prideful man, and this must feel like a rejection to him. Her eyes filled with tears she fought hard to blink away. "It is difficult to explain, Kendrick. In answer to your question, no, I would not stay simply because I had no other choice. I want to stay. I want to become your wife. Yet I feel I must have an answer to whether I can or might be forced to leave."

"You seek assurances and answers for things that are impossible to ken." He studied her carefully. "I can see there's no sense refusing you this chance to try, though I think it a most foolish endeavor. What ridiculous plan have you concocted?"

"I believe we must re-enact the scene of the day you found me as realistically as possible. I will take my things and place them on my plaid. You and the men will charge through the forest toward me, and we shall see what happens."

He remained stalwart and silent, his hands lightly holding hers. "You dinnae expect Lorne to suffer similar injuries to those he sustained that day, nor recreate your head injury, do you?" The asperity of his attempted jest confirmed his discontent with her.

"Of course not," she huffed. "If it is any comfort to you, I promise if this attempt fails, I will never try it again." A piercing intensity blanketed his expression but he uttered no additional protestations.

"Perhaps you will ask...?" She quickly clamped a hand over

her mouth and dropped her head stopping the words about to spill forth. They should not discuss a future together until it was determined whether she would be staying.

His arms clamped around her like a vise as he pulled her hard against him. He breathed deeply, absorbing her scent. A breath never sounded more cheerless. "Let us get this over with then. We will go before first light tomorrow. You'd best get busy preparing for our trip. I'll speak with the men."

She turned to leave, then turned back, "Do the men know what I disclosed about being...?" She lowered her voice and leaned in. "About being from the future?"

"Rabbie knows, and Lorne suspects something unusual is amiss, but telling Struan is another matter. You handled his superstitious reaction at the river, but this revelation might cause him a fatal fit of apoplexy." He laughed at the thought.

"Perhaps we should just say that I lost something very important and want to search for it."

"Aye, I'll think on that. But if I say we go, my men will obey without question." He turned her away and smacked her bottom, none too lightly, "Now off with you. I must see to my men and prepare for our departure."

That evening she joined the family and clan in the great hall. If others noticed her state of quiet reserve, no one mentioned it. After the meal, Kyle pestered her about teaching the children a song of their own. She finally relented and took them aside, settling the girls on one side of her and the lads on the other. This song is about Old MacDonald and his farm of singing animals. The children burst into guffaws and giggles. She gave each group a number of animal sounds they would sing and then the refrain, "Old MacDonald had a farm, EIEIO," which they would all sing together. It didn't take long before the children eagerly practiced their lines and ancillary noises mimicking the animals mentioned in the verses.

When the song ended, the audience awarded their efforts with much applause and pounding of feet. After she declined to sing additional songs and excused herself for the evening, Kendrick escorted her from the hall. "You have made the bairns and their kin verra happy this evening, Andra. These songs you sing, they are well kenned where you're from?"

"Oh, yes. All the songs I've sung are very popular."

When they reached her room, he followed her in and went to stoke the fire. "May I sit with you a while?"

She tilted her head and gave him a lopsided smile. "We must be up early and should be well rested before we leave." While she spoke, she fumbled at the ties of her stomacher then dropped it to the floor.

With no further preamble, he removed his brooch and folded his plaid neatly over the chair by the hearth. Wearing just his knee-length linen shirt, he approached her, a smoldering heat in his eyes.

"Will you help me with the ties to my gown?"

He growled in compliance and helped her strip away each piece of clothing with exquisite tenderness. Then she removed his shirt.

They stood toe-to-toe, naked and glowing from the fire's light. She placed her hands on him, trailing her nails up the sculpted muscles of his chest to cling behind his neck. Leaning into his strength, she lifted her legs and wrapped them around his hips. "I need to feel you inside me," she breathed into his ear.

A responding groan rose out of his throat. With hands firmly gripping her buttocks, he walked her to the bed. They made love with slow, exploratory touches, and she saddened over what they might soon lose. Before long, they both cried out in a frantic rush of passion. They quickly plunged into the oblivion only sexual congress afforded.

Later that night, Andra woke to find her bed empty. She rose and carefully packed all of her things in her bags.

Chapter Thirty-Eight

The men gave little more than cursory greetings to Andra as they strapped on their weapons and tied their gear to the horses. It was still dark when the guard lowered the bridge and opened the gate for them to ride out of the castle. Heavy swirls of misty clouds draped the upper ramparts and towers. She cast one final, longing gaze on the place that had become her home and refuge during the past months. A worried, forlorn ache welled in her chest, and she could not prevent the tears that slid down her face. No one had come to see them off. Kendrick left the castle's defense in the hands of his chief guard, Alec. The previous evening, Kendrick had informed the family they'd be gone for a few days. His manner of declaration informed everyone he would not tolerate questions about their absence.

Under a steady drizzle of rain, they rode fast and hard. The ghost-gray sky seemed to droop against their heads making it impossible to judge the passage of time by the sun. A somber mood enveloped the now well-wet travelers.

"We'll rest here to refresh ourselves and the horses." Kendrick announced as they approached a small clearing beside a copse of young saplings and a few scattered pines.

The area was not familiar to Andra. "Is this a different route than we took to return to the castle from the cave?" she asked, stretching her stiff back and legs, pushing off the sopping plaid she had worn over her head.

"Aye, 'tis a much steeper and harder ride, which was not possible when we carried the bairns and Lorne with his grave injuries." He scanned the scraggy peaks shrouded in fog.

"Don't blame it on me." Lorne chided, his mood more jovial once they stopped. "I did just fine. 'Twas Cormag and his renegades that you sought to avoid on the ride home."

Andra flinched, sucking in a breath as if the words had punched her in the stomach.

"Och, beg your pardon. I dinnae mean to remind you of any unpleasantness."

Struan piped in on the subject as well. "Dinnae fash yourself over the likes of him. You did the world a great favor wiping that filth off the face of the earth."

She doubled over, bile burning her throat, feeling as if she would hurl everything in her stomach.

"Hold your wheesht, you fools," Kendrick admonished.

"Well, 'tis nothing to be ashamed aboot is all I'm saying," asserted Struan.

Andra stood up abruptly. "I know all of you are accustomed to killing your enemies and the blood and guts and violence don't faze you, but I still find it overwhelming." Kendrick moved to comfort her but she lifted a halting hand.

"I'm not saying I would not do exactly the same thing if faced with similar circumstances. I'm certain I would. I'm just not ready to discuss it, if you please." On that note, she turned and stomped a few feet away.

She caught a few of the Gaelic phrases they spoke. As far as she could tell, none of the men raised a question about why they were traipsing over the countryside. She hadn't thought to ask Kendrick what reason he had given them for the trip, if any. The powerful connection she felt for these men surprised her. They had shared hardships, laughter, fear, passion, and love, all of it at a visceral level. It stunned her that she did not miss daily newspapers, magazines and forgot about television. Why had she ever wasted time on that medium when there was so much life to be lived?

"*The hapless five.*" She laughed aloud.

Kendrick moved behind her. "You find something amusing, lass?"

"Not really." She dropped her chin shaking her head with a smile quirking the corner of her mouth. "It's just a name came to mind for our auspicious group." she chuckled.

"Och, I'm thinking it might be unflattering of me and my men?"

"I mean nothing derogatory, but the term hapless five popped into my head and made me laugh."

"Humph. No offense taken then." His attempted scowl failed miserably.

She searched the hills, afraid to focus on Kendrick for fear she would lose her nerve. "How long before we reach the cave?"

"If we ride hard and keep our stops brief and infrequent, we might arrive there by midnight. Depends if the weather continues to hold."

It had been drizzling steadily since a short while after they left the castle. "You consider this," she waved her hand and wrung out her soaked plaid, "to be *held* weather?"

Rabbie had been quiet the entire ride, but piped up with a smirk, "This is a veritable bonny day in the Highlands. Winter will be upon us soon, and then you'll think on this day as extremely pleasant."

A frown quickly replaced the brief smile. She thought Kendrick had advised his cousin of their purpose, and the possibility she would not be here come winter.

They made only two other quick stops. For the most part, she thought they made them for her benefit and not their own. Her back ached; her butt and legs had grown numb. It seemed as though she'd ridden her blasted horse for a lifetime when they came around a small loch and started another assent. Night had slipped its dark fingers around them hours ago. The men seemed capable of riding indefinitely without conversation. They could doubtless ride in their sleep. She'd suspected they were simply riding around in circles, completely lost, until they passed a loch that reminded her of the place where they'd encountered Rabbie the night of the children's rescue. Perhaps they were not lost after all.

The drone of the horses' hooves over damp ground or rocky escarpment invaded her ruminations. Was she making the right choice? Could she turn back now and forget her past, forge a new future in this land of harsh yet exquisite beauty and even harsher living conditions? A knot formed in her stomach when she considered a future without Kendrick. She knew, without a doubt, that she could carve out a life with him by her side and relish whatever time they could grasp.

Suddenly, an even more disturbing thought punched through her consciousness. The first Jacobite rebellion would be happening in less than ten years. What would happen then? Now her mind fidgeted over all manner of horrific new concerns. Did she dare tell them what little she knew of their history? Would the consequences of such a revelation be catastrophic? Did these thoughts represent more reasons why she should not stay? Exhaustion covered her more heavily than the sodden weight of her cloak.

"Andra, love, we are here."

Kendrick's hands lifting her off the horse jerked her to the present. "Was I asleep?" she asked, placing her hands on his shoulders.

"If not, then you were verra deep in thought." He stepped back but didn't release her immediately. Tension marred his beautiful face. "We dinnae need to continue with this experiment. We can leave on the morrow after a bit of rest and reconnaissance of the area. It's not too late to stop."

"I'm weary and soaked to my bones, Kendrick. Now is not the time to discuss this further. Let us face tomorrow and see what comes."

Rabbie, Lorne, and Struan busied themselves at the back of the cave lighting a fire and laying out pallets for sleep. She wandered toward the pools and waterfall. Dropping to her knees, she splashed icy water on her face. The thoughts of their last time in the cave swamped her with kaleidoscopic visions, and heat tingled between her legs. If she weren't so exhausted and confused, she would grab Kendrick's hand, drag him to her spot under the pines, and beg him to ravish her senseless, making all her worries dissolve under his heated ministrations.

Then what, you dolt? There was no sense rehashing anything. Sleep, they all needed sleep now.

She could feel Kendrick's gaze on her. Obviously, he could not rest either. Finally, he moved his pallet next to hers and pulled her back against his chest. She snuggled against his heat until they both finally nodded off.

Chapter Thirty-Nine

Andra was running, her legs felt like lead weights. Fire engulfed everything around her, people were screaming and heavy smoke filled the air. Though she tried desperately to scream, no sound would escape her parched throat. Suddenly, the thunder of horses' hooves pounded toward her and she faced a ghostly charger carrying a golden god. They didn't see her, and in seconds would trample her under their slashing hooves. She startled awake, her brow drenched with sweat.

The men attended to their business oblivious of her terror. The smell of roasting rabbit made her mouth water while her stomach roiled in revulsion. She went to the pool, splashed moisture on her face, and gulped refreshing water from her cupped hands.

"Are you well, Andra?" Kendrick had approached silently. How did they manage to come upon her unawares all the time?

"Yes, I just need a moment of privacy." She headed to the entrance noticing the sky had turned a pale gray; it must be at least an hour or more past dawn, she decided.

When she re-entered the cave she stayed by the horses and gear and waved Kendrick toward her. "What have you told the men about our mission?"

"As yet, they only know that you're looking for something you lost," He quirked his brow at her inquiry.

"Thank you. I'll join everyone shortly." She turned back toward her gear that someone had removed from her horse the night before. She had carried a bow and quiver of arrows on the trip. She took them in hand, and then she went to Struan's pack and removed his broadsword. The hiss of his sword as she removed it from its sheath riveted eight eyes on hers.

They started to move toward her when she stopped them with a firm command. "Stand down. Hold there, if you please."

"What danger worries you, lass?" Struan asked, eyeing his sword precariously clasped in one hand while she held her bow in the other, an arrow notched in readiness. Rabbie stood back, his hands loose at his sides. Lorne stepped toward him, a worried look on his face.

"I have something to tell you, Struan, and you too, Lorne. Rabbie and Kendrick are already aware of what I'm about to disclose."

"Andra, what in God's name are you on about?" Kendrick yelled. She almost laughed at his shocked expression, but now was not the time for levity. Besides, she suspected he'd be even more shocked before she finished her speech.

She tossed the broadsword to land close to Struan's feet and then raised the bow and arrow, aiming it directly at Struan's heart. "Don't reach for it yet, just listen to me."

He pulled his arms across his chest, stood to his full formidable height, a fierce scowl wrinkling his brow. "Now, what is this nonsense? You think to threaten me with your wee bow and arrow. You'd be dead a'fore the arrow pierced my heart assuming your aim is true." He cast an anxious glance toward his companions, perhaps not quite so certain of his claim. He bluffed, as he well knew she possessed excellent aim.

"I have no desire to harm any of you. I love you all as though you were my family, my blood, and I think my actions have proven that sufficiently. But…" she took a deep breath and focused steely attention on one man.

"Struan, do you see that I hold your life in my hands?"

"Mayhap, mayhap no," he grumbled lifting his chin boldly.

"Good, now pick up the sword at your feet."

"Andra, stop this!" Kendrick started to move and she swung the arrow toward him. "What are you doing? I can see your mind awhirl with some mad scheme. Put down your weapon, Andra, before someone is hurt." His rigid stance suggested he might be questioning everything she'd told him. Perhaps he wondered if she was insane or a witch after all.

"I will do this my way, Kendrick. Please just hold your peace and give me a moment." Swinging back to Struan, she said, "Pick up your sword, Struan."

He warily reached for his sword without taking his eyes off her. She released a sigh of relief because so much hinged on the wild tactic she had decided upon. Struan was the most superstitious of the bunch and what he would shortly witness could have devastating consequences to her and possibly to everyone else.

"Will you allow me to speak without threat, until you've heard everything I wish to tell you?" She stared at Struan and glanced quickly to Lorne. Lorne lifted his palms in supplication.

Struan answered, "Aye, whatever grave news you have to impart, I will listen. You needn't threaten my life for the consideration."

"Good." Never wavering, she dropped the bow to the dirt and lifted her arms wide. "You now hold my life in your hands, my friend. What I'm about to tell you will be shocking, no doubt, but consider that Kendrick and Rabbie have already been apprised of this information and have accepted it as truth."

She squared her shoulders, keeping her arms outstretched, she took a great gulp of breath and plunged ahead. "I am from the future, from many, many years and a place far away in the future." So began the saga of her time travel to when they found her and why they had returned here today. Before she half-finished the story, Struan tipped his sword into the ground, his mouth agape in astonishment.

When she finished, she lowered one arm, fisted the other hand, and pointed a finger at Struan. "And I do not want to hear you accusing me of being a witch again. Do you understand me, Struan? I won't stand for it. I do not understand how this happened. We have come here today to find out if this time travel thing can be reversed."

"Is this some sort of crazy joke?" asked Lorne. Struan stammered incoherently.

"Nae," Rabbie laughed. "'Tis no joke. Andra has shown us information that makes her story plausible, though downright astounding."

"Have all of you completely lost your minds?" Clearly, Struan could not grasp Andra's disclosure. "I do not find this amusing."

Kendrick burst into raucous laughter. He turned to Andra shaking his head. "You'll have to grant him that you are a wee bit mad. After all, who in their right mind would hand Struan his claymore and then rattle his senses with such an outburst. You might have considered a more orthodox method of disclosing your story." Then he burst out laughing so hard he had to gasp for breath.

"Well, 'tis unbelievable. Absolute madness and nothing less," Struan sputtered, his face blanched of all color. "I cannae comprehend what you're saying. If ever there was witchery..." He stopped abruptly as both Kendrick and Andra glared daggers at him. Struan continued to stare at Andra as though a fearful apparition had appeared in their midst. "Mayhap she has bewitched all of you."

She did not want this to end in an altercation between Kendrick and his most trusted men. She must convince Struan, so she marched up to him and stood, once again toe-to-toe in challenge. "There is no witchery, and no one has been bewitched. Can we just agree that there are many mysteries in this universe that no one understands and due to some bizarre quirk of nature I find myself inexplicably here—in your time—a time that is not my own. I am not a witch. I am only flesh and blood, no different than you."

"Do you think I'm insane, Struan? Do ye doubt your laird?" Kendrick had adopted his most lairdly timbre, and she could feel the heat of him as he moved to stand behind her.

Struan did not look at her, but at a point over her shoulder. "Well now, that 'tis not exactly what I meant. I would ne'er disparage you, Kendrick, but I'm having great trouble accepting her declaration."

He blew an exasperated huff toward the roof as if he would

find an answer etched in the rock above his head. "Mayhap the wee fairy folk are playing mischief with us." He finally turned his gaze on Andra. "However, I'll not dispute the matter with you. I owe you a boon for leveling the odds against my opponents in our recent battle. And if there's magic in you, it has only been to our good. Though I'll not deny it unsettles the mind, but if Kendrick and Rabbie believe this wild story, then I will not argue."

Kendrick turned her toward him and swung her into his arms, pressing a firm kiss on her mouth. "You're going to be the death of me, woman. I am not in favor of this scheme you've set your mind to, but now we're here let us see to it."

By late afternoon, they had arrived at the place by the boulder where Andra had landed that fateful day. The men reluctantly left her alone while she laid everything out on her plaid. She pulled the urn onto her lap and rubbed its smooth surface like a talisman.

"Well, Dad, it's now or never." Her voice sounded loud in the sudden quiet around her. "I wish you could advise me because to tell the truth, I don't think anything remains for me in San Francisco or my time. Everything I've ever wanted seems to be right here. Does that sound completely ridiculous?"

"Of course it does, but you are the one who sent me here. Perhaps you didn't specifically plan to toss me through a time portal into 1705, but that's what happened." She removed the lid and held up the urn listening for the rumble of horses' hooves.

* * *

She was a wild one, and Kendrick would never be the same if she left him this day. Yet, he could not suppress the delight she elicited with her antics, no matter how unorthodox her methods. The hardest moment in the last few days came when he led his men into the forest, leaving Andra sitting on her plaid with all her possessions spread around her. It took considerable will not to beg her to reconsider, not to grab her onto his horse and hare into the hills. Unfortunately, he knew she had to get it out of her system and he must allow it, even though a part of him wanted to throw her over his shoulder, carry her back to his castle, and tie her to his bed. An erotic image jumped into his head at the thought of her lashed to his bed, naked with her auburn hair spilling across his pillow.

The men had not talked between themselves since leaving Andra. They stopped the horses about a half-mile from where they'd left her.

Uncharacteristically, Struan spoke first. "Why in bloody hell are we doing this? If you truly believe she's from the future, and you obviously don't want her to leave, what are we aboot? What if this is the work of some witch—" Kendrick glared at him. "All right, all right—fairy folk or the like? What will happen to her if she ends up somewhere terrible with no family and no one to take care of her? This is bloody well the stupidest thing we've e'er done, and I'm not fookin' in favor of it. Not at all." His agitation caused his horse to dance and jump under him.

Lorne and Rabbie vociferously agreed with Struan.

Kendrick rubbed a hand through his thick hair, making it stand up on end. "I am not in favor of this either, but it must be done. She will not let it go. It plagues her night and day. She'll never have a moment's peace if she does not try this experiment. We're here. It will soon be done and over with."

"And if she doesn't disappear through the threads of time, brother?" Lorne asked. "What then?"

"Although it is none of your damn business, I intend to marry her, and I'll not be naysaid on the matter."

"It's aboot fookin' time!" exclaimed Struan, startling everyone. The other two men chimed in, resolute in their agreement that he and Andra belonged together.

"Let's get it done then." Kendrick spurred his horse through the trees at a full gallop.

* * *

The rumble of horses' hooves reached her ears. "It's time, Dad!"

She tilted the urn with her right hand, rubbed the ruby in her father's ring with the thumb of her left hand, and let the ashes drift on the wind. "As you requested, Dad, I leave your ashes on the soil of your ancestors. Speak to me, please; help me know my course."

Originally, she had planned to withhold a small portion of ashes, just in case. Now, as she watched the men approach, a shaft of light penetrated the trees, illuminated Kendrick's blond hair, and shimmered around the horses. The filtered sunlight lent the air a burnished orange like fire. It was a replica of the previous night's nightmare. Kendrick looked like a bronzed god atop his charging horse.

Holding her breath, she fully upended the urn. "All, or nothing," she gasped. Andra awaited the crushing blows from the horses' hooves or their passage, like a whisper of air, through the vacant spot where she had knelt only moments before.

The scene appeared to her as a dissolving palate of form and color as they roared through the trees; a bit like a Monet painting when standing too close. She wondered if she was already gone, no longer visible to them, just a dissipating vapor on the wind.

The horses pulled to an abrupt halt a few yards in front of her. Kendrick was the point man, Lorne slightly behind on his right, Rabbie and Struan the wingmen. Kendrick's horse huffed, tossed his bridle, and stomped his hooves, turning in tight circles, rebelling against the cessation of their gallop.

The entire vista swam before her in a watercolor wash. When Kendrick slipped off his horse and threw the reins to Lorne, she dropped the urn. "It is done," she whispered. She could barely see him now.

His hand reached in her direction. "Saints alive! Andra?" He flicked his wrist, fingers imploring her, "Lass? Is it over? Are ye finished?"

She sucked in a gasp of air, only then realizing that the watery vision was due to a torrent of tears streaming over the rim of her lashes.

"Oh my God! I didn't leave. I'm here." In a flash, she ran to Kendrick and threw herself into the arms of the man she loved as she had never loved another. "You are here. I am here." She laughed, cried, and slapped her hands to his face and shoulders, needing assurance that he truly held her in his arms.

He swung her around, threw back his head, and roared. "You'll never leave me Andra, I will not allow it. Do you understand me? You are mine. We belong together." He set her down, the leaf cover of the forest floor thick about her feet. Gripping her wrists, hands crossed one over the other, he asked, "Will you take me as your husband, Andra, freely and without reservation?"

She gripped his wrists in return, their hands clamped like vices. "Yes, I will marry you, Kendrick. I will marry you and love you for all eternity as God and your clansmen are my witnesses." She flicked a glance to the men still mounted on their horses.

"I think this demands a celebration and a good night's rest." Lorne exclaimed, and the other men hooted their approval. He pulled out a flask of *uisge beatha* and they all took a drink, even Andra, who choked a bit on the slow burn that followed.

They returned to the cave, bundled their belongings and secured the supplies they intended to leave behind, everyone anxious to return home.

When Kendrick and Andra retired to a room at an inn along the road, he stoked the fire in the brazier and then stripped her slowly, touching her so gently she thought she might melt.

"My beautiful, fierce, wee banshee. My wife." He slanted his lips over hers sliding his tongue tantalizingly at the crease, seeking entry. Meeting his urgent strokes with her own she clutched him to her naked body.

"That bed looks a bit small for two." she smiled wickedly.

"Nae love, it will do for tonight, but when I get you back to the castle, I'm tying you to my verra big bed and not letting you leave it for days."

"I think we should wait until we make this marriage official before you start tying me to your bed in the castle. There would be no stopping tongues from wagging over that."

He stepped back, his hands on her shoulders. "This marriage is already official, wife."

"What?" Mouth agape, eyes wide; she had no idea what he meant.

"Your words earlier, you said you took me to husband and that you loved me. You swore before God and the men, did you not?"

"Well, yes, but…"

"That is all it takes in the Highlands, *mo chroi*. You are mine, we are wed, and no one will take you from me. However, if it's official you want, we can repeat our vows in the keep with the rest of the family present. I suspect my mother and Isabel will demand it anyway."

She realized that he'd laid her on the bed and climbed over her. Heat flamed where his hands roamed, then cooled when they moved to other regions. Their first joining of the night was unrestrained, hot, and fast. But oh, the second time, they came together in sumptuous, slow delight. They nipped and tasted their fill, finally falling into a deep and restful sleep, her lying atop him, her head nestled into the crook of his neck.

Chapter Forty

After the evening meal on the first day following their return to the castle, Kendrick stood and with a deep reverberating voice called for silence and the clans' attention. "I wish to announce that Andra Heather Adair Cameron, daughter of Angus Brian Cameron and—"

He never finished the announcement. Alith rose from her chair, clutching her throat and gasping for air, then fell to the floor.

The crowd rumbled with hushed strains of concern and frightened looks at Andra. Obviously, a few had not embraced her as much as surmised. Perhaps more than a few would not rejoice over a union between their laird and a Sassenach who also carried the Cameron name. Enough of them would see Alith's collapse as a bad omen to the union.

Andra swooped down to check for a pulse. "She is alive, her pulse strong and steady. Whatever do you think happened?" She gently patted the old woman's cheek while rubbing her arm. "Alith, can you hear me."

Jane knelt beside them and pulled a vial from her skirt. She uncorked the vial and waved it under the old woman's nose. A strong astringent odor accosted Andra. Alith's lids fluttered open. Her eyes, milky with age, latched onto Andra. Raising her hand to cup Andra's cheek she said, "I kenned you were ours, lass, as sure as I breathe, I kenned it. My verra own sweet lassie."

Beatrice knelt beside them, "Hush now, Alith. We'll take you to my rooms where Jane can attend ye." She tipped her head, a signal to Kendrick.

Alith refused to relinquish Andra's hand, grasping with a clawed grip. She kept saying it was in the eyes, and she should have seen it right away. Andra wondered if Alith had suffered a stroke.

Once settled on a bed with pillows behind her, Alith asked for a sip of wine.

"Won't you allow Andra to leave while Jane examines you, Alith?" Beatrice pleaded.

"Nae, she must stay with me; I have many questions for my Andra. Don't fuss now. I'll be fine, just a bit of lightheadedness 'twas all. The rest of you may leave us, return to your meal. We'll send for you if you're needed." Despite eyes rheumy with tears, the strength of Alith's voice brooked no refusal to her request. The others departed, but Kendrick stayed by the bed near Andra, "I will stay with you as well."

"Aye, of course, MacLean. What I have to say might interest you"

Alith's thumb trailed over Andra's hand seeking the ruby ring on the middle finger of her right hand, panting slightly as if that small effort exhausted her. "Ye said this ring belonged to your da, is that nae right?"

"Yes, my father said it had passed down from his grandfather to his father then to him. It's a family heirloom." Andra recalled how Alith had expressed great interest in her rings when they first met.

"Why did ye not tell us, my dear?"

"Tell you what?" Andra asked, keeping her voice low and soothing. Alith's agitation concerned her, especially since she'd sent Jane away.

"Did ye not say your father told you his family had died, that he had nae clan remaining in the Highlands?"

"Yes, his parents died fairly young. My mother's father met him—I don't remember where—and invited him to live with my mother's family for a short while before he attended university. In fact, my mother's parents helped pay for his education."

"And what were your parents' full names, Andra? I don't recall we ever discussed that, did we?"

"I can't say that we did, Lady Alith. My mother was Gillian Edna Adair and my father was Angus Brian Cameron, although everyone called him Brian."

A choked sound rasped in the old woman's throat. "I am not familiar with the Adair clan," she whispered, shaking her head, her hands trembling.

"There is no one left in my mother's family, they have all been dead for many years now." Andra answered.

"Do you ken the names of your father's parents?"

"Why yes, his father's name was Donald James Cameron, and his mother's name was Davina Alith Cameron. Until I met you, I had never known another woman with the name Alith. But I'm told it isn't an unusual name in the Highlands."

"There ye have it!" Alith exclaimed. "I kenned it must be so." She kept shaking her head while rubbing the ring. Andra's fingers numbed from the clutching pressure. "He remembered our names yet he told you his kith and kin had died? 'Tis that the right of it?" Before Andra could respond, she added, "Mayhap he tried to contact his uncle's clan and they told him we were both dead."

"He...wh...what? You're not suggesting he is a relation of yours?" Her father had been born in 1953. Andra shrugged her shoulders, turned to Kendrick with eyebrows raised in question, and then turned back to the old woman. "That could not be possible."

"Aye, I am telling ye, 'tis. 'Tis more than possible. When we first met, your ring reminded me of Donald's ring, but then I hadn't seen it in a long time. I imagined someone else could have had a similar ring made. Now, I am sure 'tis me Donald's ring you wear. We had one surviving son, Angus Brian Cameron." An anguished hitch caught her voice before she continued. "He would have received that ring upon his father's death just as Donald had received it from his father."

"But...but...my father's parents' names...."

"Aye, Donald James and Davina Alith Cameron. 'Twould be me dear, departed husband, Donald, and meself. Although, everyone here kens me as Lady Alith MacLean, me full name is Davina Alith Dunbar Cameron MacLean, you see. Dunbar being me father's name. When Donald died in battle, they returned his body which was missing his ring. Our youngest and last surviving child, Angus Brian Cameron, fought in the same battle, but they ne'er found me boy. No one ever heard from or saw him again. They buried many of the lads in mass unmarked graves. 'Twere a terrible thing to do, but that was the way of it, and no one remembered seeing Angus after the battle."

She took a deep shuddering breath, still clinging to Andra. "Mayhap your father suffered a head injury during the battle that took his da. That could explain it. Saints be praised for your mother's parent's generosity toward a lost, young man. He must have sworn fealty to your family's clan for their kindness. Was that the way of it, then? Did his memory ne'er return?"

Flabbergasted, shocked, bamboozled. How many words existed to describe baffled and bewildered? This couldn't be; her father would have told her if he had come through time, wouldn't he? Andra was as shocked as Alith.

With eyes as wide as saucers and a stupefied expression on her face, she simply stared at the old woman for several seconds. "Alith, I'm completely lost. I don't doubt that you believe my father was your son, but I can hardly make sense of it." This astounding information made Andra light-headed and queasy, so she redirected the conversation back to Alith's history with the MacLeans.

"How did you come to live with the MacLeans?"

"Oh, 'tis a long story, but I'll shorten it for you. I blamed my husband's clan for the loss of my family, me sons and husband. I could not forgive them. Me own father and mother were long dead by then, and I had no surviving siblings. I could have returned to the Dunbar clan, but Edme MacLean and I had been friends since we were bairns, and I desperately needed a friend's comfort." Her parched lips puckered as she reached for the wine and took a long drink, then continued.

"Donald, God rest his soul, had left me with a few valuables: a fine horse, a few jewels, and enough coin to make me way if ever something happened to him. He understood my unhappiness with the clan. I held great anger in me heart following the death of our first two sons in a foolish skirmish with a border clan. Shortly after they returned Donald and the other senior warriors for burial, I left the Cameron clan and made my way to me dear friends, Edme and Ailbeart MacLean, Kendrick's grandparents."

Kendrick had pulled a chair beside Andra and rubbed gentle circles on her back as they listened to Alith's story. When Andra glanced at him, she could see this new development had rocked him on his heels as much as it had her.

Except for the quiet hitching sobs from Alith, they remained silent for several moments. "Please. Tell me, you…m…my father… Oh God! I don't know how to phrase this question. Please, tell me," she sucked in a breath, "that there is no connection between us and Cormag Cameron or his clan?" All the air left Andra's lungs in a whoosh.

Unfocused eyes spilled a stream of tears down the old woman's face. "No. Well, mayhap, but the northern Camerons severed their connection with the southern clan, of which Cormag was laird, many generations ago. 'Twas me understanding verra bad blood existed between them for as long as anyone remembered." Alith swiped away her tears and took a calming breath before continuing. "To the best of me knowledge, Donald's people never associated with the southern Cameron clan."

"Well, at least that puts my mind at ease." However, Andra could find no ease with this new discovery about her father. Though the more she listened, the more her father's heavy brogue, the odd turns of phrase, and things he'd said over the years, came back to her. His reluctance to provide more than cursory details about his family, though he loved to regale her with stories of the Highlands and their people, confused her to this day, but now made more sense. Andra barely registered that Alith spoke again.

"When I arrived at Ruadhstone Castle, Edme was gravely ill. I nursed and cared for her until she recovered her strength. My gift in the healing arts made me a valuable asset to the MacLeans. When Edme recovered, I took the clan name. I knew only sad memories remained with Donald's clan. Besides, I dinnae want to see the Camerons again, nor did I want them to seek me out."

Kendrick interrupted at this point. "Lady Alith, you look pale and wan, I think you both need to rest. Could we assist you back to your own room for the night? We can talk more on the morrow. Andra still recovers from her ordeal in battle, and I dinnae want her to suffer a relapse."

Andra raised her brows in consternation. She felt fit and hale, albeit in total shock. Still, she did feel the need for space to process this new revelation. She could not comprehend the potential repercussions from this discovery.

Alith gripped Andra's hand, "You won't leave us, girl? Give me your word that you'll stay and meet with me on the morrow?"

Before she answered the question, Kendrick responded, "She won't leave us, Auntie. She is my wife. We are handfasted. That's what I planned to announce when you collapsed. But we plan to repeat our vows before kith and kin verra soon. I'm sorry we caused you such a shock with the announcement. Let us meet again on the morrow. You have much to discuss, but there will be plenty of time for those talks after we rest."

A brilliant smile lit the old woman's face. "Handfasted, you say. Och, it makes me heart glad to hear it." She placed rough, gnarled hands on either side of Andra's face. "To this day I mourn the loss of me husband, Donald, and me wee bairns, especially Angus, your father, as he was our last and youngest son. I tell you true, granddaughter, you are God's dearest blessing. I am so proud to call you me own."

* * *

Back in Kendrick's rooms, Andra stared into the fire speechless and numb. She couldn't wrap her mind around what she had heard from Alith. How could this be possible? How had her father not told her about his time travel experience?

"What do you think this means? I am more confused than ever. Do you think what Alith says is true?"

He remained thoughtfully silent, and then took her hands into his. "You've nae told me much about your father and mother. Isn't it possible that if you could come here, your father could travel to your time? Mayhap that is why you weren't meant to return; mayhap you've replaced your father here."

"I honestly don't know what to think about any of it. I can't possibly explain this to Alith. We cannot tell her the truth, do you think? Of course not." she answered her own question.

"Still, I don't want her to think her son did not love her or want to return to her for he definitely loved his family. He spoke about them with such high regard, but in this new light, I now understand his reluctance to reveal more. He always seemed terribly sad when he discussed them, and I learned not to press him."

He handed her a glass of whisky. "I think you need to drink this and rest, Andra. This has been a shock for all of us."

Without a moment's hesitation, she knocked back the whisky and barely choked on the after burn. Kendrick helped her disrobe and laid her on the bed. He climbed beside her and pulled the covers over them. She curled tightly into his warmth. Andra's stomach clenched in knots, and her head ached. She wrapped her arms around his neck and sought the relief she always found in his kiss.

"Dinnae fash yourself, my love, we'll figure this out. All will be well; you can put your worries down now." He kissed her temple and she melted into his strength assured of his love.

He rubbed her shoulders and back, breathed her scent deep into his lungs until they both relaxed. His need for her pressed hard against her thigh. His touch, like liquid fire, burned away her anxiety. "Make love to me, husband."

"I like the sound of that, wife!"

ABOUT ALEIGHA SIRON

Following an accident several years ago, Aleigha's road to recovery was paved with the adventures and excitement of romance novels, inspiring the creation of her own tales. Recently learning about distant Scottish ancestors, she traveled to the land of craggy peaks, mists, bogs, and the ubiquitous heather, where she fell in love with the setting for her first full-length time-travel romance novel.

In her lengthy business career, Aleigha wrote and derived an array of management and other technical training programs until she turned her writing efforts to her true loves: fiction, and poetry. Her poetry has been published in numerous anthologies and university presses. Most recently, her poetry was included in an Escondido Municipal Art Gallery collection, merging art and poetry, a form known as ekphrastic poetry. The San Diego Poetry Society also selected a poem for publication in their 2015-16 Annual Anthology.

Currently, Aleigha is busy working on two new novels and plans to revisit a Children's Book written years ago for her many nieces and nephews. When not writing, reading, or attending poetry workshops, she often walks along the shore at sunset with her husband and her trusty Labrador helper, Strider, breathing in the ion charged air while seeking inspiration.

Find Aleigha online

Website
www.aleighasiron.com

Facebook
www.facebook.com/profile.php?id=100010744560568

Twitter
twitter.com/AleighaSiron

Tirgearr Publishing
www.tirgearrpublishing.com/authors/Siron_Aleigha